HASTEN DOWN THE WIND

CU00482538

"...stories of past courage...can teach, they can
offer hope, they can provide inspiration. But
they cannot supply courage itself. For this each
man must look into his own soul."

> John F. Kennedy,
> *PROFILES IN COURAGE*

PART ONE

It was Stanley's day off, much appreciated. The slow current of a sunny summer Saturday in Los Angeles drew him to the park near his apartment. He had stayed in bed late and eaten breakfast at Jim's Café around the corner on 7th Street. There was not much else to do in the morning. He briefly thought of church--his church had Saturday services--but he decided it was too late to make it. Maybe next week.

So Stanley strolled MacArthur Park. No cakes melting in the rain, no rain, even, but a myriad of denounced humans, struggling to maintain life on a very few dollars. They ate, drank, talked, laughed, stared at their thoughts. Stanley walked near them; he felt tranquil.

There was music coming from a small car parked on Alvarado. Two Mexican men sat inside, relaxing and evidently enjoying this peaceful mid-morning. There was some traffic. A dog questioned whether or not to cross the street to the origin of a food-cooking smell.

Stanley walked down Alvarado Street after leaving the park. He had no specific direction today, no plans--only to relax and think about this week and think about what lay ahead and how it may transpire. He enjoyed attempting to figure out his life, in this way, and then to see how it developed. It was a fascinating question: What will happen? Would he "make" it? Would he be "happy"? Would he work too long at his present job until he got tired of it? Would he become a boxing champion?

He thought of Amy. He wasn't picking her up this weekend as he normally did. She'd wanted to come up but Stanley had a fight this Thursday, and seeing her didn't seem like a good idea. It would be difficult to resist having sex. Or, perhaps, he was getting tired of her. He didn't know. He liked her, even loved her. But she didn't seem to understand him. Stanley was almost 30, Amy had just turned 22. She was lovely, a real California girl, not gorgeous, but pretty. Sandy blonde, pure Southern California, good sense of humor. But...

He walked. This section of Alvarado was always busy, weekends or not. <u>Muchos</u> Latinos, doing things they needed to do, getting clothes, food, beer. And some Anglos. A few derelicts. Older people. Stanley liked them: they seemed to have an interesting attitude about life. They had history. Stanley enjoyed seeing people, seeing their faces, hearing their words, watching their interaction. He went further south, slowly.

A few birds had flown past, as he walked, making him suddenly realize he was getting away from the crowded part and on to less busy parts of town. Time to turn around.

It was a warm day, warmer than usual. The summer was here. 1977.

What was he to do? It had been three years since he came to L.A. Three hard years of training at the gym--with a few extended pauses--and working at several gas stations. Twenty amateur bouts. Thirteen wins, after losing the first two, getting scared, deciding to quit, then talking it over with a friend. Sitting alone up in the hills, thinking. Boxing was hard. What if he wasn't going to do well? The thought of not doing well depressed him, so he prayed, and gave it another chance. It was like getting over a barrier that had been deliberately set before him. Stanley had needed that obstacle; it made him work harder, and improve. He won twice and lost in the finals of a novice tournament, but then won more and took the open-division tournament championship with a streak of 3 knockouts, but lost in the semi-finals of the Nationals. He moved up in weight, from welterweight to junior-middleweight, and lost. The decision was close, but he lost it. The guys at the gym advised him to return to welterweight. But he felt he was too thin in that division. He was taller than his opponents, sure, and had a reach advantage, sure, but he didn't feel strong enough. He felt weak as a welterweight, always having to keep a shorter, stronger opponent away with a jab because if he got inside the guy could beat him. Stanley wanted to fight inside, too; that meant being stronger--and being stronger meant moving up in weight. So he'd made the adjustment. But it took a while to gain the necessary strength. That was what he lacked in the fight he lost. He hadn't developed properly with the extra weight. It took months to turn that weight into fighting power. That's why Ali lost the first fight to Frazer in his comeback. Ali had been off so long he wasn't truly ready. Simple. He wasn't in _proper_ shape. Sure, Ali was in good condition, but not for Smokin' Joe's stuff. And he'd only had two fights to prepare--one of which only went three rounds. That's good, but not good enough. And Stanley learned this lesson as he worked out, got into shape, and lost again.

Why? He didn't know. He felt he could have beaten the guy, but he didn't. Why not? Amy was sympathetic. She encouraged him. He fought and lost, again. <u>Three</u>. He gave up, stopping for several months. Larry, his coach, told him: "Don't quit. You can do it." So he came back and trained longer and finally got into proper shape and started winning again. After all, he <u>did</u> have a "reputation" to protect, even though it was only amateur. So he won four fights as a junior-middleweight and found himself about to try for another win Thursday. It was Saturday now, as he walked up Alvarado, and he was thinking about this.

Stanley knew his world depended at this moment on boxing. It was what he loved, what he cared about. Over these past years it had become, improbably, his entire existence. <u>Only boxing mattered</u>. When he was doing it, he felt alive, fulfilled. It seemed that God had given him this ability and this challenge, and what he did with it was up to him. Stanley didn't know exactly what the purpose of it all was--or where it would take him--but he was willing to go with it and find out. How could he know where it would lead?

<u>Thursday</u>. It was getting close; it scared him. He was always afraid before a fight, but apprehension seemed

to help. Being afraid was galvanizing. It got him going in a way he'd never experienced previously in his life. And after a fight he felt more complete than ever. He loved "getting ready," training, sparring in the gym, going to the arena, getting dressed, going down the aisle and into the <u>ring</u>. What a beautiful, breathtaking, breath-giving place. There would be his opponent. And a referee. And his trainer, with Stanley, helping him. How good it felt to be there and be in shape and want to do it and to be scared and to wonder what was going to happen...

2

     Stanley went back to his tiny apartment. The rest of the day he read from a book of John Keats' poetry, listened to music, flipped through some old boxing magazines. In the morning he would run, and after a rest, go to the gym. And go to the gym Monday, and Tuesday, and Wednesday, waiting for Thursday night.

     It had been a good day off. Stanley felt a non-gym day was his day off (even though he didn't work Sundays, either). Maybe he'd call Amy. She said she didn't have plans this weekend, so she'd likely be at home.

     Calling her was always fun. She had a blithe manner of speaking, a fertile imagination, could joke about almost anything. Sometimes the conversation turned to sex, and she'd make a provocative comment to get him going. Once she said sleepily, "I'd like to suck on your balls." It had surprised him, although he hadn't believed her.

     Mostly, however, they talked about their lives. She had, at present, a not-so-enriching job as a counter-girl at a laundry in a small shopping center on 17th Street near where she lived with her divorced mother in rural Costa Mesa, an hour's drive from Stanley's apartment--but she didn't have a car.

By three p.m. he was asleep, the small plastic record player emitting romantic rock-and-roll--a pleasant-voiced singer, Anne Murray. Light wind gently moved the curtains of his corner apartment, a soft breeze flowing through his room. Outside, the afternoon's activity continued, unaffected by Stanley's nap.

At one time this district had been called, for obvious reasons, Westlake, there being two lakes and a park-like, easygoing feeling.

Now, in 1977, it was more crowded, busier. Just another part of L.A. People worked, bought necessities, exchanged opinions, ate, drank, argued, and some stole. A diverse district: not only Latinos, but Orientals, blacks, Anglos, living together in the basic American tradition. Here Stanley, in fact, was a member of the minority which was, in the rest of the nation, a majority. But he enjoyed it--he felt at home, for some reason. To him, America had begun as a working struggle with honorable goals, and he felt a part of it all.

The sun set, the air cooled, the lights came on. It was Saturday night. Beer-drinking evening-talk and laughs and love and hate and joy and sorrow. Somehow it--all of it--woke him up. In a few moments Stanley Larson was out the door, down the stairs and out of the building, his cowboy boots clunking on the sidewalk. He went to 7th Street, west to Alvarado, and turned right in the direction of Bob's Steak House. He wanted dinner: boxers need healthful, substantial food. Their systems work hard--this he had learned over the past three years. He'd found that a boxer's food was wonderfully utilized: when some dude is trying to hit you, it's essential to have had proper portions of protein. So he ate, hungrily, slowly, after the smiling waitress brought his meal. Bob's Steak House was full, although Stanley ate alone.

In the morning he woke early, put on his T-shirt and Levi's, drank a cup of instant coffee, and felt good. He drove his red '57 Chevy to Belmont High School, parked, climbed the fence, went onto the track--the football field. A few people were there, running. He liked to run alone, when no one was there, but on Sunday that meant getting up before dawn--he didn't feel like it, today. He needed the proper amount of sleep, with the fight this week--and he'd stayed up until midnight, listening to the radio. Stanley had discovered since he began boxing that he needed extra time to be quiet, to rest, to enjoy his life. The almost daily training and "road work" demanded much from his body--more so than average life--and that meant hours of plain rest in order for his body to build and rebuild. Many people didn't understand the severe work involved in reaching and maintaining boxing condition--and the resultant relaxation needed. But it all fell into proper place: exercise, rest, nutrition. The time he spent reading magazines or sitting thinking or soaking a sore hand or listening to the record player or radio was very enjoyable--more so than in his past. Somehow his body and mind and spirit and soul responded to it, needed it.

So today he felt good. It was a brilliant, sunny Sunday, nine a.m. But as he ran Stanley became increasingly fearful. Couldn't help it.

He ran hard; he was in good condition. Not the best, but pretty good. Many fighters encountered a disturbing tendency: overconfidence. Stanley was no exception. It becomes difficult to get into top shape once you have some fights and begin to do well. You lose the passion to get into great shape--it doesn't seem necessary, anymore. Part of you says, "I can do it. I can do well," because you can. But then you fight like that a couple of times, overconfident, and realize you could have used that extra conditioning; you get tired, you can't throw that right or left the way you want. You get hit more often. The coach complains, the fighter trains harder. But naturally his

opponents become better ones, and it's not so easy to win.
Discouragement sets in. At that point having faith and
strength of heart become very important--crucial. Only
that will keep you going. It gets tougher; you know it
won't get easier. That's another hurdle: the more you
fight, the better opponents you face--a simple equation.
So...one day you find yourself in mediocre shape. Perhaps,
for some strange reason, you don't want to do well; you
lose, and blame it on lack of condition, rather than the
fact that he was better. It's a good excuse: you just
weren't in proper shape. Somewhere inside you know if you
don't do well your <u>next</u> opponent won't have to be any
better than this one. It's a self-defeating process. Just
slow it down a little, you tell yourself. Stanley had felt
that impulse, on occasion, and hated himself for it. But,
as his trainer and others at the gym told him: He can't
slow down, he can't wait, he must get going and keep at it,
now. He's almost 30, beyond the customary age. Too late
to wait.

So, he ran hard. But the fear was there.

Stanley had a bowl of cereal in his room, rested,
worked on a poem he was writing; he forgot about calling
Amy.

Later, in the gym, it was noisy and crowded. He
didn't like it much on Sundays--there was an unprofessional
atmosphere there, on weekends. Sure, anybody was welcome
if they paid to work out, but Stanley preferred weekdays
when the attitude was more concentrated on boxing.
Saturday and Sunday brought in the guys who weren't real
boxers. Of course during the week some came in who weren't
boxers, either, but they seemed to have a different
attitude--respectful, or something. Maybe they were into
the sport more--maybe they loved it more and Stanley could
sense that, hear that. Questions they asked or remarks
they made seemed appropriate, not tinged with jealousy.
But on weekends it was different.

So, it was too crowded. He did his usual warm-up. No
one was there to train him or work with him--Larry always
took the weekend off. Carlos, a stablemate who normally
came in Sunday, was nowhere to be seen. He worked by
himself, hitting the bags, moving around the floor,
shadowboxing in front of the mirror. Then a friend of his,
Tony, a lightweight, asked him to go a few rounds. They
helped each other put on their headgear and gloves, put in
their mouthpieces, and boxed three rounds. Stanley took it
easy. Little Tony was a good amateur, though, and hit him
a few surprise pops to the side of the head. Left hooks.

Stanley worked harder the second round, but not much. He had the weight advantage, didn't want to hit the guy too hard. It was a nice, easy workout. He showered, dressed, and took off in his Chevy, feeling fine.

It was a pleasant day in Palm-tree land. Stanley drove along Sunset Boulevard, cruising west, toward the sea. But when he got to Highland, he turned south and headed toward a familiar coffee shop. He hadn't eaten much in the morning, and what with running and going to the gym, he was quite hungry. Being at the correct weight, he wasn't concerned about eating too much--he just needed to get the right stuff.

Inside Stanley sat at the counter. He got a hamburger patty with scrambled eggs, and a salad. Tasted good. He also had a cup of coffee, but decided against a second one. Shouldn't have too much.

A pretty girl was sitting at the table to his right, behind him. Stanley looked at her several times, and she seemed aware of it, but wouldn't look up. It bothered him. He always wondered why girls acted as though they weren't aware of you when you were very aware of them. How come they couldn't just look over and smile or something? Did he have to have a Cadillac? What was it? Was there something wrong with him? Maybe she was married. But it isn't just her, he thought--it happens a lot. Maybe I scare them. And yet, they act like they aren't scared. Someday I'm going to just walk up to one of them and say, "What's the matter? Why are you unable to look at me and nod hello? What are you so afraid of?" But he didn't have the courage. He could get in the boxing ring (although with difficulty), but he couldn't say anything like that to a girl he didn't know. But he sure wanted to.

Afterward Stanley walked a few blocks, before returning to his car. It was important to walk after eating, something fighters always used to do. Now it wasn't done much. The experienced trainers taught it, but not everyone, anymore.

Stanley drove his '57 back to his room, rather than to the beach--he'd had enough activity for the day. Inside he put on a Linda Ronstadt album and sat by the open windows, listening to that sweet sound. He loved her songs, loved her photos, even loved her words in magazine interviews. Last September he'd seen her perform at the Universal Amphitheatre--so alive, so beautiful. But he knew she was out of reach.

"Heart Like a Wheel" came on, one of his favorites. He smiled and closed his eyes, feeling the cool breeze as Sunday's afternoon entered his small apartment.

"Some say the heart
        is just like a wheel
  Once you bend it
        It can't be mended"

--sung softly and yet with strength--revealing an abundance

of emotion. He wondered if she was actually like that,

inside.

3

In the morning instead of running he went on a long walk, after eating cereal and toast. Stanley didn't feel like having breakfast at the café, or anywhere--just a bite at the apartment and a walk, then back to his room to sit for an hour or so with the radio on, hoping to hear Ronstadt, or the Eagles. He got lucky--a song of hers did play. Stanley didn't always have such luck. It was a melodic, tender story of a girl who left home and friends, and now yearned to return. She sang it with such heart, Stanley felt her yearning, too.

He went to the gym around twelve, when it opened. Larry, his coach, wasn't in yet--couldn't make it that early on Mondays. In fact, no other fighters were there, at first. Just the old doorman, sitting in his chair. It was a comfort to work out in an empty place. Stanley liked to be alone in the gym. He could feel its decades of history. Many good fighters had been through there; it had character.

Sunlight came through the windows and down from the skylight, creating a church-like atmosphere. He trained hard (three days to go), then boxed when his friend Lonnie came in--a black middleweight. Since the fight was

Thursday, Stanley would go a few rounds today and tomorrow and that would be it, except for a light workout Wednesday. On the day of the fight, nothing. And no work. Luckily his boss let him off on days when he had a bout. This was the semi-final of a tournament. If he won, he'd go on to the finals.

Stanley showered and dressed, said goodbye to his friend, thanking him. Lonnie was a pro with a slightly marked-up face. Stanley felt good, but he was thinking about the fight. He went to the coffee shop on the corner of Third Street, a hangout of his. A kind and gentle guy worked there, Jerry. Big guy. Always asked Stanley about boxing, about <u>his</u> boxing. Stanley told him of the fight coming up; Jerry said he'd watch it on TV.

Stanley had a cup of fruit and a hamburger. Nothing special. His weight was fine, so he wasn't worried about eating the bread. Or the excess grease. He was one-half pound over the limit, and that would be gone tomorrow, inasmuch as he had increased his running this last week. Eating requirements were tricky. At first, when you're out of shape, you can't eat <u>anything</u> that's not right, but you <u>crave</u> what isn't right. Then you start getting in shape and begin to eat more--good stuff, but more. So you try to cut back--even though it's good food. Then you get into good shape and you can eat <u>anything</u>. You use it and get rid of it. But if that training doesn't lead to a fight, you start to lose drive and don't train as hard and the extra food starts to add up because you keep eating like before. So you have to start over again losing weight, trying to eat salads and vegetables, staying away from beer.

Sitting quietly at the counter, he thought, as usual, about boxing. It fascinated him; it was exciting. And he recalled his first fight. His opponent had been more experienced. Stanley went in there and kept swinging, but the guy knew what he was doing, so it didn't matter much. In the last round Stanley landed some good shots, and almost got the dude. But he didn't. And, man, was he tired. In between rounds he was aware of how tired he was. It seemed that as hard as he had trained, he was still not in good enough shape. <u>Next time</u>, he told himself. After the fight the decision was announced. He lost, of course. But it had been a great fight and everyone had cheered when it was over and again as they left the ring.

But now Stanley had to go to work. Back to the vaporous gas station, an old-style place on Wilshire Blvd. Back to the hours and hours of getting up from the chair in the office (a nice, comfortable place for a guy training and running 6 days a week), going outside in the heat to ask how much they wanted, to take the hose from the pump, hit the handle to get those numbers back to nothing, find the tank opening, put in the nozzle, fix the nozzle to flow slowly (if it's two dollars or more) so Stanley could get around to clean the windows with the small spray bottle and paper towel (to look busy so the customer felt good and would return) (although Stanley would prefer none returned so he could sit longer) and then shut off the hose at the proper number, put it in the pump, collect the money, if necessary give change back from the ancient cash register at the pumps or fill out the form if they handed him a credit card, take down the license number, add up the price if he'd given them any oil, hand it to them to sign (funny how most customers smiled at that moment), take back the pen and the holder, stare at the car as it pulled away, off into the world going anywhere and maybe to return, maybe not, and wonder what was going to happen, how long was he going to work here, when might he get away, when might he finally turn pro (an exciting and scary thought), and when when when in the life of Stanley Larson would the future actually be: was it the next fight, the next day, the next

car to come in, the next thought? Just another day at the
gas station.

That night he drove to Belmont High, always a still,
eerie place around midnight. Stanley liked to run there
after work. He climbed the tall, locked fence near the
empty grandstand, walked to the track, loosened up and ran.
The property had been built along a steep, sloping street,
a few feet up at one end, many yards at the other--in order
to be level. This field, supported on the street side by a
long concrete wall, indeed was unnatural. The dark school
itself sat adjacent to the football field, behind the
stands. One end of the field was high above a boulevard,
and from there Stanley could see the downtown skyline, the
flashing red light on top of the City Hall building. He
could see other buildings, some with lights, most without.
It was a strange, esoteric sight, dark and beautiful and
quiet.

Afterwards he climbed back over the fence, jumped into
his car and took off. He was sweating well. But the radio
wasn't working--Stanley's life wasn't exactly perfect. He
couldn't buy everything he needed. But he didn't want new
clothes, or a new car. He wanted some free time, some

music, some rest. He didn't want to have to work and train, both. He just wanted to box. It would be great to not have to go to work. He could run in the morning, eat breakfast, read, listen to music, write a little, go to the gym in the afternoon, train hard, come home, maybe have someone cook his dinner. Oh boy. And rest. Have a couple of beers and go blissfully to bed.

Oh yeah.

4

Stanley wished that it was football season. He enjoyed watching the games at his friend George's. Sometimes he went into a bar for a beer to see one--but bars were trouble. There was something that happened when people around him were drinking. They seemed to get hostile. Not everyone, and not always when they drank. It was mystifying. But, now there was baseball. That was okay, although it didn't have enough action for Stanley. He wanted to see more hits, more running on base. And certainly more home runs. Of course if you changed the rules you'd have to fix it so the old records didn't get messed with. Have a day when the new rules came into being, so Babe and Roger couldn't be diminished by a 200 home-run season.

Tuesday he boxed several rounds with Hershel, an amateur Larry also trained. He had quick hands and forced Stanley to throw a lot of jabs to keep him away. The more you hit Hershel the better things were for you. If you let him get through, though, his quick punches would occupy you far too much. It was an excellent sparring session. He kept going after the guy, not letting him punch often.

Larry was there, instructing them both. Afterward Stanley was happier than Hershel, but they were both satisfied. Hershel was preparing for a semi-final on Thursday, also.

Stanley drove to work. Did not want to go. He was thinking about the fight and he didn't want to work. Cars went by him in the other direction, and he wished he was going with them. He headed westward, wishing he was going anywhere but to work.

Football had true excitement: seeing a touchdown pass in the final seconds--what's better? Or recovering a fumble. A long field goal. A long run. Yeah.

He felt moody at work. Didn't want to eat when he normally did, didn't want to talk to his co-worker when the kid showed up at five, an hour late.

It had been a good workout, but he couldn't dwell on it. The fight was coming up; Stanley dwelled on that. Maybe...maybe he would die.

He always felt a vague foreboding prior to a bout. He should be pro. If he was, he wouldn't worry. These amateur fights are peculiar; you get odd feelings. Can't relax; too tense. A regular pro fight is better. At least it seems like it. But something about these amateurs...maybe it was the incomplete sense of them. You fight, but you're not <u>truly</u> "fighting." Fewer rounds than pro fights. You're an amateur. Just that.

"Are you pro yet?" "Hey, Stan--turn pro yet?"

He was tired of that question.

But yeah, he was still fighting amateur. So? Lots of guys have had two times as many amateur fights. What about them?

His trainer wanted him to get through the tournament and have a few more fights and then go pro.

The Olympics were too far off. 1980. Didn't seem worth the work. If he turned pro he could make some money, get out of this job. If he waited for the Olympics he'd have to stay amateur all that time.

Last year he'd come close. Made it to the National A.A.U.'s, but lost a close decision in the semi-final. Good fighter from the East Coast. Real hard to hit. Kept slipping Stanley's jabs. Kept sidestepping his right hand. Bastard! If Stanley had won <u>that</u> tournament he'd have gotten into the Olympic Trials, and then on to Montreal. Oh, that fighter had been good. Black guy. So relaxed. What was his name? Couldn't hardly hit him.

But now Stanley needed to do <u>something</u>. He couldn't just hang around any longer, fighting amateur. Life waited in the pro ring. He had to go for it.

In the evening he thought perhaps he would give Amy a call. She was a sweet girl, but kind of weird. Didn't follow along with your normal pattern. She was her own girl. That is--imagine anybody going out steadily-- singularly--with _him_, while she lived 40 miles away in simple good old nice pleasant gently conservative Costa Mesa? And liking it?

How could she be happy seeing him on weekends, and not each weekend at that? Three out of four at the most.

But she loved him, and he loved her. At least, they thought so.

Stanley decided, however, not to phone her. It bothered them both when they weren't going to see each other, soon, and just talked. If two people are together each day and then apart once in a while, talking by phone is good--nearly impossible to do without. But in this case it hurt--because they couldn't see each other much, and the week before a fight not at all, and it didn't feel good to speak on the phone under those conditions.

He wanted to be free enough to think about the fight and enjoy some peace and relax a bit in the days preceding it. With Amy he'd be concerned about her, about keeping her pleased, making it nice for her. She understood.

Boxing was important to him. She was accommodating in that respect.

So he strolled along Alvarado, after work, deciding not to run that night. Instead he'd go to the firebreak above Elysian Park, at dawn. There were still quite a few people out. Although this was not the safest place in town (what was?), it was okay. For him, at least. Mostly pleasant, working people. Not a bunch of criminals. Further over toward Hollywood it was more dangerous, late at night. The ones you saw there made you think. They were strange-acting. Here maybe a few were drunk, but not so much. When you have to get up to work the next day or to look for some work, you can't get too crazy the night before.

So Stanley walked; he looked at the people, studying them. Mostly Mexican-Americans, some Asian, some standard-looking Americans, some eastern-European (who spoke similar-sounding languages), blacks, French, and even east-Indian and probably American-Indian too. But mostly, people who just did not have a lot of money, yet had a quality that he admired. One might say it was persistence. It was something that kept them going. It was something that he responded to, and sensed was a quality <u>he</u> needed, also, to do well in the ring.

Sunrise in the hills had a wonderful effect on Stanley whenever he ran there in the early morning. It was an experience unmatched by any other except, perhaps, falling in love. He felt the slowly enveloping warmth, saw the slowly gathering light. He felt the brand-newness of a day that had never been, the glory of God's grandeur, the freshness of life, the clarity of morning air, the pure wonder in his being for this all--<u>how</u> this could be, <u>why</u> it should be. A terrific happening--the dawn of the new day. <u>Right</u>, he thought, as he ran, it's like being in love. The poet Keats had fallen in love. Perhaps he'd felt like this, too.

Afterward he ate breakfast, napped in the heat of his apartment, worked on his poem, went to the gym. His workout was light, "just enough to break a sweat," as Larry would say. He moved around, jabbed, weaved, threw a few combinations, loosened up. He never trained hard the day before a fight. He was in good shape, anyway.

At work that afternoon he tried not to do too much. Since the boss always left shortly after Stanley arrived, he had the remainder of his shift to sit and let his co-worker take care of the majority of the customers. It took a bit longer, and Mark worked harder, but Stanley would make it up to him--and anyway, Mark liked doing it. At least, he said he did. Mark was on the football team in high school and seemed to understand the requirements of Stanley's current circumstances. Also, Stanley would work on Mark's old Dodge truck, sometimes, as his part of the deal. Another employee, George, worked at the station part-time. He was taking automotive classes at Trade Tech and advised Stanley regarding the truck. George wanted to become a full-time mechanic. Because he had a wife and child, and one due in several months, he studied hard.

Actually his name was Jorge, but his friends in high school in El Paso had named him George to simplify things. Not tall, but strong and powerful, he had played as middle-linebacker while only a junior.

Mark, however, was big, near-sighted, and planning on a good senior year as offensive lineman, hoping later to play football in college. The three of them got along well, although George only worked on the weekends, now. Such was the finite and simple world at Barry's Lo-Gas.

Wednesday evening went. Stanley strolled Alvarado, again. He played Ronstadt's "Desperado" on his little record player and then fell asleep. Sometimes he ran the night before a bout, but he didn't feel like it this time.

It wasn't necessary--he was in good physical shape,

knowledge which allowed him to sleep well. And he'd

decided he wasn't going to die in the fight, after all.

5

The morning was fresh and lovely. Stanley walked a bit, in the sun, ate a healthful breakfast, went back to his room, and read--Schlesinger's *A THOUSAND DAYS*. It helped him to explore someone else's courage, someone else's pain, their work, their effort--it coincided with his. He enjoyed the book--found it inspiring and encouraging--except for the tragic end he knew was coming.

Stanley loved to read, but this day it was difficult. He wasn't relaxed. He always felt odd the day of a bout-- sure. There was no running, no training, no work at the station. Yet today he felt more disturbed than usual. There was quiet, fresh air, but many thoughts.

Putting the book down, he turned on his radio to hear a disc jockey that came on at noon--Russ O'Hungry. He was wild and fun, played good music, and made interesting comments about the world, between songs. Russ temporarily lifted Stanley's spirits.

Later, after a small meal of steak and salad, he lay on the grass, in the park, trying to keep his mind off the approaching contest. To no avail. Finally he went to his room and read, once again.

Larry picked him up before seven. Duke, a beautiful, big, old-style trainer, was also in the car. Duke was going to "second" the fight. He asked: "How you feel, Champ?"

"Good." That's all he could say.

Larry drove, nodding his head in silent approval.

Stanley was scared, as usual. He couldn't figure out how to prevent it, so he tried to hide it by silence and steady breathing. They drove to the arena without much talk. Duke sipped from a small bottle and spoke about fighters he used to train. But Stanley wasn't listening.

He thought about his shape. Seemed alright. He thought about his Chevy, about the disc jockey, about poetry. He tried to think about <u>anything</u>, but he couldn't get away from the bout. There was a measure of excitement, joy, and fear at the same time. He wanted to do it, but he was afraid...

Oh well. What do I have to worry about? I can beat this guy. I have a better record, I trained hard.

Funny, that didn't mean a thing at the moment. Plenty of guys with good records don't win. And <u>he</u> must have trained hard, too.

But it wasn't about <u>winning</u>, so much. What was it? Something...just getting through it. That's what mattered.

Then, the auditorium. Walking through the parking lot, in the door. Smiles and hellos. On down the hall, beside the arena. Stanley glanced inside. Not many people there, yet.

Then down the steps to the dressing rooms. It was called "the dungeon." The floors were cold, the walls yellow-green. Not a window anywhere. Other trainers in the dungeon greeted Larry and Duke, some said hi to Stanley, asking how he felt.

"Fine."

"Great!"

He managed to smile.

The formalities began: showing his license, being examined by the doctor, undressing, getting on the scale, redressing. Larry half-kidded with someone in the doorway while Stanley underwent the process. He appreciated the way Larry wasn't too serious, how he seemed to sense Stanley's feelings, assisting him by being relaxed. It was difficult to describe, this quiet assurance that Larry provided. But it was valuable.

And then Duke sipped on his brandy after they all got into the dressing room, finally, talking of Charlie Burley, the "uncrowned champion." Larry took a few sips also. Stanley undressed again, put on his gear--supporter, protective cup, trunks, socks and shoes. This was always a tough moment, going from one thing to another. So final. Once he was in his "stuff," getting his hands wrapped, the fear increased. Duke wrapped his hands, as usual. He was good at that. Must have done it thousands of times. Did it for Archie Moore, he'd said. Duke had fought in the twenties, but didn't look that old. Said he'd met the great Joe Louis. He understood the sport, the way only experienced black fighters seemed to.

Larry spoke with another trainer in the room. One other fighter was there, waiting. Stanley's opponent was in a different room, fortunately.

Noise outside, loud voices in the corridor. Someone opened the door, looked in, and not finding who or what he searched for, went away, closing it.

Stanley breathed deeply, purposefully.

"How you doing?" Larry asked, walking over to him.

He smiled. "Good. Nervous."

"Yeah!" Larry took it easily, as usual. He had fought; he knew.

The room was warm. The other boxer flexed his hands, looking at nothing. Larry was speaking with the trainer, and Duke was talking, too, out in the hall somewhere. He was always happy to be there, happy to work with Stanley. You could hear it in his voice.

Stanley sat quietly, Larry glanced over at him, then back to the other trainer.

Crowd sounds came down from the arena. After a while a bout started. Larry left and returned, telling Stanley he was going to be the third bout so he should start to "get ready" soon. He didn't want to warm up. Warming up was just about the hardest thing, next to facing the guy during instructions. Warming up was painful. It meant you were really going to fight, and there was no stopping it.

But in a few moments he started. Of course he didn't want to fight <u>without</u> being warmed up. So he stood up and moved around, throwing jabs, shaking out, kicking his legs. Oh yeah, he felt that sick feeling now. Oh yeah. He moved quicker, but it didn't leave. Oh man. He bent over a couple of times and told himself it would be over soon.

Larry watched him. He must have been nervous too, but he didn't show it. An official came in with the gloves. Larry looked them over while the official examined Stanley's hand-wraps, marking his "ok" with a red pencil, watching Larry rather violently pull, then adjust the gloves on Stanley. <u>Why did he always do it that way</u>? Oh well...

The official left. Stanley continued to warm up. Why did it always take so long? He started to think: had he trained enough? He should have run more, he should have--

Then a man was at the door.

"Larson! Next bout!" He went down the hall, calling to someone else.

Larry, looking serious, said: "Okay, keep moving." He threw the robe over Stanley's shoulders.

"Now just jab this guy. Just jab him the first round. You understand?" Stanley nodded. He was breathing well now.

"Just keep sticking."

"Okay."

So, they went into the hall. Larry placed his hands on Stanley's shoulders and pointed him toward the stairs that led to the arena. Duke followed with a towel, a bucket with items for the corner--water bottle, Vaseline, mouthpiece. They started up the stairs; a few people wished Stanley good luck as they left the dungeon.

There was noise. They got into the auditorium proper, Stanley bouncing on his feet, keeping warm as the three of them moved swiftly down the aisle, and there was the ring. Oh boy...but excitement now exceeded fear.

A couple of people were climbing out of it. Stanley didn't look at the ring--he never wanted to prior to climbing in. He heard a few encouraging comments as they went down the incline. Oh boy...

He breathed strongly, deliberately, as they walked. Then they reached the ring, started to climb up into it. Larry helped Stanley through the ropes, and suddenly, he was in.

So he moved around, tossed a couple of punches in the air, kicked out his legs, just kept moving. He was warmed up.

His opponent, a shorter, white guy, was climbing in also, along with his handlers. This was it--they were over there, in their corner. A referee was in the ring. The announcer was there. Larry told Stanley to get some rosin on his shoes. So he went over to the little wooden box, rubbing each foot in it, putting a gloved hand on the thick rope for support. Then he returned to his corner. Larry put some grease on Stanley's face. Duke was just outside the ropes, his look passive. They were ready.

The announcer, microphone in hand, announced who they were, the fact that this was a Silver Belt semi-final, junior-middleweights. Duke stayed outside on the apron, Larry and Stanley approached the ref, the opponent and his trainer approached. The referee said his normal stuff about the rules and clinching and good luck and Stanley didn't want to look at the other guy but then again he didn't want him to think he was scared to look at him so he did but he couldn't look for long so he looked away and man he was breathing well and Duke yelled something as they shook hands and Stanley felt a strange lightness and they went to the corner and Larry repeated himself about jabbing, Stanley nodded, Larry put in his mouthpiece, took his robe, and Stanley wondered what was he doing here? like he always wondered just before the bell and Larry started to climb through the ropes and then there wasn't anybody there but him and his opponent and of course the referee and then the bell rang and he turned, and moved toward the open, and it had begun...

Stanley jabbed once as they met in the middle, vaguely connecting, and then backed away, thinking what to do next. He went to the left, bowed a bit, and went to the right, jabbing again. His opponent ducked, threw a slow right to the body; Stanley blocked it. Seemed like the guy was taking his time, too--but you never knew for sure. He might be planning on a surprise. It wasn't usually until well into the fight that you could count on your opponent settling down to box--and even then his corner may have told him something else, like: "Wait for him to get a little tired. Take your time." But normally Stanley began slowly--not the other guy. Weird.

They went around the ring, Stanley jabbing more, from too far away, mostly missing. His opponent moved away and Stanley went forward, sticking, and then threw a right, which was blocked. The force of it, however, made his opponent retreat. Possibly he realized that this Larson could hit. They slowly circled, waiting. The opponent's corner yelled, the crowd booed. Stanley stayed easy, beginning to sweat--the bell was a ways off, still. Instead of jabbing, the guy threw a lead-off right hand. Weird. The two of them were just solving a couple of problems: how to get at the other one, and what to expect from the other one. Once you figured that out you kind of relaxed, then, and just boxed.

It took a while. His opponent finally jabbed, and threw some long rights, one connecting, clinched a few times and hit Stanley with another jab--not too hard. Stanley wasn't worried about that. But those long rights...He popped a quick left to the belly, partially blocked, and ducked one of those long rights, fortunately.

Usually short guys throw short rights. But both types can be dangerous.

They were both breathing deeply now. It was a fairly even round. Toward the end Stanley stung him with a left hook, but before he could follow up, the guy came back swinging a bunch of punches and Stanley had to back up, getting hit by a few, blocking and covering. That was interesting, but not alarming. He obviously had something in him and if you hit him hard he went at you--so you had to get to him first--and often. When the round ended Stanley sort of had an idea about it. He'd have to bang the guy with several good shots, not just pop him now and again, and then move away quickly. He'd have to get in there and hit him because the guy seemed to wait, and then attack.

At the corner he stood instead of sitting, something Larry advocated. Duke reached over the ropes with the sponge, wiping his face. He held the water bottle but Stanley didn't want to rinse yet. Larry took it, removed Stanley's mouthpiece, poured water over it, glancing at the other corner and then back at Stanley.

"You're doin' fine. You're doin' fine. But get busy."

Stanley took in a deep breath. "Yeah. Okay."

"How do you feel?"

"Good." He exhaled, watching Larry.

"Okay. This guy is being careful. I don't want you to be. Move in on him. Two jabs and then the right hand behind it. Understand?"

Stanley nodded.

"And jab on the way out. Throw a jab while you move back. He's gonna go to you when you hit him so keep moving."

Stanley nodded again; Larry put his mouthpiece in. He was right. His opponent always attacked when Stanley landed a punch or two. Duke looked very serious. He displayed his own right hand--turning it over strongly-- boom--as if to say, "Go get him and don't play--you can do it," smiling a near-toothless smile.

So then, the bell. Stanley moved out--trying to remember what he had been told, with the thought of Duke's example. It seemed as if Duke, who knew a lot, was telling him he could get this fight by doing just that.

Larry's words made an impression. But, they were fighting again, and obviously the other corner had advised his opponent to do more. He went fast at Stanley and tossed several shots. Stanley blocked, but one hit him hard in the nose. Umm.

The crowd liked the improved action. Stanley stepped back, popping a straight jab into his opponent's right eye, as Larry advised. That made the guy drift back a second. But instead of going after him, Stanley moved away, resting; then suddenly Larry yelled:

"Stanley! Two jabs and your right!"

The opponent's trainer yelled too: "Get off, get off!"

Stanley went in. He did it. He banged two jabs, the first one didn't hit but the second one did. And he threw the right hand. Hit. He ducked a long right; the guy moved away.

Stanley chased him. He jabbed and hit him again. The guy attacked, but Stanley caught most of the punches on his gloves, returned with a hard right.

They were boxing well, now. His opponent started to jab but Stanley moved in anyway. The opponent grabbed him and they held for a moment until the referee broke them apart. It was a nice breather. And the dude wasn't attacking him now--though his cornermen were yelling. They weren't supposed to yell very much but they were getting worried. Stanley was winning this round. His cornermen were quietly watching.

Stanley kept his jab in; the guy seemed less
interested in getting close to his right hand now. He
wasn't responding like before. Stanley knew, however, he
had to hit him with his right. The guy might get smart and
start punching more--a situation that could increase in the
next round, the last. So Stanley kept at him, and they
boxed to the bell, both trying to do well--Stanley trying
to get in his right hand, the opponent trying to avoid it
and throw a few punches back in the meantime, some of them
landing.

In the corner Stanley took a rinse and spit it out.
Duke sponged his face. Larry started right in at him about
how he was going to win and had to keep at the guy and
throw that right and watch out for his long punches and
keep sticking--the crowd seemed to like it. He was
breathing hard, and then remembered how Sam, his first
trainer, always got him to take big breaths between rounds,
so he did, and the sweat was pouring off him. And somebody
yelled "Come on, Larson!"

Soon Larry dried his face with a towel and put in the
mouthpiece and the bell rang and they started again. This
time his opponent wasn't as fast, so maybe he was getting
tired. Stanley sure felt tired. They boxed for awhile and
Stanley got after him with two jabs and a right, which

missed, and then he threw them once again. This time the right landed. His opponent didn't flinch, however, but came forward in the pause and threw that long right of his, scoring; Stanley moved back and pulled away and Larry yelled the loud way he sometimes did--so he jabbed twice and punched solidly with his right and the guy leaned against the ropes and didn't hold his hands up and Stanley hit him with a left hook and a right cross and another hook but the guy only tried to move away a bit, and couldn't get his gloves up to protect himself, so in came the referee who went between them and took Stanley's arms and lifted them up and people yelled and the bell was ringing over and over and Stanley smiled and in came Larry and Duke and the opponent's trainers and Larry grabbed Stanley and put his arm around him and then Stanley went to his opponent who was now in the corner looking sort of unhappy and he put his arms around him and the guy half-smiled and his trainer said "Congratulations" and "Real good. Real good."

And so the crowd hollered. They liked that kind of fight. And with his arms held high, Stanley went over toward his corner as the announcement was made: third round knockout.

6

Stanley hadn't stayed to watch the professional bouts. Instead he went to George's apartment after the fight, when Larry dropped him off. Larry had made his usual speech-- "Keep at it, kid; you know what it takes." He and George sat on the floor in the bedroom and drank beer from quart bottles while Alicia sat on the bed. She had beside her, asleep, their three-year-old son. When they would laugh at something he'd start to wake, but her kind, gentle hand would soothe him back to sleep. They discussed the bout, pleased with the result. George and Alicia had watched it on TV. They went over various parts of it, excitedly. George loved the way Stanley had been so persistent in his "pursuit of the guy." How he'd kept at him when he got to him, until the referee had to step in.

"Sometimes you're not aggressive enough," he pointed out. "But tonight--" Alicia interrupted, laughing: "You were aggressive enough, hombre!" George laughed too, agreeing.

"But he put up some resistance, let me tell you," Stanley said seriously.

They discussed the fact that the guy didn't fall down. Stanley said: "Oh, I don't care. He was tough." George agreed: "True, that's true, but I wanted to see you knock him down." Stanley drank from his big beer bottle, shrugged. "No, it's the way to end a fight," George insisted. "I wanted to see you do that."

"You don't think I was trying to?" They laughed.

Alicia said: "At first I was worried for you, he came on strong, you know, but--"

"Then he got hit a few times!" George offered. "Man, he didn't like that."

Stanley kept nodding, smiling. "Lucky for me." As he started to take a drink he banged his front teeth with the bottle. He pulled it away quickly. "Ow! What the--"

"¿Hombre, qué pasa?"

"Are you hurt?"

He felt one of his front teeth with his finger. "I chipped it!"

"What?"

"You okay?"

"Yeah. Yeah." It was a lesser-sized tooth next to the very front ones. "Little chip."

George stared at him.

Alicia admonished him for it. "¡Estúpido!"

George asked again: "Are you okay?"

Stanley nodded, feeling it with his tongue. Then he looked at them sheepishly and took a sip with a flourish, laughed. "Man, I go through the fight, and it's okay, and then I'm sitting here and do this!" They all laughed.

The boy on the bed stirred and woke up, staring at them.

7

Boxing provided certain advantages. One was the way in which it brought people together. It made friends of many diverse types. It brought so much out of a person that he was less afraid to open up, to let others know him. Fighters expressed things to each other that everyday life did not require, or even allow. An adventure or a crisis could do the same for a group of people. But with boxing this personal bonding occurred over a period of time as trainers and fighters became friends, mutually acknowledging the struggle, the ups and downs.

Another advantage was the seemingly endless array of backgrounds and cultures that manifested around a gym and in an auditorium. Stanley's first "gym" friend was a small Irish pro who eventually returned to Ireland with enough money to live well. Or, at least, he claimed to have enough. Stanley's second friend was an old white fighter who, though long retired, hung around the gym dispensing advice. Women, too, were starting to box. It hadn't always been so. Little Tony was Anglo, Lonnie black, Duke part American Indian, part black, Carlos Mexican-American, Larry, Sammy, Hershel black.

Boxing also had an essence of hope and longing, of searching for a way to express, to excel. In an action sport one could find solace in effort; it eased the occasional discouragement inside. Oh, there were setbacks, there was weariness, at times, physically--but not the kind the world hands out in daily living. Not the weary-worn-hurting pain of trying and failing, the standard result of striving toward a goal and not obtaining it. In boxing, if you stayed healthy, you could work hard and find a joy in that, regardless of your degree of success. You could be out there really boxing, loving it, and life was yours each moment of the experience. At least, Stanley thought so.

The morning after the fight he awoke, and felt good, with the minor exception of a swollen lip and a slight headache. Grateful, Stanley said a prayer of thanks as he got up from bed.

He glanced in the mirror before going out to the bathroom down the hall.

He was happy, not minding the dark bruises he discovered on his forehead. So?

Boxing had always fascinated him and when he began doing it he felt full. He believed the Lord had given him something to do, something to be. Everyone else had plans, he'd thought. Either they enjoyed going to work or had an idea of what they wanted to do. But not him, before boxing. Stanley hadn't been satisfied. In school others had goals that satisfied them. Although he'd read about people who weren't happy with what they were doing, it didn't seem that he was like them either. Now, he saw it differently. People weren't as happy as they pretended. They felt inner weariness when confronted with failure and loss. It had taken him years to learn that, for some reason.

Returning from the bathroom he heard loud music from the next apartment. Were his neighbors satisfied with life? He'd have to ask them, sometime. They often played their radio in the morning. Was that a sign of fulfillment or of unhappiness? Most likely they weren't satisfied, but he didn't know. Maybe they were. Or maybe they were searching for something, as he had. Stanley sat in his chair by the window and looked out at old Westlake, thinking: those people who weren't satisfied weren't him, they were normal people. He had something to do, something to be. Perhaps they needed to seek the unusual, as he had. Perhaps then they would find satisfaction. Unless they already had it. But most people didn't seem to. His head hurt. Maybe he'd gotten hit harder than he thought.

The question was, who was he? What was he? What was he going to do? Yes, he'd found boxing. He'd been given boxing. He fought and found feelings of accomplishment and joy. The running, the training, it all gave him something. A life. A way to live. But was there something more?

In the past he had tried to avoid acknowledging his searching, because it meant he'd have a rough life ahead of him. If he could only be happy and satisfied with something <u>regular</u>--then he'd have fewer problems. But it wasn't to be. He'd gone to college and quit. Prior to that he'd served his time in the Navy, but gotten out. He was compelled to seek, and seek, to search for himself, for life, for God. Now he was happy, in this city, doing these things. He wanted to go ever further. He wanted to stop working at the gas station, to get a better place than this little apartment. But more important than that he just wanted to fight, to feel alive and affirm the life he had. He wanted to continue to be, to sense God, to be aware of the world around him, in the heart of him, in the soul of him--to exist.

He drank a glass of water, returned to the chair. <u>Need an aspirin</u>.

The strength he had now, in his body, made him feel happy. It was a pleasant thing to know you were strong--

and healthy. Sure, his poems weren't much, but he liked writing them. Sure, he missed an old girlfriend from college, but...so?

He responded to music, to the "California Sound," to Linda Ronstadt, Jimmy Webb, Fleetwood Mac. But why? Was it that he felt so much more than anyone else? No. He was not the only one. Others felt it too. Eagles' music, Jackson Browne--seemed to touch him personally, touch that place in him that searched and longed and cared and thrilled. No, he wasn't the only one. Myriads were touched that way--they had to be. They bought the tapes, didn't they? Well, best get breakfast. What was it his teacher had said? "You're too introspective, Stanley."

On the way to the little café, Stanley enjoyed the sunshine. It was a lovely, warm, Southern-California morning. Things looked good to him. So he was introspective. Big deal.

"Praise God," he said to himself, looking around. Everything had a gentle cheerfulness: the trees, the sidewalk, birds, people, wind, the traffic, even.

He paused at the top of the street. Usually he thought of this area as crummy--but not this day. It looked, it seemed...hopeful. Sure, people were struggling, but not without direction, scope, or future. They could accomplish something. He had, hadn't he?

He turned toward Skinny Jim's Café, east of the corner. Stanley liked it there. Many of the surrounding sports-political-social-interest locals wandered in there. Hanging out, listening to the news on an old radio, hung over, making jokes, drinking coffee, arguing over political events.

Inside the shack Stanley took a seat at the counter, which was all there really was. The place was a small hut made over into a spot to get eggs, coffee and toast, or at night a cheap steak with fried potatoes. There was one small table beside the counter. The radio was on, as usual; a newsman was speaking, as usual. A couple of men were at the table, talking, as usual. The cook, apparently a drunk who was in recovery, who was sober and happy to be working, gave Stanley a cup of coffee from the large urn against the wall. Who knows what was inside the contraption--but pretty good coffee came out of it.

There was a discarded newspaper at the corner of the three-sided counter, and Stanley, as the cup was set before him, reached for the sports section with joy. He wanted to see what might be there about the fights the night before. He took a sip of the hot stuff and, feeling a warm breeze from the screen door in the back, hearing the news reporter go on and on, and aware of the cook slowly preparing an order for one of the other customers, he opened up the paper, looking for the report.

There it was. Not very big, of course--just a few paragraphs, but it was there. He put the paper down, took another sip, and then looked with genuine interest at the story of the bouts at the Olympic Auditorium. At the bottom, in small print, were the amateur ones. Tournament semi-final bout, light-middleweight class, open-division: Stanley Larsson TKO 3, Don Frankenhiemer. Larsson? Ha!

He took another sip of coffee. The sensation that was enveloping him now was in no way intruded upon by the minor fact of his name having been spelled incorrectly. He didn't care!

There it was, the fight result.

So the guy's name was Don. Guess I heard them call him that.

"What can I do up for you?" the cook inquired, with a certain zest.

Stanley had fried eggs and toast. He also luxuriated in a bunch of their greasy fried potatoes that tasted so good. Another benefit of fighting was the pleasure of eating that which you could not eat before a fight.

Stanley didn't really have it too bad, though. Some
fighters suffered tremendously trying to take off pounds.
But if he ran enough he didn't have to worry. Sparring in
the gym really took the weight off too. If you run and
then box at the gym you can keep your weight where you want
it. The other thing to think about is that the food be
good for you. That's important. If you eat good food,
you'll be alright. Simply having your weight down doesn't
mean you're in top physical shape.

He ate the eggs, putting ketchup on them. He ate the
toast. He shrugged when the cook said that the Dodgers
would probably lose to New York should they get to the
World Series. There was something on the radio about it,
even though it was still only July.

Then a loud, weird-looking man came in, his hair
askew. He was rude, making crude remarks, then protecting
himself by laughing as if he were just joking. The cook
got him his order, but the discourse was coarse and the man
was vulgar. He proceeded to attack every race, and life,
outside of his, vehemently.

Stanley was unhappy about this. He didn't want
someone's sick ideas to damage this wonderful morning. The
man was jealous about many things. He seemed deeply
bothered, and expressed his anger to the people around him.

The cook tried to make the best of it, smiling and nodding when he could. It was obvious he knew the man, who must have come in often. But Stanley began to get mad.

"Yeah, and--and--and--," the guy slurped, trying to drink some coffee and speak simultaneously. "You know those fucking assholes are like that! Ain't worth nothin'!" He tried to eat a forkful of spaghetti but it fell to the plate before it reached his mouth.

He was quiet for a second, attempting to eat. Then: "Sure, you can't get any good Mexican food down in Mexico. You gotta get it in America, that's because--I'll tell ya-- that is because, you look and see, you go in the back of a so-called Mexican restaurant and you'll find a Jew owns the place. No shit!"

Somebody at the table laughed, the cook nodded; the man was being encouraged. Stanley decided to leave. He wanted to stay there and enjoy his breakfast and coffee but this was no good. Then the man said, "Mexicans ain't worth nothin'! Huh! They steal a wrench from somebody and call themselves a mechanic."

That brought Stanley off the counter bar-stool. He took a breath, pulled some singles from his pocket, put them on the counter and turned, getting out quickly, oh so quickly.

8

As his food settled down, as the sun heated up L.A. like it did during summer, as cars moved normally up and down the street, as a few people with small children proceeded normally up and down the sidewalk, as Stanley thought comfortably of the story in the newspaper, as he considered continuing the walk or heading back to his room or calling up Amy right then--although he would see her soon--or buying a magazine, or what, since he could take it easy until three when he had to be at work which he sort of liked because it was something to do since he needed something to do the day after a fight, rather than just sitting around or driving around, because he liked to keep active, he liked to do something. It wasn't a good idea to have a fight and then sit around without exercising or anything for the mind and for the body to keep your emotions together so you can go on from there, because a fight is such an extreme, remarkable event that you could have a let-down which might affect you the next time you fought. That was something you wanted to avoid, to keep free of, and try, rather, to have your life be beautiful and relaxed and going smoothly so you could work at the gym and run and be in good shape physically, mentally, emotionally and spiritually for your next bout without worrying about anything or having an adverse afterward-reaction-effect when you weren't able to protect against it or, anyway, that was how it was explained to him on a few occasions in the course of his training; that's what led him to think it was a smart idea to go to work, since it was familiar and sort of fun and provided him with a kind of workout that wasn't too difficult yet was steady and, in fact, interesting in the sense that every order was a little different because each car was a little different and each particular spot they pulled into was a little different for him to go over to...yet, all-in-all, it was basically similar so he wasn't troubled by unusual variations that might cause excess effort or stress beyond what was acceptable in order for him to gradually proceed, to function, to make his life what he wanted it to be.

On the other hand, there were those songs of Linda's, and Eagles music, which carried his life along like a flowing breeze, the kind of breeze that brought happiness and health, provided you joy and softness and warmth, while you wished its return as soon as it was gone, and its tenderness gave you hope that everything might be as beautiful, someday, as gorgeous, as lovely--if the world could only figure out its problems and correct them, if it could gain the knowledge it needed, if the Lord would allow this to occur, then, naturally, this world would become as true as the music, as the breeze.

George had found a loose wire and fixed it for him, so the makeshift speakers were working again. Stanley searched his radio until, luckily, he found an Eagles' song, "Peaceful, Easy Feeling." That's what he wanted. It made the ride to work more pleasant. It wasn't so much that he didn't like the job--it wasn't bad, really. But a sharp disparity existed between winning a boxing match in a tournament and taking an order for a few bucks' worth of gasoline. It wasn't that he minded it. In fact, with the unemployment rate as it was, Stanley was happy to have regular work. It was the bizarre difference: going from people cheering him to people saying "you missed a place" on their windshield. From sitting in the dressing room to sitting in the little office. Then again, when the bell rang he'd go to the center of the ring as when the bell rang he'd go to the car that had driven over the signal hose. Not so different after all.

It was the same old gas station, though, and the same old activity. He put on his white "Lo-Gas" shirt and funny blue-grey pants and old work boots, walked out to the pumps, and began. Getting the request, taking the hose down, removing the gas cap, putting in the gas, and so on. Credit cards, cash, smiling at the customer, looking around the station. Sometimes a familiar person came in, sometimes a girl who said hello and kidded a little. The girls didn't open up too much, though, because no matter who they were, no matter how he tried, there was always something there between them, something warning them: watch out, keep back, this is only a gas station attendant, don't bother with him. In the beginning Stanley had tried to overcome it, in many ways. It was so subtle. They were nice to him, but not open, not responsive. He didn't try as hard now. He had Amy.

Women were raised to look for a man who merited approval, who could give them the things they wanted. A gas station attendant was not on the list.

On the other hand, Stanley didn't hold it against them. He was sorry, though, that the social order could rule a person's behavior to that extent. He felt it should be the other way around--that people should do what they thought was right and then the social order would adhere to that.

It was frustrating to know you could be friendly to a girl but she'd still drive away, and even if you should say, "Please come back in again" or even if you attempted to get her phone number, she'd be worried, because you'd barely met. And how could they, yes, how could they? After all, you were in a gas station.

The sun set. Wind was making the colored pendants flap, and by eight it had cooled off. Not that he minded the heat. In Southern California summer didn't normally get that hot, anyway. It got hot in Atlanta, where he had spent a summer working, and in other places. But in Southern California, though it could definitely get warm--real warm--there just wasn't the intense heat one felt in other areas of the country.

He put his foot up on the desk and looked out at the gas pumps, and at the boulevard. It was a going-out night. It seemed like everybody had dates and they were heading for movies, restaurants, parties. Not everybody, of course. Some people had other things to do. Some had to work. Some were ill. Some were alone. Some were afraid.

Stanley had to pump gas.

His headache was gone, but his lip was still sore. No concussion, at least. Wonder how "Don" is feeling.

The station, being on a corner, afforded a good look at the cars going by.

<u>Too bad I'm not in one</u>, he thought to himself. <u>Going to see a movie with Amy, getting something to eat</u>. But then Stanley smiled, remembering how he'd won the bout, that he'd advanced to the finals. If he could stay in shape--even get in better shape--he could take it.

So he sat in the office and thought and watched and planned. Mark was there now to help with the customers.

What would he do <u>after</u> this tournament? Win it or not, he had to make a decision. Many at the gym were telling him he should turn pro.

Why wait? That was a big step, however. Was he ready? Pro boxing was tough. His opponents would know what's what.

With the amount of amateur fights he'd had, most anyone would say he was ready. Only it wasn't the kind of thing you leapt into and just took your chances. It had to be done right.

So--on Friday, July the 15th, 1977, Stanley wondered what to do. He sipped some of the coffee he had left from his takeout dinner. The day before, the 14th, he had won. Today he wondered what to do. And again, the thought of winning the bout made him feel fine. But already it was becoming just a memory.

9

The morning was hot. Someone was hammering nails, down the alley, outside his window. Stanley didn't feel like going to the café. What if that jerk was there? So he went to a coffee shop near MacArthur Park. He looked through the newspaper and listened to people talking nearby as he had toast and eggs. The Cincinnati Reds, a team he liked, were not doing too well. That's the way it was with professional sports. You start to root for somebody and they don't do so well anymore. Not always, but it seemed like it. After the great World Series in 1975 it seemed like this was the team. And last year too. Now, however...it occurred to Stanley that a couple of years, actually, was good. Then he thought about himself. If he waited to turn pro he might wait too long. No, no, he had many, many years left. Didn't Sugar Ray Robinson fight until he was 45?

The thing, however, was not the fact of time slipping by. It was something else. Some...fear or something. But what was he afraid of? Or was it really even fear? Sure, he was excited and concerned when he got in the ring, but that was natural. Even before, waiting in the dressing room, or walking toward the ring and thinking about getting up there. Everyone felt that, it seemed. Maybe after enough fights that wasn't as strong a feeling, but it was there. That wasn't the deal, though. It was...somehow, Stanley held back...he would be apprehensive, and hold back. He wouldn't go ahead with what he wanted to do or say. Why? Maybe he should see a psychiatrist.

The waitress refilled his cup and removed his plate. Did she feel that way too?

Other people must have fears that kept them from doing the things they wanted--kept them from saying things they wanted to. Stanley had felt he was alone with this, but no, that wasn't the truth. Many people stopped themselves from doing what they could--what they should--what they might. They'd told him so. But it shouldn't be like that. People should do, say and be what they could, what they were supposed to.

Why was it? Why did he lack aggression?

Try, that's what he should do. Take a chance.

It wasn't easy, of course. A decision to take a chance was one thing and doing it was definitely another. He could decide to do a lot of things, but doing them, well...

Stanley got up suddenly and went to the phone to call Amy.

PART TWO

She was happy for him. He'd picked her up that Saturday and they drove to L.A., talking a little, joking, kissing. Except for his run on Sunday there was time to kid around and have dinner and go to a film and talk about things and, of course, spend the night.

But Amy had been miffed he hadn't called sooner, and asked him about it on the way to L.A.

"Only one phone call. That's it. Why did you wait until today?"

"I can't explain it. I mean, Thursday I went over to George's, and we drank some beer and I...it was late. I'm sorry."

"Okay, but yesterday?" When he didn't answer: "Oh, never mind. It doesn't matter. I'm happy you won."

What else could he say? They rode in silence. Then: "I was in a funny mood yesterday."

She laughed. "How uncharacteristic of you."

"What does that mean?" he asked, looking over at her. She didn't say anything for a moment, staring ahead at the freeway traffic. Stanley began to repeat his question but she quietly said:

"I know how moody you can get. It's why I like you."

"Are you serious?"

She smiled at him. "Do you doubt me?"

"No, Amy...I guess I am moody."

"No kidding."

She warmed up to him as the afternoon progressed, as they had dinner, as they decided not to take in a movie, as they wandered Westlake. By nighttime they were in bed, making love.

It was good. She held on to him tightly, as usual--it was the only time Amy would reveal her desperation. They knew each other well and spent little time finding each other, finding the excitement their bodies produced. It was passionate, then gentle, then rough. She repeated a line from *MIDNIGHT COWBOY:* "You're the only one, Joe," as usual, lovingly.

When it was over they lay in the heat of the room, feeling the cool air from the open windows, holding each other.

At three Amy awoke. She tried not to disturb him. His body was outside the covers. Since the moonlight and the glow of the city came partly through the windows, she could see him well, and she watched him.

After a moment she slowly lit a cigarette. He didn't move. Amy smoked carefully, not wanting to wake him. Her gaze passed over his body, reaching that part which had been active, but now rested.

Amy was tempted to apply a kiss, but she didn't--it wasn't something she did, ever; she didn't know why.

Stanley had asked her to, at one time, but she couldn't. She'd wanted to...it was just that something, somehow, was stopping her. She wanted to, and yet...it wasn't him, it was a resistance, within.

As her cigarette burned slowly, Amy thought. She looked down at him again. It looked pleasant, she thought, so what was restraining her, so secretly, without her understanding? Things did that. Things pushed at you, and they held you, and you tried to figure them out, but you couldn't. It was something from her past, but she wasn't able to recall it. You should let the good be with you and the bad not be with you, was her philosophy.

In the morning, after separate journeys to the bathroom, they held each other and joked about nothing. He told her of the fight, and chipping his tooth. They had only spoken briefly of those things the day before.

"Want some apple juice?" he asked, getting up and reaching to the tiny refrigerator.

"Okay."

He poured her a glassful, gave it to her, and began to dress. She watched him. "Where do you think you're going, hotshot?"

"Have to run--'road work'--the finals are coming up in a week or so." Amy nodded, not disagreeably. But she didn't like it.

"Hurry up then. I want breakfast."

Stanley went to Elysian Park to run on the firebreak. A path went up through the woods and hills above the park. At the top you could see parts of downtown; running there always raised his spirits, brought him in touch with God, gave him a strong uplift. He thought of Amy, though, and hurried.

He had the finals to look forward to, and he wanted to win. Doing road work here made him believe he was accomplishing something--doing what was required of him to win.

It was mid-morning and hot, but the air was clean. Stanley felt, as he made his way along the curvy path, as healthy and happy as he had felt when he was in the Little League, years ago.

So he ran, enjoying the sunshine and the fresh air and being in the hills, close to the trees and dry brush.

He saw a few birds, felt the earth under his feet--strong and real. He was sweating and breathing well. He thanked God as he reached the farthest place and turned for the return run.

After he'd gotten back and showered, they climbed into his Chevy and went to Bob's Steak House. Stanley had coffee first and asked her about the night before--was it okay? "Yes, of course it was," she laughed. "What are you asking that for? Do you think otherwise?" She read the newspaper and pointed out a couple of articles. Amy was interested in events taking place around the country, and in world affairs. She had been in junior college for two years but had not gone on to a four-year school. A question of money, fear, and making a decision.

They ate breakfast while Amy read. Stanley liked her intensity; it was good to see. She cared about various issues; she had strong opinions. "What about the government?" he had asked her once. Why didn't she go into it in some way? Yes, she thought she should.

Her interest in events, trends and developments gave her face that look he loved: capable and fresh.

She commented on the state's current shortage of water. Due to the drought, water was no longer served automatically--you had to ask for it.

"And I need it more than most people," Stanley remarked, lifting up his glass.

She gave him a sardonic look. "And I need you more than most people."

Afterward, they walked. It was always good to walk after eating--a boxing tradition. The idea being that the food got to where it was supposed to go in your body faster.

They strolled along Alvarado, holding hands. Their presence added something of value to the street. It was always good to have a couple walking on Sunday in the summer--wherever they were.

A lot of people were in the park so they decided against going there; they proceeded, instead, down Alvarado past Wilshire.

"Do you believe there really is a water shortage?" Amy asked.

He thought. He didn't take her questions lightly. "I don't know. Do you?"

"Well, if there is, how could it have happened so suddenly, without anyone being prepared? I mean, we have agencies or something to be watching for that stuff."

Good point. "Yeah. It is funny."

"Maybe they want to scare us, to control us. Maybe they have a law they want to pass and this is a way to get everyone to go along with it. It's a tactic that's been used before in other countries."

He thought about that too. "Really?" He didn't like to think his country was doing such underhanded things. "That's chickenshit!" It made her laugh.

They crossed Seventh Street.

"But what about the governor--he wouldn't go along with that."

"Oh!" Amy laughed again. "He only wants to be president. He doesn't care about this state."

"Are you serious?" Amy shrugged. "Just because he wants to be president doesn't mean he doesn't care about California. Jerry Brown is a good guy, he's--"

"You wait! He'd leave office tomorrow if he could become president!"

Stanley thought about this too.

They turned, continued east on Eighth Street, for awhile, but stopped and decided to go back. It was pretty hot, and his car was still at the steak house.

On the way up Alvarado they paused by the theatre to see what was playing. Not too interesting. Then they stopped at the bookstore and went inside. Amy found a book she wanted, and Stanley bought it for her. They made their way to the car, and he drove to a shady spot near Melrose, parked, put his arm around her and smiled.

"Let's not talk politics."

Amy looked through her book. Stanley liked this restful time. He was a little tired from his run that morning. Amy had slept when he had gone to run and when he returned she was up, dressed, smiling and happy, her light-brown hair clean and brushed.

"Take a shower?" he'd asked. "You look good."

"I had to, the way you slobbered all over me last night."

In the car he started to doze, and Amy read. But before long it was too hot, and he couldn't rest, and she couldn't read. So they drove back to his apartment. Neither of them wanted to do much this weekend--both were interested in just taking it easy, being together.

So they went up to the room and relaxed. Amy took her shorts off, got on the bed and read her book. Stanley sat in the big chair and rolled up his hand wraps. He seldom had the opportunity to do this, but he wasn't going to the gym today. When he put his wet stuff out after training he normally didn't get to it again until he put it back in the bag to go to the gym. There he would wrap his hands by letting the "bandages" hang down loose as he put them around his wrists and hands. It was his routine. The only problem was keeping the ends from hitting the dirty floor, which was almost impossible. But Larry had told him to take Sunday off, giving him the luxury of rolling up his hand wraps.

Amy put her book down and turned on the radio.

"I'm bringing you a little fan next week."

Stanley shook his head. "Can't see you next week, remember? The fight's going to be Monday or Tuesday."

"Oh, right," she said, returning to her book, not looking at him.

Then she glanced up. "We don't have to have sex."

"Yeah, sure, good luck."

"No, really. I can resist. You don't like it as much as I do anyway."

"You think?"

"I wish you had a tape player," she said, after a while.

"I like sex," he said.

"Not as much as I do."

In his car, however, there <u>was</u> a tape player, so she could hear what she wanted--of what they had--when he took her home that afternoon.

Amy played "Still" from a Lionel Ritchie tape, over and over, while they drove.

The sun was beginning to set--a goodbye glow. The windows were down; Stanley could hear his muffler leak. He'd have to fix it, but it sounded good--like a hotrod.

All of a sudden Amy said: "Hey!" and when he looked over he saw she had undone the middle buttons on her blouse and pulled it open, and there were her lovely pink-pointed breasts revealed in their natural simplicity to him, and he thought how funny she was, and laughed. Then she did the buttons up, and the display was gone as quickly as it had appeared.

They kissed goodbye in front of her mother's house like teenagers on a date. She said: "Call me, asshole," and went inside.

2

When he drove back to L.A. he thought about her. She was something else, Amy.

It was a peaceful ride. He played an America tape. The wind was warm and the sky was a rich blue, even after sunset--delaying the approach of evening. Because of the ocean's flat horizon, he thought. You could see a few stars, but it wasn't quite night: the "magic hour," as they say.

When he reached L.A. it was dark, however, and he parked, went up to his room, pulled his boots off, put them back on, went down to the street, and walked to the coffee shop at Eighth and Alvarado where he had some dinner. A light dinner because in the summer in the heat he didn't always want to eat much, and that was how it was, then.

Stanley reflected on their short weekend together, on boxing, on how some people didn't like it.

Maybe they were right, maybe he was wrong to do it. Who was a boxer these days, anyway? A boxer to most people was a broken-nosed, undereducated simpleton who would be washing dishes if only he was smart enough to dislike getting hit, and if he was white he didn't have to be just a dishwasher--so Stanley had no excuse at all for doing it.

There was always someone he'd meet up with who felt it was wrong. He flinched inwardly when he told anyone what he did. They almost invariably reacted negatively, except some tried to hide it behind a fashionable curiosity. The first year was the easiest, because most people felt it was okay to be starting out, or "dabbling" in the sport. But, stand back, when it was that he was serious, when he was doing it the second year, and planning on keeping at it, now, that didn't take too well with folks, especially friends he'd had before he started. They didn't understand and didn't want to understand, for some reason or another-- which Stanley couldn't figure out. For awhile he tried talking them into it, explaining the excitement, the benefits for your mind and body, how it was safer than driving your car, good for this or that reason, but they always put up an inexplicable barrier, shaking their heads, forcing a smile and saying something like: "If you really want to do it, go for it," but not meaning a word of it. They understood auto racing for the "need to compete" and skydiving for the "thrill" or deep sea diving, with only some air in a tank on your back, for its "beautiful sights," all more potentially dangerous than boxing. But they couldn't tell him why, so he quit trying to explain it, for the most part. Occasionally he'd try again, and be unsatisfied with the outcome. Even people who hung around the gym, even <u>they</u> were not exempt from making demeaning remarks. "What are <u>you</u> doing here, anyway?" You'd think they could understand. <u>I mean, what were they doing there</u>? And when he would suggest he wanted to turn pro, well, that was really too much. That was hard for them to believe. He'd get more encouragement if he said he was going to skateboard to Tucson.

3

"Well, we have to have a champion."

Larry nodded. "Yeah, we do, but I won't choose between them. If they fight each other, I can't be in one corner or the other." He looked away. Stocky Sam, the heavy black man he spoke to, looked away also.

The two men were standing inside the gym, near the front door. It was Monday; they had come in early. Sammy watched some fighters who were training, and thought it over: two of Larry's boys had made it into the tournament finals. They were in the same weight category; they would have to fight each other, no question.

Larry didn't know what else to say. He had worked with both fighters for some time now, and he was happy they were up for the title. "They'll have to do it," he shrugged, "but I can't be in one corner or the other."

Sammy, a member of the association sponsoring the tournament, agreed. He knew both fighters well: he had taught and trained Stanley when the kid first came to the gym, years before, and coached Hershel, on occasion. "Should be a good fight, anyway. We'll just get somebody else to work with them."

Meanwhile, in his room, Stanley had some juice and cereal and peanut butter on wheat toast and geared himself up for the approaching week, for the fight. He had no idea he had to fight his stablemate. They'd known each other from the gym--boxed together and listened to Larry and used each other's equipment and gone to each other's bouts--sometimes.

Neither of them had experienced fighting a friend, or even thought about it, for that matter. Hershel had had a few more fights than Stanley, but neither of them had been around long enough for this prospect to present itself. Nevertheless, fighting a friend was something many boxers eventually encountered--a fact of life.

Hershel was good. He was fast, he was slippery. But he didn't like to get hit.

An hour later Stanley arrived at the gym, walked upstairs, said hello to the doorman, went directly to the dressing room and started taking his stuff from his small bag. He wasn't going to spar today, so he'd brought only his wraps, bag gloves, jump rope and workout clothes. Larry walked into the room. He had been out on the floor when he saw his fighter come through the door.

"So you decided to get back to work!"

"Yeah! How you doin', Larry?"

"Oh, real good." But there was something j
voice. It didn't sound carefree. "Listen..."

By the time Stanley had his shoes tied and his
wrapped he knew he was boxing his stablemate next Tuesda
knew Larry was unhappy about it, knew he was going to have
to go at Hershel plenty in order to win. Even though he
had more power than Hershel he wasn't as fast, or slick.
Why were the black fighters always so fast? Also he knew
the idea made him uncomfortable, but accepted it.

"We've got somebody else to work your corner. Bill
Cox. I won't choose between you two. Pancho's going to
work with Hershel. I'm sittin' in the auditorium, and
going to enjoy it, I hope." Larry was trying to be casual
as they walked together out onto the floor. Stanley smiled
at him and started to warm up. By the time he had
completed his workout five people--trainers, boxers,
hangers-around--had complimented him on his last fight.
One even commented that he'd won twenty dollars on it.
That made Stanley feel good, and he forgot about fighting
Hershel.

After his shower he went to the hamburger spot up the
street, as usual. It had been a good workout; he was in
good shape. A couple of days off don't hurt you when
you're there.

He had a cup of coffee. The big friendly counterman was happy to see him.

"How'd it turn out?" he asked him. Apparently he'd missed it.

"Oh, I stopped him in the third round." Jerry smiled at this. "The referee stopped it." Stanley drank the coffee, relaxing, and Jerry began serving another customer. Traffic went by on the street. Things were pretty nice, for Stanley--except he had to get to it with Hershel, next week.

Amy, at the same time, stood behind her counter at work acting cordial, taking orders, returning clean laundry, taking money, looking out the door every now and then, sighing. She missed him.

The rest of the week was unmercifully slow, for her, but it was mercifully fast for Stanley. He trained and ran and sparred and worked, and Larry helped him, and he only saw Hershel once, but it was an unpleasant experience. If he intellectualized it, it was fine--hey, they both wanted to box, they both wanted to win, they both wanted the title. No big deal.

Yet--they could hardly talk to each other, only say hello. Lucky they weren't any better friends than this, they both thought.

Finally, it was Tuesday. Stanley felt like running in the very early morning, so he did. But he didn't go to work or to the gym, of course. He listened, instead, to old records, read *A THOUSAND DAYS*, napped, and spent time in the park near the lake.

Larry didn't pick him up--Stanley drove this time. He did pick up Duke, although he wouldn't be in the corner either, and they went to the auditorium silently, only discussing things not relevant to the night. But Duke wanted to see the fight.

Larry was in the dressing room, waiting, with Sammy. It was unusual for Sammy to be there, and he said: "Good luck, son." Simple, but Stanley appreciated the gesture. He said the same to Hershel, when he arrived, and Larry told them: "It has to be this way. I want you to treat this like any other fight. Good luck to both of you. Better get ready." The trainers went out, so they undressed, put on their gear, laced up their shoes, sat in chairs--all without talking--and stared at the door, floor, and walls.

Things were happening upstairs, bouts had begun. They sat and waited. Bill Cox came in, wrapped and taped their hands, and left.

After a while Hershel looked up and said, "I'll be glad when this is over."

"Me too."

A tournament official entered, checked and marked their hand wraps, and went out. A moment later he returned with Pancho and Bill, with boxing gloves, watched them put them on, and left. Pancho had to go upstairs. Bill asked: "You guys alright?" They nodded; he left.

Then, the yelled announcement from the hallway: they were on after the next bout.

Pancho came in, sweating from having worked a fight. He nodded at Stanley and Hershel. "Come on, guys, warm up."

They warmed up, moving around awkwardly. Bill came in and led Stanley out to the corridor. "How do you feel?"

"Fine," he lied.

Before long they all went through the door, down the hall, and up into the auditorium proper. It was not as crowded as regular Thursday fight nights. This evening was only for the tournament finals, no professional bouts, no television.

But there was noise. Shouting, whistling, even from the smaller crowd. And there, up ahead, was the ring.

Stanley knew Bill, the man who was helping him, but he didn't recognize the second, who said hello, holding the ropes apart. Stanley bounced into the ring and over to the rosin box to rub his shoes in, moved around for a minute, taking deep breaths, generally getting used to the fact now but still not excited about it, wishing it was Larry with him and not near-strangers, but, hey...

--then the referee with his instructions happening too fast--way too fast--and Hershel never looking at him, even once...then back to the corner with Bill telling him to keep his left going and his hands up, and there went the bell...

--there went the bell, and the handlers suddenly climb from the ring and Stanley goes toward his opponent. It has started, with Hershel shifting to and fro with his head pulled in and Stanley attempting a couple of sticks but they are not close and he can hear yelling and such from the auditorium, not something he could usually do; and now Hershel is in on him close throwing some glancing blows and Stanley covers but he can't block them all, and throws his own right but it doesn't hit as Hershel is away, already...

--Pancho yells from the other corner and at the same time in comes the fast black opponent again and Stanley knows he must protect himself from this quickness and blocks a jab and drops to the side of another one, no time for him to counter...

--as he moves around to the left he tells himself to get in there and tries to jab but he's not balanced and Hershel slips back and then that noise from the auditorium. Why does he hear that now?

--but this very fast kid is at him again and Stanley grabs him and takes a breath and the referee pushes them apart and they move around a bit...

--what should he do? He tries to think, and knows what he should do--not wait, and let this happen, but keep his jab going--so when Hershel heads toward him again he gets ready and BANG, hits him with a good straight left, like he can...then Hershel stays away and Stanley watches him...

--and this time as his opponent comes in Stanley is ready with BANG, another solid jab...it stops him, so Stanley throws his right but Hershel gets his glove there to stop it, although the punch strikes his face a little, hard, so he grabs Stanley, knowing he, Hershel, is vulnerable now and in close flails with several un-aimed throws, holds again, and the referee pulls them apart...

--the crowd yells but Stanley doesn't hear it now, he feels better and knows this will be the way...his opponent doesn't move toward him now, but waits, so Stanley goes toward him, looking out for those quick moves, jabbing, connecting...

--but he feels something on his face...something...on the left side of his face...hot sweat, or...

--he misses with a right and a left both--Hershel is slick--steps back, begins to throw another one-two...

--in comes the referee, toward them, putting his arm in front of Stanley, halting his advance, looking somewhere on the side of his face...then he takes Stanley's arm, leads him to the ropes as Hershel backs up, gestures into the seats and there is the ring physician, up on the apron, examining Stanley's brow--but it's only slightly moist, it can't be enough to stop the bout--and the doctor says the word "Sorry" and looks at the referee and says "That's it" and Stanley stares, breathing, at the doctor, and the referee goes away waving, signaling that it's over and the doctor says "I'm sorry, Stanley" with true regret in his voice and puts something on Stanley's brow to stop the bleeding...

4

The City of Angels was quiet, but at four in the morning he woke up, thinking about the past evening's events, and remained awake. The curtains, as thin as they were, showed no movement. The moon didn't appear to be anywhere around; it was too dark outside.

Stanley sat up and put his feet on the floor. He seemed excited, of all things. He felt alive and ready to go. What was this? he wondered. Alert and anxious, he felt like there was something he had to do. He walked to the table and looked at the clock. He felt like going somewhere, anywhere, so he got his Levi's on, got a shirt on, got his boots on, grabbed his keys, went out the door and made his way downstairs.

For a change the landlady wasn't up, prowling. She oftentimes roamed around during the night muttering and writing strange things on the lobby walls with chalk, only to wipe them off the next day.

He went outside into the black night. It was almost cold. He felt so awake, so alive. Why?

There was his red-and-white car, looking like a tiger, poised in the rich darkness. Stanley went to it, got in, fired it up; it roared to life, thrusting its authority throughout the night.

He drove to Main Street, which was empty and still. The area that he knew so well had never appeared so unusual to him. The gym was closed, of course. He saw only one person walking nearby.

The coffee-shop-hamburger-spot he frequented sat as a solemn, barren enigma. Yet, as his car approached, Stanley saw there was a light inside. He pulled to the curb and could see the owner working behind the counter in the empty coffee shop.

The car went silent. A few noises could be heard on the street, from somewhere. A truck rumbling, a voice in the distance. Stanley jumped out, still propelled by a strange energy, and went to the door. He knocked and Dino opened when he saw who was there.

"Hey! Come in! What the fuck you doin' around here this morning?"

Stanley smiled, shrugged, walking in. "Well--"

"Want some coffee? Here, have a cup." He went behind the counter after rebolting the door. "Man, it's pretty early. You're not working out this early?" He poured a cup of hot black coffee, put it on the counter, waving Stanley to sit.

As he did Dino saw the bandage over his eye. "Hey, what's that? What happened to you?"

"Oh--" Stanley sipped from the cup. It was too hot. "That's, uh, two stitches. You know, it's a cut." He looked down.

Dino stared at him. "A cut? You got cut?"

"Yeah. In a fight."

A car ran by on Third.

Stanley proceeded to tell him about the fight, and getting cut, and that he thought it was from a butt maybe, from one of the times they were in close, that Stanley thought he'd been butted when his opponent was clinching to keep from getting hit since Stanley had just started to hit him with his left and his opponent couldn't keep away and probably thought he was going to have a tough time since Stanley can hit and--

"They stopped it?"

"Yeah."

Dino shook his head.

He sat quietly as Dino worked, getting ready to open for the day. Stanley drank his coffee.

"He butted you?" Dino asked him. "How come he wins, then?"

"I don't know. The referee didn't see it. He probably thought I got it from a punch. But, man, I don't think he hit me <u>once</u> with his right hand." Pointing at the bandage, Stanley was trying to explain it to himself also. "Maybe he did, though. I don't know. I never got cut before."

Dino was cleaning the stove. He'd stop when Stanley said something, return to his work when they weren't talking.

He liked Stanley. "Too bad," he said. "That's too bad."

"Yeah." It was unnerving to lose early in a bout when you were just getting started and you shouldn't have to stop. Then he realized that was why he felt so energized: they'd only just started; it didn't feel over, but it was.

After a bit Dino made him some scrambled eggs, once he had the stove on. They tasted good.

"It was for the championship, too. For the Silver Belt championship."

"The tournament's finished?"

"Yeah."

There was more traffic on the street. He was feeling better because of the coffee and the breakfast and the talking. Stanley wanted to say other things about his frustration, his sensations, his loneliness.

"I wanted to win," he finally said. Dino nodded, stacking up some cups for the day.

"It's--well, I had him, you know. I wasn't going to lose. I had him every time he came in, I was stopping him." He showed Dino the method, sticking out his left a few times. Dino watched. "That way he couldn't get close to me."

In a little while Stanley went over to the window and sat on a stool. The owner was in the back. On the sidewalk a few people were walking, most likely going to work.

His cup was empty, but he didn't want any more anyway. He'd had too much. It was time to pay and leave.

Dino unlocked the door, turned over the "Open" sign. It was getting light outside. The sun rose even on this bleak downtown area; even to this bleak and forlorn place the day came, in the midst of broken lives, dragging footsteps, sorrowful countenances. The sun even rose here.

Stanley went outside. No big thing, he assured himself. Adversity makes us strong. He put his hand up to the small bandage. Still, he was troubled. All the time and effort, and "that it should come to this." That was a line from somewhere...who said that? Shakespeare.

He drove around the city, aimless. He thought: maybe I should go to church. He went sometimes to the Seventh-Day Adventists Church. They worshipped on Saturday, which, they said, according to the Bible and history, was the true Sabbath. But, this isn't Saturday, this is Wednesday.

He continued west on Hollywood Boulevard, driving by the church, reading from the sign in front that the Saturday service would be at eleven.

He wanted to drive for a while. Later he should go to the gas station and tell them what happened. But it would be in the paper; Stanley didn't want to tell them.

Anyway, he'd go to work later. They don't really care, he thought. They talk like they do, but I'm only another person working there and, sure, there's something fascinating about boxing, but they don't really give a shit. In fact, there's something about it they don't like. Maybe they're jealous, and hate it that somebody is an athlete. But Mark is an athlete.

Two stitches. Wasn't that much. They don't let amateurs fight that long if they get cut. If a fighter is cut or getting hit a lot, they stop the bout. They won't prolong it. They let it continue if pros are doing it, because with pros the importance of winning influences any decision to stop. Even though getting cut or being hit a lot may appear crucial, often the contestant can fight back and end up winning, if given a chance. But that's the pros.

Maybe he'd call Amy. She'd be up by now. But on the other hand he felt embarrassed about it. He had to tell her sometime. It wasn't on TV, thank God. She might see a newspaper. He was getting confused, and tired. What was he doing? Why did he drive downtown and sit there all that time? He had sat in coffee shops before--but usually when they were open for business and not that time of morning. It was only a fight. Sure, it was the championship, but--

That was it. The year before, he had been in the tournament and won in the finals, and had gone to the Nationals. And now his coach was talking about him turning pro, so there would be no championship this year. He had wanted to win. He had wanted to be the 1977 Champ and <u>then</u> turn pro. Oh, how sweet that would have been. But they took it from him! He was going to win and he was butted and they took it away from him forever.

That was what mattered. <u>Justlikethat</u>, all the effort and sacrifice and time--and it was over. What now--turn pro having lost it? Of course, maybe he hadn't been butted. Hershel did have fast hands. Maybe he'd zapped

him one...

All those days training, running...now everybody will

say he should turn professional and "get that money" and be

what he's supposed to be.

As difficult as it was to box--the work on moves,

punches, blocks--and the constant negative reaction on the

part of some people--for that to be added to a loss, a loss

from nowhere, and the let-down at the termination of a

tournament, put him in a bad mood. Athletes, he thought,

whatever their endeavor, engage in an unusual, tiring,

romantic, unromantic, rewarding, empty life.

And as he drove that day, novice-division welterweight

Silver Belt semi-finalist of 1975, open-division

welterweight Silver Belt champion of 1976, open-division

light-middleweight Silver Belt finalist of 1977, gas pump

jockey, hotrod enthusiast, book-reading God-fearing

straight-talking music-loving Los Angeles resident Stanley,

cried.

5

Eventually he went all the way to Santa Monica, saw the ocean, returned and cruised by the gas station without going in. There were a couple of people there, the owner, Barry, and the daytime attendant-mechanic, Harold. Day and evening people were different. Day workers were only there temporarily, and were aware of it. But the evening workers had a more settled, relaxed attitude; though their stay might be brief, it felt permanent. It could be because the day men wouldn't accept the night work, feeling it was too dangerous. But the night men, Mark, Stanley and George, on weekends, didn't think they could get another job so quickly, and accepted the work. Anyway--robberies were rare.

The owner tried out a girl once, in an attempt at fairness, but concluded that she was not as fast because the work was too difficult, physically. Stanley wondered about that. It wasn't like the station had cars zooming through every moment. It wasn't like they lined up waiting to be taken care of. So, how was it she couldn't take a slightly longer time to do the job? It wasn't like she couldn't get it done. Stanley decided the boss had been uncomfortable with the idea.

Harold had been working for a few months. The previous mechanic had quit, unwilling to pump gas when it got busy. But Harold didn't mind. He came in early, worked on the cars, pumped gas, ate lunch and left long before Stanley arrived. But they spoke when Stanley stopped in to get his paycheck. Harold had told him: "Who cares? I'm grateful for the job."

"Barry should hire another attendant."

"He will. This is okay for now. I don't care."

That was the attitude, Stanley thought. Harold was right.

Why grieve? It was merely a fight. Against a good opponent, one who'd advanced to the finals by defeating several other men.

He parked at Melrose and La Cienega. There was a good restaurant there and he had to get something to eat. It always happened after he fought. Residual hunger.

Stanley went in, saying hello to the hostess and sitting near the front so he could see out the window.

He asked for decaf and a glass of water. A friendly busboy brought it to him. Stanley drank the water first.

He sat for some time, watching a few of the customers. A more-or-less Hollywood crowd came in there. People who either wanted to do movies or were doing them or had done them.

A fairly loud man at the table next to him was talking about someone he didn't like, loudly enough for everyone to hear.

A lot of that took place in Hollywood, Stanley had noticed. A person would be treated badly in a business deal, and would be angry and apparently have nothing to do except tell anyone he was with the story. There was often very little that might be done to salvage the situation, so they would complain bitterly. These business deals seemed to continually happen, and there wasn't time to work a problem out, especially afterwards. It was similar to boxing. If you were in shape, and you fought, whatever happened was fair (barring judge or referee bias). But due to the nature of the process, results became effective immediately--and if a person was tricked or cheated, there was little he could do about it. So the man was mad.

Stanley ate a delicious, well-done cheeseburger. The waiter who took his order was from Texas, and kept people laughing with his good-natured humor. He saw that Stanley was unhappy, and respectfully adjusted to that, although he did attempt to make him feel better. At one point he whispered to Stanley, referring to a waitress wearing tight jeans: "Looks like she <u>painted</u> them on!" After a while Stanley felt as relaxed as he had at any time since the past night's events.

He left after an hour, with a nice feeling, saying "See ya later, Cowboy," paying the check at the door, walking into the warm, sunny day, supposing that life wasn't <u>that</u> tough, after all.

The '57 started right up. It was a powerful car, thanks to George's help. Why grieve?

He drove up the wide and active La Cienega Boulevard, toward the Hollywood Hills. At Sunset he took a right, going toward his part of town. The movie world seemed to end there, and he had to head back to his own world, like it or not.

He put an Eagles tape in the player. Gradually, going eastward while the Eagles sang, the sun behind him, with last night's activity behind him, with the sound of headers and leaking pipes beneath him, Stanley struggled to accept his fate.

He remembered a fight he'd had, one of his early ones. He hadn't trained hard enough and he wasn't strong enough and he lost. For many days he'd grieved and felt stupid because he hadn't expected the fight to be that difficult. After all, he'd won his previous two, he knew he was good,

it was only a tournament for boxers with six fights or
less, he'd had four, it was only the novice division...

And he recalled his very first fight. Sammy said:
"He won't have any more experience than you." Direct
quote. But his opponent had had many fights in the
category of "junior," under age 18, before technically
turning "amateur." Stanley didn't know that, and neither
had Sam, apparently, so he lost.

That had been depressing. He'd considered giving up
boxing, but he wanted to do it. So he trained harder, ran
more often, and eventually got in there again with
confidence and strength, and lost. Once more his opponent
was too advanced. But he'd learned a lot. He won his next
two. Then he lost, too overconfident.

It's an ongoing process. You hit the bags, move
around in front of the mirror, you work as your coach tells
you what to do; he holds out those mitts, you go at them,
jab, hook, right hand, uppercut, some days you spar. You
do sit-ups. You take a shower, put your things in a bag
and say goodbye and then drive, tired, home. And if your
car isn't running, you take the RTD. You sit, pitching
back and forth as the lumbering machine rolls along on its
assigned route, and hope it goes to the right place, and it
does.

You go to your room, get on your bed so your body and mind and soul can relax. You wonder how you will fare in your next fight.

Okay, he hadn't fared too well this time.

So, you must live with what is, you must accept and adjust and go on, adhering to the simple truth that your life is what you make out of what you have.

Stanley stopped outside his apartment building, but he didn't want to go in. The huge pink building waited, mysterious and benign. He didn't want to go in, but he didn't want to go to work, either.

At that moment Amy walked into a much newer building on the campus of the University of California, Irvine. She was feeling a combination of fear and excitement, like Stanley felt so often. What she was doing, in fact, was not that extraordinary, but the implications of it were. Providing, of course, she follow through. It was, after all, only a pre-admissions day event. But as she looked for, found, and then stood in the line that would lead her to the applications, her excitement and fear increased.

It was the table for new admissions and information. The line moved, but not hurriedly.

Amy was dressed nicely. She had taken care not to be in shorts and an old blouse, attire she often wore when she wasn't working. This was her new life. This was her effort to become what she hoped to become: a college graduate.

She finally arrived at the front of the line. A pleasant, 40ish man sat at the table with several stacks of papers and a few pencils and a tired smile. But Amy's smile was full of energy.

"I'd like an application for admission to U.C. Berkeley, please."

Stanley sat pensively in his car, then finally managed to get out. He had to call Barry to ask for the day off-- that much was certain. From his perspective working today was <u>out of the question</u>. Anyway, the doctor had advised against strenuous exercise for at least a week.

He went to the pay phone in the old carpeted lobby, and called his boss.

"Hi, it's Stanley...well...I got cut over my eye...a couple of stitches...can I skip today?...yeah...see you tomorrow...thanks."

The landlady was nowhere to be seen. Good. At least that worked out to his benefit. She could be a problem when she was in one of her crazy moods. She'd pester you until you felt like swearing at her, which was something Stanley tried never to do to a lady. She had a way, though.

He went to his room, only then remembering he had to go shopping. But he sat for a moment trying to rid his mind of the despair he felt. Rational thinking didn't seem to shake it. He'd have to wait for it to go away on its own. Sometimes things were like that: no matter what you told yourself or what your feelings should be, you felt the way you did for the reasons you did, period.

At last he made his way to the corner market to purchase a few necessary items, including beer.

6

The next morning Stanley decided he would take a few days off from boxing. Perhaps even a few weeks. Just to relax a little, to think things over, to re-examine his whole life. Larry would understand. Anyway, he couldn't spar until his eye healed, so all he could do was hit the bags and shadowbox around the floor, and do light road work.

So he ate at Jim's Café, walked a bit, read awhile, rested, then drove to work with a sense of relief inside. Maybe the pressure had been getting to him. Yeah, a few days away from the gym. Have some beer, visit George and Alicia, go around the city. He parked behind the vaporous gas station, reluctant to get out. He just simply did not want to get out and go into the place. He'd have to tell about his eye, explain about the fight. He didn't want to. Maybe he'd take another day off.

But he should have called earlier. He should have said his eye hurt and he couldn't come to work. Now the boss had probably seen his car--how could he just drive away?

But he wanted to drive away. He didn't want to go in there and put on his dumb shirt and tell about the fight and put gas in cars and put can after can of cheap oil into them.

So he put his transmission into first and drove away. He would have laughed but he was too worried. As tough as a job was to get these days--and he does something like this. Was he crazy?

But, he felt good. It was what he wanted to do. Stanley drove down the street feeling better than he had since the night of the fight.

It was just one of those things you did and felt good about, whether or not it seemed like a smart move, logically. So he drove along Wilshire, trying not to think logically, trying to accept what he'd done. As his Chevy made its path down the street, he convinced himself he was participating in a free act, something supported by the Constitution, something people have a right to do, something he'd gone to Vietnam in order to preserve.

Of course, he'd phone. He'd have to phone in. But this was startlingly enjoyable--throwing off a burden, albeit temporarily. When you did it you threw off its claim on you, showing there was no claim, that you were a free human being. As he drove farther away he almost wanted to sing, he felt so good. His parents must have been right--he was irresponsible. Ha!

But now what? He'd say he didn't feel well enough, yet, and that was the truth. He'd say when he got to work, faced with the prospect of it, he just couldn't go through with it, that work represented a physical activity which appeared too difficult to him. Also true. The owner would not like it--he seldom liked anything that meant a customer might have to wait and possibly leave without being serviced. But that was how it had to be, and that was exactly what Stanley said when he called. And of course Barry didn't like it, asked him to come in. But Stanley was firm.

"Alright, kid. I'll have to stay until Mark shows up."

"I'm sorry."

"See you tomorrow." It was like a warning.

"Tomorrow, for sure."

Stanley drove to Sunset Boulevard and cruised along the so-called "Strip." This time of day there was no action whatsoever. But he didn't need the "action." He didn't want to see crowds on the sidewalk, expensive cars, neon signs, beautiful people.

The sun was bright. Elvis was on the radio--"Heartbreak Hotel." Two men waited at the curb and crossed the street when Stanley stopped for a red light.

A well-dressed woman crossed from the other side. She didn't look at Stanley, but he looked at her. So did the two men, as they passed by.

Larson, you got nothing to worry about. And you can see Amy this weekend. Cool. The light turned green; he drove on, feeling free.

7

L.A., during summer, was unlike other parts of the nation. It had its unclean factory air combined with the best of all air--from the nearby sea--mixed with the dry tasting desert air from the east, held in place by the "emersion layer," giving the "basin" an atmosphere that practically defied description.

On windy days you felt refreshed and full of life--on non-windy days you wondered if you were indoors or out-- whether a transparent top had been placed over the city-- which, in fact, was true: the emersion layer, a temperature phenomenon.

Windy days this unclean air was blown away, providing starry, warm, clear evenings, welcomed by the denizens of Angel-town with smiles and inner longings. They consciously appreciated this quality of living, and unconsciously sensed the past--of Indians, Spaniards, pioneers, men and women who walked the shores, grew crops, hunted, fished, made adobe to build missions and homes in order to live in this bountiful length of land on the edge of a peaceful sea, a land alive with timber, deer, eagles, lakes of quick fish, with rocks to sit on, and rest.

Non-windy days this unclear air clung to the hills, to the trees, to the buildings, and the denizens of Angel-town felt depressed, choked by smog and heat, questioning their decision to live here. At least, so it seemed to Stanley.

Lying on his bed that evening, Stanley attempted to figure out what he should do. He wanted a change from the gas station, but how? He wanted to get away from the gym, for now, and yet it seemed impossible. There wasn't much in his bank account, and finding another place to work may not be easy. Larry would be upset about his getting out of condition and would be concerned that his fighter may not come back.

He had to do something. As he put his beer bottle on the floor he closed his eyes, visualizing Amy's soft blonde-brown hair and her tender mouth. A horn honked in the street. He thought of L.A. with its water shortage, its gasoline shortage a few years before, of the substantial earthquake a few years before that, of the occasional hill fires, burning brush and long-worked-for houses so rapidly, of the political assassination and riots in the 60's, the crime, the grime, the traffic.

Rain had not come to Southern California for a long time. Water was being diverted from upstate in order to supply the people in and around L.A. The drought was making people think things weren't as good as they had believed. An uneasy feeling accompanied the realization that something as important and basic as drinking water was in any way difficult to obtain.

He thought how these events made people strong, able to withstand difficulties. And the penniless, brave Latinos who come to L.A. to improve themselves, to help their families back home; they have the strength of the Padres who came before them, empty-handed but strong-willed. Stanley opened his eyes, picked up his beer, took a drink, put the bottle on the floor again. He stretched out, feeling sorry for the Indians who had been here first, who had been displaced, shunned, killed.

There were hardships all around that many people didn't care to endure--imperfect air, distances requiring time and effort and expense, rush-hour, winter fog that shut down airports and patio restaurants with ease and made driving a danger above normal, unusual characters who roamed the streets at night, hitchhiking and hustling, selling and buying drugs, stealing, murdering. But the Santa Ana winds would come suddenly and blow away every imperfection, it seemed, the filth and dust, removing it to the sea in a rush of warmth, and people would dress as on a tropical island. You knew you were embraced by the desert and the sea and the mountains and the sky, you saw happiness in place of weariness, you sensed potential rather than weakness. At least, Stanley did. He fell asleep, the night air circulating.

Amy walked to the door, at work, looking across the parking lot, wondering how to tell him. Behind her the noise of the dry-cleaning plant droned on. She had to tell him she was going to leave for Berkeley, to start the fall semester. Even though it was less than a thousand miles away, it might as well be ten thousand. He won't understand. He'll think I don't care about him. He'll say it's my way of running. But he's wrong. That's not the truth. I'm not running away.

She watched a car pull onto the street, lit a cigarette, took a drag. The place wasn't busy today, at all.

PSALM 109:23   I AM GONE LIKE THE SHADOW WHEN IT DECLINETH: I AM TOSSED UP AND DOWN AS THE LOCUST.

She remembered it from Sunday Bible Class, years ago. She'd memorized it.

Just have to tell him. Just have to explain it to him. It's not him, it's me. I have to go ahead, have to make something of myself.

Stanley parked behind the gym and tried to prepare himself for the talk. He got out, gave a dollar to the parking attendant, went to the entrance of the old building, went up the cold, familiar stairs.

Larry was working with a young fighter at one of the heavy bags, a towel in his hand. Stanley felt strange. It shouldn't be this hard. Larry won't like it, but he'll say okay.

Amy sat in her chair behind the counter. No one was in the front now and, anyway, she felt like it. You have to sit down sometime.

He'll understand. He knows that we're different. His boxing and the things he does are very important to him. I need to do something that's important to me.

Stanley explained how he wanted to take off for a while. How the training and the tournament had gotten to him. How life sometimes leads you to things that might not appear right, from the outside, but were right, after all.

Larry shook his head. He plainly didn't like it.

"Shit, man. You've been coming along good. This is a mistake. You've made a lot of progress, especially this year."

"I know, but...what I want to do is, ah, wait awhile. To relax a little."

"You don't need to relax now." Larry watched his other fighter pound the bag. "You need to keep at it. You're built up now."

Stanley looked around unhappily.

"Let your cut heal. Take it easy for a week or two. All I want you to do is be in here every day. You won't have to do no hard training."

"I know. That's not the point. I need to get away from it for awhile."

Larry laughed his loud, friendly laugh, a laugh Stanley had become accustomed to. But it had an edge to it now. "Oh man! This is really something."

The bell sounded. The young fighter went away, moving around, breathing in and out.

"Shit..." Larry looked Stanley straight in the eyes. "I know what you want. You just want to do some soul-searching. Isn't that it?" Stanley smiled in agreement. He was relieved. "I know, Stan, I know. Some soul-

searching." He stepped over to his other fighter to wipe
his face with the towel.

Amy sat quietly at the wooden table in Elysian Park
and looked at him. Stanley's face revealed the unhappiness
he was feeling. He, in turn, was looking at the empty
wrappers and milk cartons on the table.

A few children were playing softball nearby. Their
shouts were the only things the two could hear. Around
them the tall trees waited and the wide sky watched. Amy
was holding firm. "It's not you, it's me."

Stanley sighed. "Yeah, I know. It's been tough on
you, only being here on weekends, not having a real life
down there."

"But it's more than that. We're just too different.
You live one way and I live another." No, that wasn't what
she wanted to say. Too coarse. She wanted to say it more
gently.

"<u>Ahhh</u>, you don't have to explain it. You feel the way
you do. Simple." That wasn't what he wanted to say. He
wanted to stop her.

"We had a lot of great times--I just have to get away.
I have to go back to college. I can't sit around doing

nothing for myself. Not that being with you is nothing.
What I mean is, my life is at a standstill."

He understood--it was more than her going to Berkeley.
"We're breaking up, then." He glanced at her, waiting.

"I suppose so," she said, and sat silently. If she
said she loved him, that would make it more difficult.

"I love you," she said, anyway.

"I know."

There were tears in her eyes, now.

PART THREE

Stanley had also taken Friday off, before seeing Amy. On Monday he went back to work. The boss, who came on cordially to customers, was particularly insensitive when Stanley returned. Instead of accepting the explanation that: "Some things went wrong but now it's better," he demanded more information and was hostile when Stanley reluctantly offered a few well-chosen words about "personal difficulty."

"What?"

"My girlfriend left me."

"That all?" he laughed. But he took him back, because he knew he had a good worker and he knew what kind he'd had in the past. Not that he let Stanley in on it, not that he would say how much he appreciated him. What he would do was use it as an excuse, in the future, to not give him a raise.

Standard b.s., thought Stanley. People, men mostly, were often jealous of him, for some reason, and took it out in secret ways. They would pretend something else was the problem, but Stanley knew the truth. They would overreact, or say something that didn't make sense, or try to trick him one way or the other. He'd seen it many times. They would struggle to win a victory over him that had nothing to do with what was going on. At least that's how he figured it.

Stanley had few friends, as a consequence. Hidden jealousy set him apart from most men; they were unable to sustain a relationship. He didn't think it was his fault. This had occurred even in elementary school and remained a pattern throughout his life. They would try to trick him or cheat him or defeat him in some way--financially, physically, mentally, socially--and he wouldn't understand until it was nearly over. They would hurt him, and he wouldn't know why. He found most men were unable to be with him or talk to him with any true closeness because of their fear or hate or whatever it was, which essentially ruined any possibility of enduring friendship. He didn't know what caused it. Once, in high school, a classmate had confessed he was jealous of him, but didn't reveal the reason.

That's why Stanley was grateful for George's friendship. Here was a person who did not have a problem with Stanley, who could be a friend, could offer help when needed, could spend time without cheating him or hurting his feelings, like others. While others would express sarcasm, even ridicule, George was supportive and kind and wasn't bothered by Stanley's success. And he sympathized with his losses. But George (and Alicia) were exceptions to the rule.

Once at a party in college a drunk student asked him: "Hey, how does it feel to have everything?" Stanley hadn't known what to answer--he certainly didn't think he had "everything." He just laughed it off. But it was a clue to the mystery: others believed he had "everything." Like the boss's reaction. What really bothered Barry was something else, something that was <u>not</u> Stanley missing a few days because of a problem. He wanted Stanley to think that was it, but it wasn't. He should have readily understood that something had occurred to cause this diversion from normal habits, but Barry was unwilling to let it be that. He scoffed at the reason. He had to make Stanley the bad guy, had to come off like the bigshot. Why? Did he think Stanley had "everything," too?

Only God must know, Stanley decided. It's a dilemma he'd faced all his life, in school, in the military, even at the gym. Better fighters took pleasure in pounding him inappropriately, trying to hurt him when they were only supposed to be working with him. The first few times it had surprised him, but then he learned: don't get in there unprepared.

The previous Saturday night he lay in a tired condition in bed in his room. It was quiet outside. He'd dropped Amy at her house, driven back sadly. This was no fun. He wasn't boxing. Amy was gone. He didn't have much more than a hundred dollars to his name.

He looked at the old centerfold picture on the wall-- "Barbara." Wonder what she's doing? He reached under the covers, grabbing himself. But stopped. He didn't really want to do that. He needed something else. It seemed like that was it, but that wasn't it. He tried to sleep, and finally did.

Sunday morning was a beautiful one at the Cambria Building. The sun shined brilliantly on the old pink stone structure, and crept into Stanley's room, waking him up.

After sleeping fitfully, with confused dreams, he rose and launched into the day characteristically, with hope and fear and strength. By his second cup of instant coffee he was swept up in new thoughts about what to do.

The sorrowful outlook that had attached to him the night before returned with brazen authority and began to work him over, slowly:

Every day that goes by degrades my condition, and the more out of shape I become the more painful it will be to get back into shape, and the less inclined I'll be to do it.

And on top of that, he thought, coming out the courtyard to the street with its cars and people, what do they care?

They don't care what happens to me. Why should they? I'm just some guy trying to be a professional boxer. If that's it. Maybe I don't really want that. Maybe I want to do something else. The gas station is no good. That isn't where I should be. But what? Oh, sure, I wanted to be a reporter, once. But that requires more school. I can't just walk into the *L.A. Times* building and get a job. He headed up the street to Jim's Café.

There's carpentry. I liked that, didn't I? He'd worked as an apprentice one summer after quitting college. But how could I get into the union? Just walk in the door, say I made some stuff for a real carpenter, light-years ago? Oh, sure.

It's action I like. Something with a little action.

Working indoors would be a drag. A businessman or something. Uh-uh! Not me. There was that class on psychology--that was interesting. But what can I do with that? Spend five or six more years to get a degree? You have to study medicine first. Not to mention the cost. And then being inside all the time. Fuck it.

He ate breakfast. It was crowded inside the café.

I took pictures for the high school yearbook. But that's a hard job to get, too. Wonder how Felix got into it on *THE ODD COUPLE*. More training, I guess.

Anything but that factory! No way. All day doing the same thing over and over again. You had to stack up sheets of metal for hours, stack up cans, load a freight car with box after box. Run a wire around them, over and over, tying them up. Stack after stack. Take them off the conveyor and put them on a skid. All day long.

What am I? The last of some breed of people who didn't want to sit in a classroom? Wanted to get out in the world and do it? Or what? Do I just want to be a fighter, and that's why everything else is unattractive to me?

What if I go to the gym, get in shape, fight a few times, turn pro, fight a few more and start losing? Then what? Go back to the gas station? Loaf around the gym? Try to manage a fighter and be despondent because he's doing it and not me? Drink a lot of beer and wonder what went wrong? That's no way to end up. In a few years I'll

be way into my thirties--then what? Hope I latch on to a
good job? What about a wife? How can I take care of a
wife? And a kid? They have to have nice things. Can't
just eat and sleep.

He had some more coffee. Too much--but it was warm
and pleasant. Sammy had told him to try to drink only a
cup or so a day, but it was hard to resist. Stanley
usually had three, four, sometimes five each day. When you
run and work out all the time it must go right out of you.
But now I'm not running and working out.

What's going to happen? My life is like a long stream
fighting its way over rocks and through fields, onward to--
where? He smiled. That was pretty good. Poetic. But how
do you make a living writing poetry? You don't. Better go
back to short stories.

What will I do now? I already won the Silver Belt
tournament, last year, so why try anymore? Yet turning pro
is such a major thing to do. Suddenly they all watch you
to see how you're doing. Public scrutiny. They want to
know everything about your life. Amateurs can just run
around and learn stuff, but being a pro is a different
story. You have to be in top shape, you can't take off for
weeks at a time, you have to talk to the press if you win
because you are, after all, white, and after all, who will

be your next opponent and how come you box anyway and all that shit they'll say and ask and lay on you and grab from you. What about a reporter who thinks you shouldn't do it, and says so, and angers you, and you don't know what to say but you must--so what can you say? "Oh, I love it"? They'll want to know why and you'll say: "Well, would you ask a miler that, even though he goes through a lot to run a race? Do you begrudge him that? Do you denounce him for that? Do you have to belong to a struggling minority to love it and want to do it?" "But why," they'll persist, "why do you?" And you'll say, "I love it, it's a great sport," and they'll look amused and you'll say, "Maybe God wants me to do it and thereby reveal that hard things can be done with God's help." That should go over well.

He sat at the counter musing. Skinny, grinning Jim himself was there that morning. "Hey, kid--what happened to your eye?"

"Cut in a fight. First round." Jim shook his head.

"Well, don't worry about it. I've seen you, you're a good fighter."

"Thanks."

Stanley's thoughts went back and forth like familiar vehicles, stopping at signals, darting right and left, leaving, returning, zooming off in another direction.

He paid for his breakfast; the city was calling him to walk and look and listen, so he did. He left his car on the street near the Cambria--wouldn't get a parking ticket on Sunday--and went east, then north.

He reached First Avenue, still wondering what to do when all of a sudden he had an urge to hear Jackson Browne. So he turned, made his way to his room, switched on the tiny record player, placed one of his albums on and began hearing that beautiful, melancholy "California Sound," taking him from painful thoughts to pleasant thoughts. He sat in his chair, closed his eyes, found a little peace.

2

The rest of the week went by slowly. Stanley worked, slept late, read, hung out in the park, did laundry, and then went to church on Saturday. The structure was built like a futuristic fortress--it didn't look like a church. He followed his usual routine: slipping past the eager group at the front, taking a program from the person in the foyer, glancing at the posters and information on the walls, zigzagging by the other smiling people before they realized he was relatively new and approached him, then waiting a moment for the committee announcements to be made before going in. If he was lucky, he could enter after the opening hymn began, stand in the back until it was completed, and find a place to sit.

Everything else he generally enjoyed. Praying, reading the program, studying the people, listening to the sermon. In this church there were many minorities. Stanley felt he too was one--he could relax there, once he got in.

However, today the sermon was political. The Seventh-Day Adventists were normally concerned about freedom--and that was the topic this time. Stanley hoped the message would be broader, though. He wanted to hear something that would help him in his life, in his search, and inspire him--but the man who spoke had other plans. He was a visiting pastor, from somewhere--Stanley didn't catch it--and he tried, the entire time, to express concern for the nation's future. His sermon centered on the inevitable enforcement of so-called "Sunday laws" which would force people to worship on the first day of the week rather than the last, as had been the situation in biblical times.

"The crisis our world faces in questionable supplies of raw energy resources will bring this about," he said. "The government will require people to forego work totally for one day a week in order to save energy. Therefore, people will be compelled to work on the true Sabbath--Saturday--and worship only on Sunday.

"The world is teetering on the brink of destruction!"

Stanley disliked that sort of talk. Generally he didn't hear it during these services.

The congregation of regulars became restless. But Stanley waited, hoping something inspirational might come from the speech.

Yet it went on, growing even gloomier. The guest speaker told them, "If you didn't comply with this future law you'll be accused of being unpatriotic and finally tossed into prison." The audience was told that President

Carter had signed a similar law when he had been governor of Georgia. Well, almost. The statute <u>sort</u> of said the state could pass such a law if--something. The visitor didn't explain it fully. "But you see that basically our President is for it"--as if a thing he did years before, a thing the preacher wasn't fully explaining, constituted proof that he would follow a similar path now.

Stanley wondered if the speaker had ever done anything in the past that he today might do differently. Or was that too much to ask?

It finally ended. There was a request for money to send a magazine to government officials alerting them to the problem of possible future encroachment of the freedom to worship. Stanley wondered if anyone would read it when it arrived at their office, but donated a dollar anyway.

Outside, feeling less than inspired, he realized summer was more than half over. It was a change that occurred inconspicuously, but had an effect on the residents nonetheless, a change that disturbed people because they weren't altogether ready for it--they wanted more time to do what they wanted, to go to the beach, to sit by a swimming pool, to camp in the mountains, to picnic

in the park. They felt pressured to complete one activity,
finished or not, and go on to the next.

It was a subtle pressure. The nature of most L.A.
inhabitants, being more or less a desire to "achieve" and
"enjoy," caused them to view the passage of summer and the
impending presence of autumn as an unwelcome prospect
fraught with underlying dangers. It meant a new and a
different effort was needed, with altered attitudes and
rearranged modes of behavior. Less playtime required
adjustments. This requirement placed new, unwelcome
demands on a people who had developed successful patterns
for the summer--tanning, relaxing, party-going--and here
came the cooling remainder of 1977, whether they were ready
or not. Also, the difficulty in knowing exactly when
summer would end created consternation over this
uncomfortable, enigmatic death to defined days, a passing
as it were from this to that without a specific awareness
of how and when it was taking place. So, for a period of
uncertain weeks in the southwest, a peculiar suspense hung
in the air, as warm days grew colder. Or so it seemed to
Stanley that lazy L.A. day.

He went to a Hollywood bar, "The Little Orient,"
attempting to thwart the sensation. It was a small bar, a
distance from the major night scene. But Stanley enjoyed

it, especially during the daytime. There were usually one or two sexy dancers up on small stages. While loud rock-and-soul music played from the jukebox--Earth, Wind and Fire, the Commodores, the Stylistics--they moved and wiggled and smiled and occasionally stared off, distantly, thinking of someone or something. A lost boyfriend, perhaps. Of course there was no touching or fondling allowed.

Beer and wine, that was all. "The Little Orient" was run by two sweet girls from Formosa, Genie and Angie. Stanley occasionally forgot which was which and had to ask. Right now he wanted to sit down and have a beer and watch the dancer and smile at her and think about being in a bed with her and...

"Hi! Can I help you?" It was a friendly girl, Genie or maybe Angie, behind the bar.

"Yeah, ah, hi!" He looked at the price list on the wall. He'd seen it many times before, but always looked at it. "A Coors. A bottle of Coors, please."

She brought it; it was icy cold. He gave her a ten, she went for his change. He took a good sip from the chilled bottle which reminded him of the Philippines, eleven years earlier.

The girl dancing nearest him was on a platform behind the bar. Stanley watched her. She was wearing the tiniest of costumes, blue and sequined with short tassels. She worked away, clutching a few dollars in her hand--tips. The girls sometimes tucked them into their outfits, somehow, but she didn't have enough bills for that, probably. The bar only had a few men in it. It was early in the day. Later, in the evening, many more would come in.

"Thank you, honey." The Oriental girl--or was she Asian?--and what was the difference?--brought his change on a small plastic tray, then walked away. Stanley looked at the money, deciding to keep it there since he figured on having another.

He glanced toward the open door; there was a large curtain which billowed in the wind. He could see a car drive by occasionally outside when the wind parted the curtain. He drank his beer, he watched the dancer's legs, looked at her flashy shoes, her painted toenails, her bare belly, her smooth, soft arms, and tried to get a glimpse of her breasts beneath the fabric that hid them. They were round, small, and tender, but he couldn't get a good look at them.

He took another sip, trying to think what the tips of them must be like, must taste and feel like. The girl was wiggling, dancing, turning to the loud sound of the jukebox.

After another Coors he went onto the street, leaving his hotrod where he'd parked it, and strolled deeper into Hollywood. There was a special kind of human music to the area. It must come from the many different tourists who traveled here and then went away--that, and the eclectic assortment of shops, hot dog spots, bars, Army Surplus, bookstores, movie houses, drugstores, clothing stores, and the office buildings that were from times gone--Jean Harlow times--detailed, marble, as if the past was still here. Cops cruised in unmarked cars, looking for crimes and criminals the tourists didn't think much about--but benefited from the police presence, nevertheless.

Stanley strolled, looking at the stars engraved on the sidewalk, reading the names, not recognizing them all. Then he went into another bar. But its atmosphere irritated him. He didn't want to have a drink there. Strange guys looked strangely at him, and anyway, there weren't too many girls. He left and walked further, crossing the street. He wanted another beer but couldn't seem to find the right spot. Finally he reached Hollywood and Vine, found a fairly nice place. It was small and had

a calm sensibility. So he had a beer, cheaper than at the

"The Little Orient"--no dancers--and relaxed. Or tried to.

Things were still bothering him--his life--but he wasn't as

worried now.

It was still light outside when Stanley made his way

from that bar in search of another. He was feeling

depressed, like he wanted to be in a fight. He knew that

was not a good idea, but he felt that way.

Being in a street fight solved little. Whatever was

gained from it seldom matched its cost. However, Stanley

felt that urgency, the gloomy, frustrated anger that

promoted it. He wasn't sober, after those beers, and he

hadn't eaten supper.

Something was worked on him, though, that saved him

from finding a fight. He knew of a bar on Melrose where

the clientele might serve as enemies. He could get into

one there very quickly, but...

The Lord must have kept him from it. There wasn't any

other explanation. Something was telling him that it

wasn't fair. A street fight entailed different things than

boxing, yet it was basically the same, and he had an

advantage. Also there was the risk of getting an injury or

causing one, like when he hit that guy who was insulting

him at George's one night, two years back, and hurt his right wrist. Not to mention the guy's jaw. Stanley felt sorry about that and wished he had apologized to him later.

But did he need to be concerned about injuring himself? Was he going to keep boxing? Would an injury interfere with his training if he wasn't training? Not likely.

He got a Coney Island hot dog and a Pepsi, and went back to his room, wishing he could apologize to that guy. Maybe George knows where he is. He'd been a neighbor, or something. Love thy neighbor as thyself. Shit, he felt bad now. Maybe he should go into preaching. Yeah. But that might not be his exact calling.

He went to bed early after eating an apple and some chips. Big dinner. The noise outside helped him go to sleep--a form of therapy. People on the sidewalk, traffic on the street. Since his apartment was upstairs, in the rear, the noise wasn't too bad. It was okay.

3

Stanley awoke desiring water and drank two glassfuls at the sink. He knew that by not working out his mind and body were losing their strength, their health. He was thirsty after drinking a few beers the previous evening-- more thirsty than usual. And he craved caffeine. Of course he needed to have food also, soon after coffee, but now it was the quick "lift" the coffee would provide that he desired.

"Lift," he said and laughed as he walked around his room, stretching a little and moving his head. Was he going crazy? He looked at the sunlight on the curtains, closed his eyes and said a prayer, asking for help in what he did this new day.

He made it to the shack around the corner after getting dressed and going out into the sharp sunlight. Skinny Jim wasn't there this morning. He overheard talk about the sports of the day, of the current political situation in L.A., the heat--and naturally, the water shortage.

"Man, you gotta <u>ask</u> for a drink of water, even on a hot day like this!" The complaint came from a tired-looking, unshaven customer at the counter.

"Yeah," the cook agreed. "It's a shame," he said as he put the water the customer had requested on the counter. It was a large glass, showing the café had feelings even as it complied with the governmental request for California restrictions. The disgruntled customer accepted it gratefully.

"Tell ya, Joe, this is just bull," he said after awhile, looking over to Stanley and back at the cook. "There's no problem with water. No way. The government is trying ta control our lives."

This remark caused a slight sensation among the other customers. The cook went to his stove, quietly.

"Sure," the man continued, glancing around again. "They're just trying ta see how much they can do ta us. If we go along with this, then we'll go along with something else. How do we know there's a <u>real</u> shortage? Huh?" He took a drink of water. "They want us ta feel like we have no control over nuthin', that things are out of our hands. That way they can do a lot of shit, 'cause we let 'em.

"If they want ta get our vote on something, or build something, now they can!"

Stanley drank his coffee. <u>Amy would agree with that</u>. Another man and a woman at the counter joined in the conversation. Joe went on with his cooking. Everyone had an opinion about the man's comments.

In late summer there were mixed-up days--overcast and muggy, then hot and dry. The day Elvis died was a hot, muggy day. And it rained, finally. It was as if God made it rain on a day that was meant to be hot, as if the year's temperature plan could not be interrupted, except on that day God wanted to show His anger yet not disrupt His original plan. Elvis' death didn't seem right--perhaps someone on earth was responsible, and God was unhappy because of it.

Yes, but this particular day, a week before that rainy day of Elvis' death, was not too hot for Stanley Larson. He appreciated warm weather. It gave him a good feeling, a healthy, happy feeling. Cold made him feel unsafe, but hot weather made him feel like he was well, that things would grow, that everything would be alright. Perhaps he was recalling past summer vacations, how good it felt to enjoy freedom, for a time.

He got some gas and drove around in his Chevy after breakfast, thinking about Amy. He wasn't over her yet.

She stayed in his mind like a tropical breeze, always reminding him of what was, what is, someplace. When did she say she was leaving? He thought of her laughter-- lively, like birds going as a group from one spot to another, like rain showers dashing down briefly, leaving things clean, moist, fragrant. Poetry. He should write that sometime.

He thought of how tender her legs were, with their freckles, their gentle way of relaxing, their way of exciting, of enticing him. Where the soft panties were, always attracting, beckoning, calling. And the gorgeous mound beneath them--oh, how he would like to feel that again. But, she was gone. He had to accept that. He had to live with that.

It was difficult to get over someone; it was more unyielding than other losses. If you tried to not think about the person, you did, and if you tried to think them out of your mind it became more painful. For some reason you kept hoping you'd be reunited. It didn't settle that that was it; you constantly dreamt up ways of being back with the person--except they wouldn't work and you had to finally go along with it.

Getting through that was going to be difficult, but he had done things that were not easy before. The thing to do was ask the Lord's help--He would take you and your burden and get you to where it was okay. You had to do that: ask sincerely for His assistance.

Stanley pulled over to the curb and did just that, there on the side of the road. He placed his hands together and closed his eyes and prayed in Jesus' name for the help needed. He was in a red zone near a corner, the northwest corner, of Sunset and Gower. Cars went by without people appearing to notice. Tears began to fill his eyes when his prayer came to a close.

Then he drove up to Griffith Observatory. It was a good drive through faintly green hills and the dark tunnel and, of course, with a partial view of the city. As a result of the drought the shrubbery and trees were very dry. The road itself was hot, a fact that could be sensed from inside his car. Stanley cruised, letting his left arm hang down outside the car door. Since he was wearing a T-shirt his bare arm felt warm in the bright sun. Slowly, as he drove, he tapped his fingers, feeling the heat of the painted metal of the door, enjoying the collective harmony of driving, sunning, tapping, steering with this right hand, pushing down and easing up on the gas pedal, watching the road turning and rising and lowering in front of him, his body leaning from one side to the other as the car turned, alternating, varying directions. He applied the brakes occasionally, shifting, like some instrument introduced while a band was playing. So he proceeded, sensing his new life, appreciating the world around him, the experience of what was happening, listening to the surrounding woods and the tires on the pavement and the air blowing through the car's interior.

He stopped at the observatory and stood at the front, then walked around to the other side, to see the City of Angels. A few people were there, putting coins into and peering through telescopes. The big one stood over them all, aimed at heaven.

What were these people looking for, Stanley wondered? They were looking for peace. Now why would he think that? Because it was true, that's why. They were just people looking around, but he sensed from their talk and their interest they were looking for peace. They weren't looking at homes, at buildings. They wanted peace even though it was elusive. They had enough of trials and tribulations. Peace was there, somewhere, and they knew it.

The effects of last night's perusal through several watering holes had begun to recede. The water, the coffee, the food, the ride into the hills, the sunshine, the profound work done by the body as time progressed--led him eventually to clear-headedness, and breathing the somewhat purer air up at the observatory before beginning his descent into the swirling city gave Stanley a refreshed sensation. As he drove downward he searched the radio for a good song, but couldn't find one. Then he had the idea to go to a club with live music to see a performance. Why not? He didn't work Sundays, he had the evening free. Maybe Linda Ronstadt was performing!

As the day progressed he ate two tacos from Burrito Village, on Hollywood Boulevard, and felt the food begin its process of enlivening, strengthening. It wasn't the same as when he was training; the process wasn't as effective. But his body gladly received nutrition, even if it wasn't using the food as well.

In the paper he saw that Linda _was_ performing next month at the Universal Amphitheatre. But that was too long to wait, even if he could get a ticket. Someone named Rosy Sanchez was appearing at the Troubadour that evening. He'd never heard of her. No matter. He'd hear her tonight. But the show wasn't until nine o'clock. What to do now? Go by the gas station to talk with George? Go to the gym? No, no. It was too late, anyway; it closed early on weekends. Write some poetry?

Finally he decided to see a movie on Hollywood
Boulevard, *STAR WARS*. But it wasn't much fun without Amy.
He left before the big battle and had a beer at "The Little
Orient." Francine, his favorite dancer, was there, but two
guys were on the stools near her--although she did wave at
him. Anyway, he didn't want to drink too much--had to go
to the Troubadour later. As he drove away he recalled
seeing Linda Ronstadt there. She'd sung "Silver Threads
and Golden Needles," among others; he could still visualize
it.

Stanley cruised along Wilshire toward the Cambria, the
pink crumbling Cambria with its hacked-up plants in the
courtyard, where perhaps at this very moment the crazy
landlady was hacking them up with a hand tool in the eerie
light from the lobby. It was a frightening sight,
something he'd confronted before when returning from work.
He usually tried without success to get by her to the
lobby, but more often than not she'd notice him and assail
him with a barrage of abusive non sequiturs, improbably
charming, as if in her hate there was a plea, an attempt to
be liked. Stanley couldn't deal with that, however,
because her comments were so intrusive and scary.

Usually it was something like:

"Are you here to help, son? Wait! Are you someone who will help?"

Not responding, he'd get to the front door. But she'd follow with that gardening tool.

"So who cares?" she'd yell, sarcastically.

He'd get to the stairs.

"Why are you running away?" That was a common remark of hers.

That made him mad, but he'd go up the stairs. She'd say something else but he couldn't hear it completely. It usually sounded like a threat, of some sort.

Maybe it was, he'd think, getting his keys out and opening the door to his room. She tended to make odd threats, especially when he didn't answer her.

But she wouldn't be in the courtyard now. Too early.

He sat in his chair and looked out the window. The evening was waiting outside. He had some fear about tonight and wondered where it came from. But since he usually felt a little stress going to a club, Stanley figured this evening was no different from the others in that regard.

He worked on a "haiku" about his college girlfriend. Seventeen syllables. First line had to have five syllables: "She and me with friends." Or is it "her and me"? No, "She and I with friends." Second line had to have seven syllables: "Group at table--two alone." Cool. Third line had to have five syllables: "We drank our kisses." No--"Drinking kisses down." That's it.

Then at eight-thirty he was out the door, having put on fresh Levi's, a western shirt, his good cowboy boots, his old cowboy hat, and his lucky gold Tony Lama coin with a chain on his belt loop on the right side.

The landlady was in her office behind the hotel-style counter in the lobby, and Stanley tried to get by as quietly as possible without being ridiculous about it.

Then he was out in the courtyard in the evening air, hearing his heavy heels hitting the walk, smiling to himself, getting into his car, starting the powerful engine, turning the wheels toward the Troubadour, feeling the eagerness inside like the first time he got into the ring, wondering why he felt like this--like something was going to happen, something good.

Then he was there, parking his car, heading toward the open door up to the guy standing by the---*oh, he heard a sweet sound*...Rosy Sanchez, he guessed, singing. It was coming from inside, and the music sounded good too, better than on tapes or records because it was louder or something

--<u>live</u>, that was why it sounded so good, and she was live too. The guy sold him a ticket and said something about trouble finding a seat, but Stanley didn't care about sitting down, he just wanted to go in to see her. He got inside and there was this singing, jouncing vision of loveliness holding a tambourine in her left hand and a standing microphone in her right hand like Linda did, smiling and flashing her eyes between words and parting her lips and closing her eyes while she sang.

He made his way around and between the tables and customers and waitresses without taking his eyes off her except for but a few occasions.

When he made it as per his plan to the back near the stairs where the alleyway door was and a few people standing, he felt uncomfortable, but he took a deep breath, wondering what the big deal was. But he knew as he stared up at the small stage and watched her behind the microphone with the music loud, her voice running like a beautiful stallion over it all in the hills of the song, through the wind and grass and peaks and valleys of sound. Behind her the small band played--piano, guitar and drums. Before her sat an appreciative roomful of folks, not as vocal as Linda's crowd had been, but moving to the song, drinking, smiling, enjoying. He knew what the big deal was--it was Rosy.

He watched her sing; she was having a good time, hitting the tambourine against the palm of her right hand to the music, putting her head back and moving her body to the rhythm, moving her shoulders back and forth, taking hold again of the microphone, belting out bold, romantic phrases, looking at her audience. Stanley didn't know the song but the words "my hot love" and "kiss me again" were earthy poetry to him.

In a moment a hurried waitress asked what he wanted.

"Corona, no lime," he yelled. She wrote it down as she left.

He stood mesmerized at the foot of the staircase. Occasionally someone would bump him or slide past him, and behind him people were talking, mingling, not watching Rosy. When she finished the song her audience applauded.

"Thank you, thank you," she said, and smiled.

That was it--he was in love. Forget Linda.

The waitress eventually brought him his beer, with a lime. He paid her and gave her a tip and held the cool bottle in his hand, tossing the wedge of lime out the back door, trying not to hit anyone. Rosy began another song, a ballad. The folks outside seemed to get louder. Maybe he should have hit one of them with the fruit. No matter. He liked slower songs; if this was the price he had to pay, so be it.

She sang like a nightingale, he thought, not knowing exactly what one was, although Keats had written a great poem about one--that was good enough for Stanley. Her feet were tapping, and he noticed the soft lines of her legs. "If you go now I'll die..." she sang plaintively. Corny but at the same time expressive, because she seemed to mean it.

He leaned against the sturdy, thick banister, holding the bottle of beer in his hand, forgetting about the people around him, and enjoyed the performance.

After a while he made his way partially up the stairs to a level spot where he could put his arms on the banister, set down his beer, and watch her, no more than ten yards away, without having to worry about seeing over anyone who might happen to stand up at the tables. It was a good spot. No one could walk in front of him; they were on the stairs behind him or far enough below, in front. Stanley could lean on the banister which was better than sitting down which he couldn't do anyway, didn't want to do, because then he'd have to look around other people, possibly missing something.

After another Corona he decided she was cuter than
Linda Ronstadt, and sang more sweetly, if that were
possible. But he wished she would do one of Linda's songs,
having obviously been influenced by her. But she didn't.
As a matter of fact, she ended the set way too soon, he
thought, and only, apparently, due to the persistent
applause, sang one final number.

After that Rosy bowed and smiled and gestured to her
band while everyone cheered and applauded. It lasted a
good while but she wouldn't do another one and the band
members surrounded her as she left the stage, moving along
the side of the tables to the stairs, and as Stanley turned
they ascended, and as they passed by she looked right at
him, briefly, curiously, and then went to the top,
disappearing into what must have been the dressing room.

4

The next day he took a long drive up Spring Street, north of downtown--an old, wide street with a non-residential feeling. No large buildings, just dark warehouses and unused train tracks. At least he assumed they were unused, because he saw many silent boxcars.

He parked and strolled around the dusty area, enjoying the sunshine and breathing the air that seemed to come from outside of L.A., somewhere.

Stanley's mood was elated, uplifted. After the show he'd stopped at Melrose and La Cienega for a cheeseburger, but the waiter from Texas wasn't there. Stanley had wanted to tell him about Rosy Sanchez--to tell someone.

He walked on the gravel near the train tracks. Now and then a car or a truck sped by, creating a whoosh of dirt and air, stirring up trash from the side of the road. The trash would float down to a different location; things returned to the way they were--except something had happened, something had slightly, swiftly altered it all.

He wandered over the train tracks, musing, looking into the lonely, empty boxcars, feeling the sun on him; it was very agreeable. In the sun at work he didn't feel this pleasant--no way.

Stanley had a sense of peace, as if he'd made it through a challenge and was at the start of another, more interesting path. But he didn't have much time for reflection, having slept late. Had to eat and go to work. So he reluctantly made his way back to his car, returning to the normal world.

But he thought of her, he remembered her...those lovely lips--those lively eyes--those soft cheeks--that sexy way she danced--the way she held her head forward, as if looking for something--or someone, and suddenly threw it back, smiling. That colorful brownish hair--somehow combining the Southern Californian with the Latin, yet being in between, and something else--a beauty that Stanley wasn't sure how to describe, a beauty that had to do with her voice, with the tenderness and great passion there, the softness and the strength and the joy and the sadness she exuded-expressed-explored...

At work that afternoon he didn't mind when someone treated him like a lesser human being, curtly asking for this or that, paying in a self-important, superior manner. As a matter of fact, Stanley began to understand they did it because of something that was wrong with them, that they felt insecure, possibly about him. But why was that? He posed a threat to them--his vitality, his youth, <u>something</u>, and they were being, as it says in the Bible, "puffed up." If they could put him down a little, they felt they were up there, somewhere, above him. Or at least not down where they must feel they are for one reason or another. Maybe it wasn't him at all--maybe they just felt bad about themselves. And Stanley didn't get upset when the boss made his familiar comments as to how useless the military reserve was. In fact, Stanley, instead of going along with it and yessing him like the boss wanted him to do, said he thought the reserves were important and valuable, that tax money was well spent on them, that they served a useful purpose for the safety of the country. But of course Barry replied: "No, they don't do shit! Just sit around, waiting!" He then made a face, exiting the office as if he had something important to do. But this was a joyful day and Stanley felt good about speaking his mind.

He remembered a place in the Bible that says Jesus will return and make the things that are not now perfect, perfect. The idea was to remember that everything is not perfect on earth, so why should we be concerned about doing or saying something if it isn't exactly what somebody expects to hear? We can express how we feel--it'll be alright. God's going to make everything perfect someday,

so there's no reason to try to protect what <u>isn't</u> perfect.
The boss hadn't liked it, of course. But you should at
least try to make things as good as you can, not be worried
when they're not, afraid to say or do something that
conflicts with the way things are. That's what Amy would
say. If he can improve things by speaking up, is that
wrong? If someone is angry at him for it, that doesn't
mean he should refrain from speaking up, right?

That must be one of the ways God makes things better
for us, by achieving it through us. He does it by us doing
it, and the more we trust in Him the more we can do to
improve things. At least, Stanley thought so.

But then Barry was at the door. "What the hell are
you doing? There's a customer out here!"

"Oh, sorry."

Later Barry took off, "before the traffic," as usual.
Stanley couldn't figure out why he didn't just say he was
leaving to go home to his family and dinner and to see his
horses before it got too dark. Why did he have to pretend
there was no other reason he wouldn't stay at the place
except that the traffic would mess him up on his trip out
to the ranch? Stanley thought about it, sitting in the
office again. What he came up with was that the boss must

want Stanley and Mark to think he cares so much about the station that even dinner and children can't drag him away, and that since _he_ cares so much Stanley and Mark should too.

Pretty silly, Stanley thought. If he hired someone he should trust them, or he shouldn't hire them. And if he trusts them to do the work, like they have shown they can, why should he be concerned about enforcing some subtle influence to make up for his personal anxiety? Stanley also thought that maybe the boss didn't even think about it, maybe he just said that about the traffic because he felt guilty for leaving, even though he'd surely spent enough time over the years to deserve a little time off. But Barry couldn't relax--possibly he was worried about the increasing pressure from major gas companies to get his station. Since the Arab oil embargo independent places had been crowded out by company-controlled self-service stations where there aren't attendants or "extras." Since the price of gasoline went up after the embargo, people were more willing to frequent those places and not ask for other procedures, more willing to do the work themselves and skip things like checking water, and tire pressure, and a lot of independent full-service places had to sell out due to decreased business.

But so far Barry, and some others, had managed to stay open due to a certain popularity or special service they provided. Yet every once in a while men in suits would show up and talk to him in private, and when they would leave he'd be in a foul mood, getting angry at minor things, not telling them what had happened.

Once he did say, after another of those well-dressed visits, that he'd been told to buy a lot of accessory items --tires, gas additives--or they were threatening to hold back his gasoline allocation. If they did that he'd have to remain open fewer hours, lift prices, and lose customers.

"That's the way those assholes force you to give up ownership," he had said gruffly, walking away. He didn't mention it again, but new tires appeared in the garage, and nobody bought them, and Barry got meaner than ever.

After the boss left that day Mark wanted to go get the food early, so Stanley let him, and worked alone for a while. Normally they traded off, and it was technically Stanley's turn. But if the kid wanted to go, he could go, although it was odd--he didn't ask Stanley what he wanted to eat.

Excitement and warmth passed through him each time he thought about the night before. Who was she?

John Keats had written that "On First Looking Into Chapman's Homer" he'd felt like Cortez and his men must have felt when they first encountered the glorious Pacific Ocean. Although some say that actually Cortez didn't find the ocean first--Balboa did--the concept of finding something fantastic when you hadn't expected it resonated with Stanley. Finding something as gorgeous as that ocean, or as rich as Chapman's translation, made Stanley think of encountering Rosy Sanchez.

A car drove in, the bell rang, Stanley went out. "Hi, can I help you?" he asked cheerfully. It was a surly man with thick sideburns in a black Thunderbird.

"Four dollars--regular."

"Sure." He turned on the pump, took the hose to the tank, removed the cap, inserted the nozzle, and cleaned the windshield.

"Check your oil?"

"Not today."

He stopped the gas flow at four-o-o and replaced the hose. "Four dol--"

"Here." The man handed him four singles, abruptly, and drove off.

Stanley put the money in the old cash register. Rather than his normal reaction of anger at customer indifference, Stanley felt sympathy: <u>must be having a rough day</u>, he thought, sticking his hands in his pockets, waiting for the next one.

A few children from the school east on Wilshire ran to the ice cream machine by the office. They giggled as they put coins in and extracted items. Naturally the kids ignored him. But he didn't care. He was only a gas jockey. They had their lives to live, their plans for the afternoon. And he had his memory of the look Rosy gave him as she climbed the stairs to her dressing room.

"Bing!" Another car came in, a convertible, a man and woman inside.

"Hi, can I help you?"

So it went the rest of the swing shift--car to car, windshield to windshield, dipstick to dipstick, gastankcap to gastankcap.

When Mark returned with to-go Mexican food he seemed oddly pleased with himself, but Stanley didn't ask him what was up. They ate silently in the office, Mark taking care of any customers that came in during their dinner. Even when a second car pulled in he'd wave at Stanley to stay in

the office. Sure was in a good mood. Maybe he got laid.
But that was mighty fast, even for a high school kid.

He was still grinning when he left for the night, at
ten. Stanley closed up at eleven, as usual, putting the
cash in the safe, sweeping and hosing the front, pushing
the dirty water into the gutter with the "squeegie,"
pulling in the display racks, washing his hands, changing
his clothes, turning off the lights, locking the doors,
thinking about Rosy.

5

It was mid-August. Los Angeles was thick with smog like it was in the 1960's. Politicians were calling for more fuel-efficient cars, automakers were complaining the extra cost would damage their business. Talk in Jim's Café focused on the southland's oil refineries, how they directed toxic fumes into the basin, creating smog.

"Nobody's tryin' to put any devices on <u>them</u>."

"Whattaya mean? They have to pay fines if they don't do it."

"Oh, yeah, a hundred dollars, or something."

"That's not gonna motivate their asses."

"No kidding. Should be put in jail."

"Jail?" They were silent for a while, contemplating this.

Then an overweight man at the counter said: "There's a positive advantage to poor air quality, you know." This drew everyone's attention. "Really. If it wasn't for smog, more people would live here. It would be too crowded."

It rained in mid-August. A hot rain, the sky gray with clouds but light with sun. Stanley had gone to the

"Coffee Pot" in Los Feliz to escape the disconcerting conversation at Jim's. But it hadn't helped.

He was sitting at the end of the counter minding his own business when the female cashier walked up behind him and asked:

"Aren't you the guy who told us Elvis died?"

Weird thing to say. He turned and looked the woman in the eye. What was she talking about? He was too confused to respond.

She waited. When he didn't answer she said:

"You know who that is, don't you?"

"What?"

She screwed up her face.

"Elvis Presley. He died this morning. You look like the guy who told us about it."

Well, he wasn't the guy. It was news to him, bad news.

Stanley listened to it on the radio after leaving the coffee shop. Shit. Elvis dead. And this rain! It's like a sign or something.

At work Barry said: "He was a drug addict. What do you expect?" That pissed Stanley off, but Barry was under pressure, so he let it go by. He got a paper to look for an item about Rosy, but found no mention--just Elvis news.

That night he went to a bar he intermittently frequented. A feeling of unhappiness was with him, dogging him. Of course he should have gone to the track, but the idea held no allure for him.

Instead he pulled into the back parking lot, turned his engine off, left his car, walked in the rear entrance, sat gloomily on a stool and asked the tall, red-haired barmaid for a beer, all the while feeling wrong about being there instead of the track, but being there nevertheless. So he drank, wondering about this moroseness that had hit him.

It was nearly midnight. The jukebox was playing some old tunes, one of which was Sinatra's. It intensified Stanley's emotion. A couple of old men sat at the other end of the bar, talking it up. A younger man kidded with the skinny barmaid.

Elvis a drug addict? Bullshit.

He got another beer and was considering getting a shot of whiskey to back it up when he realized what was bothering him so much.

Sure, he felt loss due to Elvis' demise, but he felt a curious pain about Rosy Sanchez. But it wasn't even her. It was a girl named Maria he'd met on Main Street two years

before. A Latina, like Rosy. He'd thought she was
beautiful and sexy, and since someone was bugging her,
following her, Stanley took advantage of the circumstance
to intervene. It worked out. He told the guy to leave her
alone, and he did--fortunately. Maria was grateful. They
walked and talked and surprisingly she went with him up the
stairs to the gym, at his suggestion.

Normally Stanley wasn't so aggressive with females,
but she was so cute he couldn't help it. She watched him
exercise. He introduced her to Duke, who made her feel
comfortable. There had been a brief moment of hesitation
halfway up those cold stairs, but she'd accepted his
assurance that it really was a gym and that she'd be
alright. He got her phone number at the bus stop, said
he'd call. She agreed to go out. Stanley felt fantastic.
If only he hadn't screwed up. If only he'd not treated her
so shamefully, later.

He sipped at his beer, hardly hearing the music, now.

Maria had been so sweet. He'd called, invited her to
a play his friend from high school was doing at the Music
Center, and they went. It impressed her. His friend
Andrew, along with an actress in the play, took them for
coffee afterwards. That impressed her too. After all, she

was just a working girl, riding the bus, living with her parents. This was different for her.

They'd kissed good night. Perfect. Made arrangements to go out again. She didn't mind that he wanted to be a fighter.

Stanley finished his beer, the redhead brought him another. The clock behind the bar showed there was over an hour until the place closed, there was no rush to go. He asked the barmaid would she get him a shot to go along.

"Oh, my," she kidded. "Doing some deep thinking tonight?" She laughed, asking: "What do you want?"

He told her which kind of bourbon; she brought it, unfortunately.

The next time, he picked her up in George's station wagon, for some reason. Couldn't remember why, now. Maybe his car wasn't running.

They'd gone to the Forum to watch the fights. Two friends from the gym were there: Carlos, the rugged amateur, and light-skinned black pro Lonnie. Sam, his trainer at the time, was there. They all sat together. So far so good. Maria seemed nervous, of course, but relaxed after a while. It was all new to her. The guys liked her, the bouts were okay, Stanley was happy. But afterward in the parking lot the trouble began, slowly. George's gas gauge was low. No problem--have to get gas. But Stanley realized he hadn't gotten the key to the lock, the gas-cap lock. Stupid. Would Lonnie give them a ride? Sure.

How they ended up in Stanley's room he couldn't recall, now. Maybe he'd said he'd take her in a cab the rest of the way. Yeah, that was it. Anyway, it was cool she agreed to go to his apartment. Lonnie said he loved "Country Club." They got some. Mistake. Stanley never drank the stuff because it was stronger than normal beer. But...he went along with it. They talked about boxing. Maria didn't drink much--maybe one, or less.

After a while Lonnie left and they were alone. He kissed her. He got her to the bed. He began peeling off her clothes. Was he too aggressive?

In the bar Stanley slammed his bottle onto the counter a la Brando in *THE WILD ONE*, foam coming out the top. The barmaid looked concerned--he shrugged at her. If only he hadn't had that dumb malt liquor. So what if Lonnie liked it?

Maria was tender. She had beautiful, firm, little breasts. It took awhile, but he'd gotten her panties off. He'd entered her. Then something happened. She got nervous. She had second thoughts. She said, "Oh, no, please," and had gotten away, pulled herself away, up the bed, leaving him without her. He tried to reenter. No, she wasn't going to let him, and couldn't--didn't--explain. Crazy. The alcohol, if only...he couldn't accept it with civility. It bothered him too much. <u>How could she do that</u>?

They didn't talk; he just lay on the bed, defeated. She said she should go; she dressed.

"Come on, please! Get up. I have to go."

<u>She hadn't even said she was sorry</u>. Is that right? Am I remembering it correctly?

He hadn't gotten up--he was too angry.

"Aren't you going to...I have to get home..."

Did he say anything?

In time Maria left, and he'd slept. What a screwed-up night. He just let her go off by herself, a young girl, into the middle of the night. What had she done then...walked? Found a telephone? A cab?

It hurt him to realize how little respect he'd shown. So, she changed her mind. So it was strange. But to send her out on her own into possible danger? Wrong.

He finished his shot of whiskey. They were closing up. "Goodbye."

He got to the parking lot, to his car, then headed up the narrow street toward a curve that brought two small streets together, leading onto a larger one; he was nearing the turn when a fast police car came suddenly around the curve, toward him, in the middle of the street. Stanley had to swerve and decided to keep going instead of slowing because after all he had been drinking and didn't want to make a big deal out of it, slamming on his brakes and all, attracting their attention and getting pulled over.

It was looking good; as the cop car approached it seemed he had room to get by but then someone was getting into a parked car on his right, even though he must have heard the roar of the police car and seen that Stanley was trying to get by, between them--this idiot still pulled open his door and then there wasn't enough room anymore and the choice became to hit the side of the speeding police car or hit the parked car, so when the idiot who'd pulled his door open on this narrow street with two cars trying to get by and one of them a cop car going fast in the middle of the road after taking a corner too sharply began to climb in--the choice was exceedingly simple: don't hit the police car.

He struck the open door with the right side of his '57 and there was a grinding, scraping noise; but the police seemed to be going on, thankfully, and Stanley kept going slowly as to not gain their interest. But the grinding

kept up for a second as Stanley was hoping the police would
continue hurriedly down the street since he now had room to
make it; he'd be able to go around the curve, park, and
walk back.

But he saw in his mirror that the cop car was
stopping, so he wasn't going anywhere, and he had to pull
over immediately, like he was going to get out to take a
look at the damage; the cop car was backing up--they had
noticed something had happened, which they are trained to
do, fortunately, yes, for all of us, except it certainly
didn't seem fortunate to Stanley Larson at that moment--no.

Then he was telling them yes he'd had a couple of
beers and here's his license and sure he'd be glad to get
out and sure he would go across the street to where there's
more light and yes he would walk this line from here to
there on the sidewalk and oops well that's okay and could
he touch his nose with his eyes closed see there he did
that pretty good and would he please recite the alphabet
why of course it goes this way a-b-c-d-e-f ah j-i hold it
just a second let me do it again a-b-c-d-e-f-g ah h-i-k-m-
p-q ah q ah, okay, shit, will he step over to their car
please will he turn around please will he place his hands
up there, is he carrying any weapons oh no are you kidding
and would he place his hands behind his back oh no

handcuffs oh shit that feels terrible oh man that's humiliating; they were reading him his rights, <u>he was being arrested</u> and he had to get into the back seat, it was the cop car that had made him swerve in the first place and he was getting angry as they closed the door with no handle inside and his wrists hurt because he had to sit on them sort of, the bracelets were tight, too tight, and one of the officers got in the front seat and wrote down a couple of things and the police radio was making that noise that makes you feel funny well this time it was you in the car and you felt funny and dizzy and mad and tried to tell him that he no that you had to hit the other car because he was well his partner who was driving had zoomed down the middle of the road, and the officer was relaxed about it but you knew he wasn't going to let you out and his partner was discussing it with the guy at the car with the bent door and oh boy this is the shits the night is really screwed up and you start to feel like maybe crying but you hold on and oh man you could have been at your room by now if you hadn't gone the way you did if they hadn't been going so fast if the jerk hadn't pulled his door open if they hadn't been in the center of the street if the bar had only closed earlier, or...

Then in that stupid police car riding through the night, the radio talking screechy talk, the evening continuing its exodus toward sunrise, Stanley drawing in some deep breaths from his partly open window, hoping perhaps his bloodstream would be influenced and the examination at the station would only read a certain amount of alcohol content and they wouldn't charge him. Foolish, he thought to himself, taking measure as best he could of the condition of his system, realizing how dizzy he was, how tired he felt, how sick he was starting to become. So he began to accept it. He began to realize it was foregone. He had been arrested, he was going to jail, and he was not about to pass any test they would give him, and his '57 was sitting on that street and these police officers were doing their job and the night was really fucked up now.

Then in the police station with more things being written down, being led to a room by a new strange person in uniform, not liking the sterile place nor the feeling of being alone nor the lights which were sickly yellow and the atmosphere which was cheap, metallic, and empty.

Then waiting, feeling the unpleasantness of being dizzy and unable to think properly or even relax and finally being taken into a testing room and it seemed like it was the same two policemen, why weren't they out on the street somewhere doing their job? And then they had this small box on a table with a bunch of dials and switches and they put some papers in front of them and you didn't even feel like a human, you were just to sit there and it was too dark in there and unreal and they had you blow into this insignificant, scientific-looking tube so you tried to put as small an amount as possible in because you heard somewhere that the air from the bottom of your lungs would have most of the stuff in it--or did you figure that out? because it did make sense: the air you had recently inhaled would have as little as any and the air in you that was close to the walls of your lungs would have the most alcohol so don't breathe that into this thing but they were looking at the dials and they seemed confused and they asked you to put more into it and they asked you if you had a cold or something and you realized it was probably not going to work so fuck it what did it matter now you were just trying to make it seem like you hadn't really drunk that much and shit, you had, so then he went ahead and breathed into the thing and after a while they had apparently taken down enough information and they thanked him and left him there and the other policeman came in and took him for fingerprinting and then to a cell oh yeah a cell and it was down a narrow corridor and this was very embarrassing and the door was very strong and the bars were very thick, the bars were kind of green, and it was a bare place with somebody else in there sleeping on the floor and so this was it oh yeah this was the drunk tank.

For about half an hour Stanley sat on the hard cold bench in the green cell studying it all in amazement before he began to feel miserable. Another drunk from the streets was brought in mumbling and fell asleep on the floor. Stanley began to feel hunger and thirst and depleted blood sugar and his eyes didn't seem able to focus properly. He started getting angry that he was being punished in this way in this place without having been convicted and sentenced under the proper and due process of law.

He still felt those last few bolts he'd had at the bar prior to its closing. To think he could be comfortably ensconced in his room with the radio on and some cold cuts from the little ice box and the pillow behind his head and...he didn't want to think about it. One of the men was now making loud noises as he slept.

Soon another person was brought in. He was aloof and seemed to be almost sober. Stanley nodded hello to him, and then the man sat on the bench at the far corner of the cell. He eventually lay down and went to sleep, or pretended to, and so Stanley, who did not feel like sleeping, sat there, conscious of the weariness and pain in his body.

After a while they brought in another man. He was about Stanley's age and after a few words it was obvious he was from England. His accent was strong. The aloof man opened his eyes. The new man liked to talk, and kept the conversation going even when no one was responding. Stanley began to think perhaps the fellow was on a drug of some sort.

All he talked about was how wrong the police were, how little he'd had to drink but because he'd had his liver operated on the effect of the alcohol was more severe than normal, so the arresting officers had thought he was intoxicated when he actually wasn't. Well, no matter, he was a musician and his band had an attorney on retainer and as soon as he called him he'd get out and they couldn't convict him anyway because it wasn't proper, now was it?

Then the Englishman pulled a cigarette from his full and substantial head of hair. Hidden it there. This got the attention of the man on the bench and one of the sleepers who had woken up to hear his tale.

But he hadn't a match. Had anyone a match? No? Forgot that.

"Only thought to hide the ciggy."

Then he looked up at the ceiling at the large lamp which was covered in metal mesh. "Think that would be hot enough? Worth a try, isn't it?" He stood up and began to climb the bars near the door. He received a warning from one of the sleepers who had ceased sleeping who knew that was a jailhouse no-no. But he kept going and tried to push one end of the cigarette through the mesh wire onto the large bright light fixture.

This intrigued Stanley, who was getting restless anyway, and he stood up on the bench, stepped over to the bars, grabbed on and climbed up alongside the English-musician-pioneer.

This is the way to live, it occurred to Stanley, taking chances, taking action.

However, the bulb didn't seem to be hot enough. Not that Stanley cared. The guy held the cigarette there for some time, and then tried to take a couple of draws on it.

Naturally the outer door of the corridor clanged open, and the former sleeper whispered loudly, "Get down!" Stanley jumped/dropped to the cell floor which was hard, especially since they had taken his shoes. Some people were approaching the cell and the guy from England didn't jump, he didn't do anything at first, and then he began to climb down; but by then the guard and another policeman were there and saw it.

"Hey! Get down!"

He did.

"What are you doing up there? Huh?" He was very interested. The other officer seemed amused.

The Englishman sort of laughed and realized in his embarrassment there was no way out.

"Well, to tell you the truth, I was trying to get a light for my ciggy." He smiled meekly. They looked at him with skepticism. "It didn't seem to work. You wouldn't have a match, would you?"

The officers looked at each other.

"Give it to me," said the first. That was that. "Don't let me catch you climbing the bars again, understand?"

Stanley was relieved when they left, but he felt the lingering pain in his feet. The musician shrugged and said with that characteristic British manner, "Well, it doesn't hurt to try."

Later, after he'd told everyone how he'd spent all of last year's earnings, eighty thousand dollars, the musician got onto the floor and began to do pushups in what he said was an attempt to pass the time.

Stanley sat in his dazed state watching him, seeing that actually the guy was in good shape and could do many pushups, and thought sadly what would be the result if he were to try it.

It was morning in a few hours, and after trying to sleep on his part of the metal bench, after feeling wretched about the circumstances, after deciding the authorities were mistaken to make things so unpleasant for people arrested like this, incarcerated without a trial, made to feel they didn't deserve a plain bed to spend the night in, he started to feel cramped and weak and tight in his joints. The decidedly unceremonial presentation of breakfast was further unpleasantness and most definitely he could not eat considering how he was feeling, and of course the perky and verbose Britisher was more than happy to take it if Stanley really didn't care to eat; ah, too bad he wasn't feeling well.

The rest of the day went slowly and painfully. Stanley finally got out around two o'clock, after being transferred by police bus to a larger cell at another station which contained more people who had been arrested. Most of them were young, either Chicano or black. There was one Oriental and a strange-looking Anglo with an even stranger story about being falsely arrested in a men's room because he was only "kidding around" and Stanley didn't want to hear it and went to another part of the cell to listen to another story, while they all sat around waiting for responses to their phone calls, and one Mexican's story was about how some time back he had broken into a house to see what he could take and the owner had come home and he "sort of took him hostage" and was drinking from the poor guy's liquor supply and made him drink too and finally, really enjoying himself, sent the man out to buy more booze and of course the man called the cops when he was out and they came and arrested him.

That was pretty funny, but most of the listeners weren't in the greatest mood to care, although they kept at it, trying to make the conversation enjoyable to make up for the lack of things like freedom and good food and girls and money and driving somewhere, and matches. They were allowed cigarettes in this larger cell but ran out of matches quickly.

His boss came through this time, arranged for bail and even sent Mark over to pick him up. Stanley expected he'd be upset about the deposit he gave the bondsman, a deposit which you never get back, but the boss didn't say a thing.

He seemed very nice about it, including the fact Stanley
didn't feel well enough to work that day, and someone had
to be found to take his place on the evening shift.

The fun part of the experience was when an officer
opened the heavy metal door of the large cell and yelled
for Stanley, that he was being released, and, saying a
rather barren "take it easy" to the men/boys when he
departed--barren because he'd really not gotten too
involved in the talk but had instead been quiet, feeling
down and not too good physically--he got outside the cell
where there were two more police, at a desk, one a female,
something which had a remarkable significance, almost a
surprising significance, after the past dreary hours and
jail-talk. She smiled and gave him his things from his
pockets that they had taken and he thought: she has legs
under the desk, there, and he returned her smile even
though it was pretty formal, this transaction, and the
other two policemen were watching. Stanley wanted to say
something, something about the cell or whatever but
everything was so formal he just nodded as he was told of
his upcoming court date, and started to leave the way the
guard was directing when he saw some matches on the desk
and hesitated, remembering how inside the cell they were
without matches, but did have a few cigarettes and had used

up the lights a couple of them brought with them, how there'd been talk about not even being able to light up what they had and how the previous guard on duty when asked said he couldn't find any or <u>something</u>, so in what felt strongly like a surge of courage Stanley reached-pointed to the matches and said: "They could sure use those in there, they don't have any," and the female looked at the other police and said: "Okay," and Stanley bravely picked them up and the guard came toward him and he gave them to him and out of some mysterious need Stanley asked: "Can you tell 'em that Larson, you know, got 'em for 'em?" And the guard said: "Sure will." The second policeman was going toward the front door and as he followed Stanley turned toward the policewoman and said goodbye and there was something in her eyes, something warm, like maybe she thought the effort about those matches was a good thing, and then he was walking out the door saying thank you to the policeman, and it was sunshiny, the wind brought him fresh air, there was green grass around the place, and Mark waiting by his pickup. He was *free*, man, *and it felt good*.

6

Carrying on was a lot easier, then. Once you hit a low spot you really hang in there when you get up and out of it. It makes you grateful to be in a good position, again, a position you didn't appreciate as much before the fall. Of course he still had to go to court in October, plead guilty, and pay a large fine. First offense.

But Stanley felt an elated state of well-being, ate a big meal, got his Chevy which didn't have <u>that</u> much damage, put on clean clothes, put fuel in the tank and drove west in search of more of the same well-being. He cruised along the beach areas, heading south, yelled at several girls who were in swimsuits, walking, and felt the sun as it so generously, charitably gave of itself even into the rolled-down windows of his automobile.

He drove through the Marina, saw a few boats and took the long way on the beach side around the airport on the small road, watching jets take off overhead, seeing the waves coming in onto the sand, and smelled the clean fresh salty sea air.

He went to the Hermosa Beach Pier, parked and strolled out where the fishermen were, then walked back to where the guys-and-dolls played volleyball on the sand and the small stores were along the sidewalk, the "strand," alongside the beach. People walked back and forth on this concrete thoroughfare smiling and talking; some rode bikes and a few were on skates which tended to mess up the pattern of strollers and pedalers. Stanley reached the oceanfront houses which had a wide stretch of sand between them and the ocean, and kept walking, though he began to feel out of place in cowboy boots and Levi's. Girls with tan, beautiful bodies were on the beach and walking past him and he thought for a brief moment of the men/boys back in jail who would undoubtedly like so much to be here, and weren't.

The beachfront homes were nice and the people in them seemed to like their fate. One place had a large front patio which was strewn with old furniture, a beat-up sofa, beer bottles and in the middle a large man with a white beard sat typing at a little table facing the water. A large white dog resting beside him looked up with near-human blue eyes as Stanley passed by. The man looked up over his glasses which were precariously pointed at the typewriter before him, and then looked back. Whatever he was writing must have been important, considering his serious attitude. Music blasted from speakers in the open windows behind him: Gary Wright's "Dream Weaver." Another man stood inside the house. He was younger, blonder, tanner, thinner.

Stanley walked on. He saw a girl sitting on her porch reading a magazine. She had the biggest pair of tits Stanley had seen in a long, long time. She looked up as he slowed, staring.

"Hi!" he said, breaking through his shyness. She smiled, to his surprise, and said "Hello" back in a rich, light English accent, stopping him.

"How ya doin'?" he mumbled, not knowing what else to say, and trying to keep his eyes from leaping out onto the top of her tiny two-piece suit.

She hesitated, the sure sign, to him, that he had come on too strong and was scaring her away. But he stood there, emboldened perhaps by his recent excursion into deprivation, and tried to think of another, more acceptable query. But then she said, "I'm fine, thank you. Getting a bit too hot, actually," and smiled again.

That accent, those huge white breasts, that coy girlish smile, was it real? She looked back to her magazine. He stood there, wanting to say something. He wanted to do something. He wanted to take her back into her place there and lie down with her and put it in between those breasts and squeeze them together and...

But...he continued to walk.

PART FOUR

Saturday Stanley went to the church on Hollywood Boulevard; it did him good.

The preacher said: "No matter what our sins are, God loves us," referring to quotes from the Bible to show what he was getting at, how they could be applied to modern life. "God forgives," he shouted.

When it was over Stanley thought about what was said as he drove idly toward the center of Hollywood.

He was glad God loved him because he was sure a sinner.

And he hadn't been near the gym in weeks, aside from an occasional drive-by.

He hadn't been over to see George and Alicia in so long they probably think he doesn't like them anymore. Their son is probably getting so big he wouldn't be able to recognize him. And the new one's probably born already.

Wait--that can't be, can it?

Stanley liked the warm desert weather of the Los Angeles summer, and the so-called Indian Summer that was approaching, but now it seemed like the weather was not changing, it was just going to stay hot and keep at it and make everyone thirsty and keep a layer of collective brownishness overhead. Where was autumn?

The hot air came into his car as he made his way down La Brea Avenue to turn right on Sunset. He saw that people were not moving around too fast, and he felt sorry for those standing at the bus stop trying to find the shade of a sign or a lamppost as their bus made its route toward them from somewhere further up the road, about to make a turn and head toward them and finally stop and let them on, out of the sun. He drove west and didn't feel like going anywhere to relax or have a cold drink or lie down.

He just wanted to drive. He went to a gas station and put nearly all his remaining dollars in the tank.

That made him think about money, which he usually didn't do. As he pulled out of the station on Sunset across from the large Playboy building he thought about how much he had in the bank--$250 since payday, give or take a beer and a sandwich and a pack of sugarless chewing gum. All of which he immediately longed for and did not have enough cash for. But the preacher had said you weren't supposed to be overly concerned about "fleeting dilemmas," that the Lord would provide for us along the way, if we had faith.

He was getting out of shape. Was that a "fleeting dilemma"? It was happening gradually, yet he was acutely aware of it. The fact that he was still in good condition relative to other people was small consolation. He knew the sort of condition he could be in, and what he should be doing to achieve it, and he knew what he was not doing, to not achieve it. Larry's oft repeated words came to him: "Alright, Stanley, you know what it takes."

He also knew, regarding his barren financial condition, that getting in shape, turning pro and making money--a lot if he did well--was recommended.

He could do it if the Lord helped him. But was that what he should do? How was he to find out? He prayed for an answer to that right there in the car and asked it in Jesus' precious name, like you're supposed to.

Then as he drove he decided to keep faith like they say you need to, and believe. So he tried to do that. He felt better. If he really wanted he could go to Barry's and borrow a few bucks from whoever was working today, and pay it back next payday.

So that's what he did. The gas station on Saturday was usually not busy, and a weekend worker was there, the owner's nephew. George didn't come in until three.

Stanley knew him, and after a few words about boxing--
"Well, I lost in the finals and I'm kind of taking it easy
right now"--"Do you think you'll turn pro?"--"Yeah, well,
when I get back in there I'll let you know"--he borrowed
ten dollars from the kid and zoomed out after putting some
carburetor cleaner in the carburetor and a can of gas
booster in the tank. He took the empty cans with him. The
boss probably wouldn't notice.

His Chevy ran very well, then, although it needed a
real tune-up. The talk about turning pro troubled him, but
the money lightened his spirits.

It made him feel good the way the guy had asked him
about fighting, how he seemed to admire him, how he'd
watched Stanley pull out onto the street. He was afraid of
getting hit, he'd said, and wondered how Stanley could take
it.

"Oh, it doesn't hurt that much--because of the
gloves."

"Really?"

What Stanley hadn't said was that he rather enjoyed
getting hit--up to a point. But he seldom told people that
--they usually gave him a harsh, obtuse look.

Stanley cruised Sunset to the Pacific, then returned, stopping for a six-pack, driving through Carl's Jr., and headed to his apartment. Fortunately the landlady didn't appear; he got up the dirty carpeted stairs to his floor safely.

He ate a double cheeseburger, listening to Three Dog Night, drinking beer, hitting the cans on his forehead when they were empty and then tossing them onto the rug. He ate some old tortilla chips that had been around for a while. He used to eat chips when he was training to replace the salt, but right now he ate them for no good reason.

The record somehow made him think about Vietnam, for a change. He hadn't thought about it in some time--tried not to. But once in a while it came back, once in a while the memories came back, vividly. Not that he'd done much over there--not like some of those guys in-country.

By the third beer he was eighteen years old again at Sangley Point in the Philippines, working maintenance for the giant seaplanes that went out on patrol in the early mornings. They flew into hostile fire areas, in search of gun-runners, and returned, the crew tired and dirty, the inside of the plane a mess, looking as it would after being used by ten or so crew members for eight or ten hours. But during the day Stanley and other ground crew yanked the equipment, mostly electronic, that had been reported working improperly, and took it into the Avionics shop. After only one or two trips inside the plane unhooking the radar or anti-submarine gear and pulling it out and hauling it to the side door and hanging it down for his partner to put on the cart, Stanley would be covered with sweat, breathing heavily. The air was warm and wet in the Philippines. The wind, occasionally strong, didn't seem to get into the airplane on the ground, and when you were working inside it was incredibly hot. In a perverse way, though, he liked it. It took the beer he'd had the evening before right out of him.

Then he'd drop the equipment off at Avionics, pulling or driving it, on a yellow wagon, enjoying the air outside as it cooled him, and return to another plane. Later he would work inside the shop.

By the end of the day he and his fellow workers would be tired, their dungarees wrinkled, damp, daubed with dirt and oil. They would head for the usual beer-and-bull at the open-air bar on the base, and after a couple of fifteen cent San Miguels usually speak of going to town. Those that wanted to and could, would, and those that wanted to and couldn't, wouldn't.

If you had to stay on duty you weren't even supposed to be at the enlisted men's club, that day--but many did it.

The men--boys--who could go to town, or 'hit the beach' as they called it, might also get a bottle of booze so cheaply on base that it was worth it to take and keep in their possession all evening until its contents and usefulness were exhausted--events which normally occurred simultaneously, unless the container was needed as a weapon, which, not often, but occasionally, was the case. Then its usefulness outlasted its contents. But fighting was rare among the men/boys who were stationed at Sangley Point.

Stanley liked to put on his civvies, showered and shaved--what there was to shave--and ride the little tram-bus to the gate. The night air was wonderful--at least until you got near the river. It would blow through the bus, creating a sharp sense of anticipation that seemed to be carried in the temperature, the smell, and the air's touch.

At the base gate the little bus would stop, you'd get out and walk through, and then you were in Cavite City, you were walking toward familiar bars, you were seeing familiar faces, and you had that familiar feeling of joy and relaxation--even though a part of you was aware of being thousands of miles from America, in a strange country--even though the Philippinos were friends, even though we were allies against communist aggression. But you felt good. You'd have a nearly frozen San Miguel at the first place, Marie T's, where you generally stopped on your trek up the main street of town. You'd look at the lampshade on the bar, where, like many others, you had written your name, and the date, in hopes that someone would find it, someday. You sipped on the splendid San Miguel, a brew that evoked Far-Eastern jungles, pure night skies, friendly smiles and the small strong legs of female inhabitants who had, in fact, made a remarkable adjustment to the U.S. troop presence--an adjustment that showed intelligence exceeding what they generally received credit for. At least Stanley thought so.

The Philippine Islands, the P.I., were being used as a base from which to conveniently attack the enemy, as had been the situation also during World War II.

And you'd think about that, sometimes, when you were out on the town, sitting in a club with friends, and it would seem curious that here, once again, the United States was defending freedom, as if the rest of the world was so incapable of it, that we had to do so much to preserve and protect so troubled a planet, one that was in conflict endlessly, strange that soldiers fought around the globe, trying to keep a mad dog at bay, trying to ensure freedom of life, freedom of religion, freedom of speech.

Stanley would recall classes in school, how there too it was said action taken repeatedly over the years at almost exactly the same place, and for exactly the same reason was necessary to resist negative forces that wanted to claim a lofty position over innocent people, that greedy desire had to be stopped, many times over.

And here they were again. Although there was argument at home concerning the war, there was little disagreement about the threat posed by communist aggression. Almost all at home saw the growth of totalitarianism as an imminent danger to our free way of living, to the benefits of God's blessings, but a growing number doubted Vietnam was the right place to fight it.

Sometimes you'd be angry at the people back in the states protesting the war. Why not get behind us and help us so we can get this over with? Not until Stanley was discharged did he understand draft evasion and civilian protests were anything other than cowardice. Only after a year or so in college did he see that many people sincerely thought involvement in Vietnam was the incorrect method of halting the advance of communism, that they weren't merely "afraid to fight." His friend Andrew had gone to Canada, writing in a letter: "To wage war in a restricted fashion isn't the American way. It doesn't produce victory, only loss of life and national embarrassment. We should stay out or go all the way, <u>one or the other</u>."

Mostly though you tried to think about something else. You thought about the beer you were drinking or the young P.I. girl who had served it or the tender-eyed girl you were talking to who had come over to sit at your table. You thought about the missions your squadron flew, about the planes going to Vietnam, while you were stuck in the P.I., how you wanted to be with them and how the girl was asking about you, and the airplanes, and you wanted her but you wanted to be with a crew and go into the hostile fire zone and maybe see some action and know that you had done it, and she was smiling so sweetly and you hoped she wasn't a spy--no way!--and you wanted to kiss her and the evening was ripe, and so was she.

Stanley sat in his room in Los Angeles, looking through the windows at the day turning into night; he bent an empty beer can by hitting it on his head, and reached slowly into the carton for another. Duty overseas had been relatively safe: the squadron lost only one plane during his tour. But he'd known the crew, had even bunked near them.

It was almost dark now. He ate a few more of the stale chips, he sipped on the beer, happy it was now the temperature he liked--not too cold, not too warm.

The beer in the Philippines had a taste that was all its own. He'd gotten used to it being short-of-cold because after only a few sips the bottle would get warm. There was one air-conditioned bar in town, but he never went there--too crowded. Anyhow, P.I. beer seemed nourishing, as if the stuff they put in it, the grains and other ingredients, had been harvested that day.

You would drink the gradually warming San Miguel, talk to the winsome waitress, talk to friends, think about being overseas, think about the states and how they were changing, pay with Philippine money, say goodbye, get up from the table, wander out into the night...

Up the street you would go, a street of interesting people and occurrences, a stinking stream nearby--waste water?--bars on both sides, food vendors, sailors, Marines, pretty girls, old women with baskets. And the smells of Cavite City were unlike any you had encountered. Dirty, yes, but alive and real.

It felt good to be there. Your shirt would get sticky, even at night, your walk would slow, you would decide between this bar or that--usually one with a new girl you were interested in. Of course they wanted money-- who didn't?

Stanley had graduated high school the year before going overseas, and his experience with girls had been limited due to his shyness. He'd had a girlfriend in school, and shared loving contact with her, but he hadn't gotten around very much. As a result contact with these bright-eyed sweethearts of the Far East engaged and intrigued him.

They spoke with charming, innocent voices, making courageous attempts at English which produced an attractive accent that soothed Stanley's feeling of being out of place, being in a far land.

They came from various parts of the islands in search of a better life than the one they had, to make some money, to buy some clothes, to live in a more comfortable fashion, to perhaps meet and interest a serviceman, fall in love and be taken to the states where they could live an improved life. The women/girls were greatly appreciated by the men/boys from America who were used to the uptight ones they had been chasing, dating, trying to comprehend. The complex, sophisticated relationships prevalent in America were gladly abandoned for this simple, enjoyable, less demanding type. And their bodies! More vibrant, healthier, free from the societal encumbrances of home, more firm and alive, as though the plentiful food in the United States was, in fact, less nutritious than the scarce food of less substance in the P.I. Or was it due to something else? The women/girls of America seemed to have an improper diet physically and mentally in a land where the opposite should have been the case. The servicemen discussed it: how they'd been happy with American girls until they ran into these. Or was it due to the San Miguel?

Something was wrong, they felt, in America--but what was it? Stanley remembered when he'd taken leave, after boot camp, how he'd heard some of his friends were into new "things," that their summer after graduation had been less than productive, that rather than having fun preparing for college or getting a job they had been sitting around listening to Bob Dylan and smoking "grass." It had surprised and bothered him to learn this. While he had been struggling that summer to be a good soldier, engaged in the difficult efforts of boot camp, people he knew were going down the drain. Or was he missing something?

He had worked briefly as a busboy after school ended, and then decided to go into the military. When he returned in the early fall, his friends had changed, retreated, escaped.

Those who during high school had been involved in drug use were few, and they were not really his friends. But this change had come out of the blue. His friends were smoking pot, and it troubled him; they had no motivation. Stanley left for aviation training with a sense of fear, fear for his country and the dangerous direction it was headed. If people he had known, whose minds he had respected, were messing around with drugs, what was going to be the result?

In the Philippines Stanley began to develop a stronger sense of himself; he began to express himself. Earlier he'd withheld his feelings and ideas, hadn't talked much, hadn't made a lot of friends or participated in many social activities. But in the months he spent overseas Stanley grew. He wrote an article for the local military newspaper about a trip he and others had made to the island of Corrigidore. He won the George Washington Honor Medal for an essay, "On Being an American": He began to enjoy the physical, mental, emotional friendship of the girls, there.

He read books. He started writing poems. He even bought a small motorcycle from someone who was returning to the states, and learned to drive it. He traveled to Manila, took "R-and-R" for a few days in Bangkok, in Hong Kong, and, of course, went to Vietnam.

They were good days--for him.

He learned a lot about fear after finally joining a seaplane crew. He'd become friends with several of the regular crew members and asked to fly with them. They discussed it with the captain; it was okayed by the Commanding Officer. Stanley would go with them on missions as a "non"-crew member, working at various positions on board--observer, radio operator, equipment technician. He even got flight pay.

Since their missions usually lasted eight hours, the crew took a lot of supplies with them, including food. Someone was assigned to meal duty for the flight, so Stanley helped there, too. Once during a patrol he briefly sat in the cockpit, in the co-pilot's seat, a frightening experience.

The roar of the engines contributed to the adventurous feel of a mission. And the low altitude. Often the pilot was compelled to take the plane down to a hundred feet or so, where they could better see what was happening, below.

Flying like that, with the hatches open and the sea churning beneath, felt exciting and dangerous.

Tropical wind ripped through the plane, so conversation pertaining to the patrol was carried on over an intercom system. Each crew member had a headset and microphone. If Stanley saw something suspicious from his post, he'd inform the pilot or the flight captain, over the I.C.S. But it was only used for important matters. The flight deck, in the front, was kept as dark as possible to allow the radar operator to read his equipment. The navigator, an officer, would be in a slightly removed, adjacent area, working on his charts and logs.

To an eighteen-year-old it was fascinating. There was plenty of time to look out at the ocean and think about what was happening. And Stanley would listen to transmissions on the radio, or speak to the other crew members, although you had to lean close and yell loudly. At some particular point the plane would turn around, and you would be heading back to the base, half the mission completed.

The P5M, generally referred to as a "pig boat," was the largest twin-engine plane in the world, according to the men who flew her. Taking off and landing was exciting to Stanley, the propellers kicking up sea spray when they were on or near the water. After landing, sweat running down their faces, the crew guzzled ice water as the plane was towed up a ramp onto the flight line where they would complete their responsibilities, climb out, and head for the barracks or the officers' huts or the bar or the E.M. club or, as was the case with some, into town where they had a small house and an island girl staying with them, a practice commonly referred to as "ranching," a practice reserved for a specific pay rate and up. To Stanley it was a great adventure, far removed from 60's California.

To get the eight or so hours of the patrol out of your system was easy. After a cold San Miguel, and a few minutes of talk, the flight suit would begin to irritate, and the thought of getting showered, shaved, and switched into civvies crept into your mind. But the relaxed atmosphere of the club captured you, momentarily, and you knew that after another beer the idea of "hitting the beach" would evaporate in lieu of another idea, that of falling onto your rack in the barracks to sleep.

Mornings were hot and muggy, regardless of how early you got up. Chow was good, but limited in variety. The best thing in the morning turned out to be the powdered milk which, although nearly impossible to drink when you first arrived, took on a most pleasant flavor after a few weeks. It must have been the climate. The milk would be poured into a small glass, with chunks of ice, and after downing it you would return for more. After a while you grabbed several glasses to carry on your tray so you wouldn't have to return for refills.

He smashed the next empty beer can against his head and tossed it on the rug, reached into the six-pack for another, groaning a bit as he leaned forward. It reminded him that he was getting out of condition. How long had it been since he last worked out? Weeks. Months, even? Two, almost.

Funny how a couple of months seemed a lot longer a few years ago. A six-month or a year's tour of duty had seemed an astonishingly long time. But now that exact same number of days didn't seem like much. A two-month stretch went by so fast you hardly remembered it, now, but two months when he was in the service was lots of time. He'd been in Vietnam less than that, and in the P.I. for only six--yet it felt like more.

Some of the crews flew over and stayed with their planes at Cam Ranh Bay, living on the *USS Salsbury Sound*, a Seaplane Tender, flying missions from the bay. The squadron sent two or three planes over at a time, for weeks at a time. Stanley had done it once; it was a memorable experience. The most exciting aspect was, of course, combat. As brief as it was. It happened twice. They were visually checking out a tiny junk that had not responded properly by radio. When they flew in close some individuals on the boat began to fire at them. The pilot got away nicely, and Stanley, to his utter amazement, found himself firing the 50-caliber from the right rear hatch.

They radioed for the "Swift Boats"--the Marines--and stayed around, at a distance, until they arrived. Simple. It didn't seem they had been hit, but back at Cam Ranh Bay several bullet holes were found in the plane's fuselage.

That had been during the day, when they could see what was happening. The next time was at night, late night, and that was different. They got away safely, again, but it was more frightening.

One of the more enjoyable things he did in the Philippines was driving around Cavite City, and in the outskirts, on his motorcycle. It was as fast as any of the cars, which made conditions more advantageous. Using a motorcycle in the states was more dangerous due to traffic speed. But here, people drove thirty miles an hour, average, with top speed usually fifty. The old busses did that, but regular traffic went at a lower speed.

Stanley got around with great maneuverability. They all drove wildly, he noticed, and were accustomed to unorthodox manners on the road. In America you'd get locked up for things they took for granted on the roads of Luzon Province.

He liked most of all driving in the rain; it was beautiful. The rain would hit his face with great, stinging force, but he could relieve the pain by letting off on the throttle. He wore a small helmet with a strap under his chin, and roared along the none too well-built roads, blinking at the rain that struck his eyes with such strength. It never occurred to him to wear goggles.

Stanley put on an old Jim Croce album, and remembered another peculiar experience.

There wasn't much of a beach to speak of, there. Not like California. But there was a spot some of them went to when they had a free day. It was a small, foliage-enclosed stretch of sand on Manila Bay. They swam there, they relaxed--trying to feel as if it were a real beach.

Stanley went there once, nearly getting into a fight. He saw a girl that he'd spent the night with on one occasion, and heard a couple of men talking about her, at a distance. She was lying on a towel, looking lovely, and even though what they said contained an element of admiration, it was also vulgar. It bothered him. He didn't know the men, and he wasn't in the conversation. They were discussing a special ability of her vagina. Stanley felt empathy for her, and was struck by the poignancy of the moment. His experience with her had been memorable, also, but it wasn't something to analyze. What sort of a life was this when men/boys could discuss so openly things about a woman/girl they hardly knew? He had wanted to intervene, but didn't--fearful of the consequences.

He had attempted to learn as much as he could about the repair and maintenance of electronic gear because it appeared to be something he needed if he was to have a well-paying job when he got out, but his heart wasn't in it. Stanley cared that the gear worked well because it was used during missions, and that was important. Other than that it didn't matter to him. But what would he do when he was discharged?

He had an interest in becoming a helicopter pilot, but that required months of training, he'd have to enlist in the Army and add time to his service. He found it curious, also, why there was such an urgent need for new pilots. Obviously it was dangerous duty.

But he was happy with his job on the flight line, the routine, pulling gear from baking seaplane cabins, putting the weighty, funny-looking equipment on the wagon and pulling or driving it over to the shop for the experienced technicians to repair, unloading it, joking with the shop crew, watching them work, doing a few procedures himself, taking fresh equipment back to the plane, installing it inside the hot flight deck, checking it, leaving the secret anti-submarine gear to be checked out by a specialist, sitting in the radio operator's chair, contacting the tower or speaking with someone in the war zone, possibly on a ship or sub who provided the latest information, in code, telling Stanley he heard him okay which was very important because this was the person you needed to reach in an emergency, who would sometimes relay important instructions during a patrol.

Every now and then you got homesick for America, for blondes, redheads, Latinas, beach girls, for sitting in a hamburger joint watching the cute cashier's behind moving under that tight uniform. Why did they always seem to wear clothes that didn't fit?

They knew, they knew. When they bent down to get something from under the counter--what thoughts do they imagine are being thought? What _time_ it is? Hardly. How to get to the other side of town in ten minutes? No way.

The girls of the P.I. didn't pretend like that. They were friendly and real, for the most part. And the guys liked them for it.

Also, there were older, sad ones, downright hookers. They made no mistake about it. You like? You pay. You go to hotel? You fuck.

Those had stayed for a long time near the base. They had not gotten married to a soldier, a pilot, a Marine, a crew member, a sailor, a clerk, a cook. They had not gone away, either, returning to the innards of the islands to work and make do and get married. They were hard. They had been hurt. They were sad. But they could laugh, still, and retained perhaps the belief that a divorced career soldier might take an interest, might provide them with that longed-for journey to America, to a new life.

The evenings were a bit cooler than the days, and when you kept to the base there were several things to do. That was unless you were on duty, in which case the opportunities were restricted to your required responsibility: guard duty, shop work, aircraft watch,

barracks watch--the worst of all--and, of course, sobriety.
Otherwise you were free to hang around, relaxing, seeing a
movie when there was one, sitting around the E.M. club.
One night Rick Nelson even flew in to give a concert. The
sound speakers provided were not very good, but everyone
enjoyed it nonetheless. After all, it was Rick Nelson.

Always there seemed to be the noise of planes on the
line and in the air, or roaring from the water in a heavy-
bodied lunge up to the sky. And they would fly in,
touching onto the salty water of the bay, lifting off a few
feet, then lighting once again on the rippling waves, both
engines noisy, both props making the water leap wildly.

The days were long, hard, hopeful and hopeless. The
nights were short, sweet, hopeful and hopeless. One day
was, more or less, similar to the rest. The monotonous
momentum was broken, occasionally, by excitement, even
tragedy. One day a crew member was killed, run over by a
plane being towed to the ramp. And, of course, one day a
plane was reported shot down, all crew lost.

They were the days and the nights in the lives of
these men, and a few women, stranded in a spot and a time
that didn't seem as though it should have been, but was.

For a while, it was fun. You'd work until you were
soaking wet, go to chow, eat a substantial meal, head for

the open-air club, down a fifteen-cent beer or two or even,
on a very hot day, three or four. Then try to shower and
shave unclumsily without slipping in the shower room and
without nicking yourself too seriously at the sink, and
then leap into freshly cleaned and ironed street clothes,
all with the hope that in town you'd achieve a rapport with
some young lady.

This hope diminished, of course, if you had to be back
on base before curfew. Not everyone could stay out
overnight. That required a pay rate higher than Airman
Apprentice (which was what Stanley was, upon arrival). He,
like many of the men/boys there, had to be in at curfew or
be subject to military discipline. "Shit, when you get up
in pay rate you got it fucking made," was a common comment.

While there, however, Stanley advanced in pay rate
level because of the required test he had taken at the end
of flight crew training, before leaving the states. This
qualified him for overnight pass privileges.

At least temporarily, however, the company commander
withdrew all "overnights" when there was a killing in town
of a soldier by a Philippino. And a knife fight a day
later, apparently in retaliation. Two military men
wounded. The required qualifying level of rating for
overnights was raised, so a lot of the men/boys were

suddenly forced to return to the barracks before curfew, regardless of romantic rapport, sexual desire, or feminine companionship.

The way they worked indicated, to some extent, how patriotic they were; most, but not all, of the squadron seriously welcomed the opportunity to defend American principles. As this was also the way Stanley felt, he got along well on that account. But since he didn't talk much and sort of disliked the military status structure, he wasn't the center of air-base popularity, although writing that story for the paper garnered him some. He was enthusiastic about military procedures, but he didn't care for the distribution of authority which was, or appeared to be, mysteriously determined by some combination of time in and friendship and other unimportant non-specific qualities, with little accent on qualification. The result was, as he grew to believe after a few months in this unlikely tropical outpost, that too many individuals were in positions they did not deserve or perform well. But who was he to say so? In his mind, these erroneous techniques used to determine the placing of responsibility could be costly to the war.

But he did have one opportunity to improve conditions. It dealt with that upper level decision to deprive certain

of the lower level gentlemen of their overnight passes.
Overnights made any tour of duty more bearable, unless
perhaps it was in an Arctic area. Stanley believed
restoring the privilege would boost morale. So he drew up
a formal "special request" chit, quoting from the official
document he'd received when he advanced in pay rate: "In
keeping with the special trust and confidence, etc." words
which, he suggested, indicated overnight liberty. If you
had "special trust" in someone, if you had "confidence" in
them, shouldn't you give them overnight liberty?

The request went all the way up the chain of command
to the commander of the squadron, who agreed with it.

The rating level Stanley had was restored to overnight
liberty status, and the men/boys once again were being
trusted, although few seemed to realize why--there was no
great announcement about it, and their spokesman/boy went
officially unrecognized.

Of course having overnight liberty could result in
missing morning muster. But in general the men/boys were
reliable. Combat support was no joke. Sure, they had a
good time when they could, sometimes violating the rules,
but the bulk of the troops behaved responsibly. There were
incidences--a couple of guys were caught together in the
same bunk behaving contrary to military law. They claimed

they were drunk, but both were sent back to the states to
be discharged. And once someone vanished from the base,
probably into Manila. Desertion. But how could he make
it? Just get a job and hide there? Go back to America?
Then what?

Shakey Jake was a friend of his; they went into town
sometimes. He was nicknamed "Shakey" because often he
would shake while picking up a heavy piece of gear. Jake
was as nice a person as you could expect to meet. He
worked out of the same shop Stanley did; they became good
friends.

Jake was a dreamer. He would sit near the jukebox on
base and think about home, about what he was going to do
when he got transferred back to California. Of course he
had a girl waiting. Military service wasn't for him. It
had "restrictive drawbacks," he said.

Another friend of Stanley's was 3rd Class Petty Officer
Pete, a wry humorist. Almost everything had a funny or sad
joke within it. Pete, too, urgently wanted to go back to
the states. He'd been overseas a long time, was already
there when Stanley arrived. Though belonging to different
squadrons, they'd known each other at San Diego Naval Air
Station, had both taken flight-crewmember classes, shot

pool together, had gone at night to Tijuana in search of a good time. Pete often remarked: "If I die, I die. But I'd rather shoot pool."

Stanley leaned over, pulled another beer from the pack, and remembered something else. Once, on the base in San Diego, he and Pete had gone to the gym and taken turns hitting the heavy bag. It had been fun but tiring--you can't just go in there and do that the first day.

They'd also gone to the fights in San Diego. It was Pete's idea. Stanley had never been before, certainly never imagined becoming a boxer. He'd liked seeing it, though. Perhaps that was the beginning. They also read books, talked them over, and prowled the city on weekends. Stanley's shyness kept him from getting girlfriends, but Pete's attitude was to go ahead and try. It was difficult to find female companionship, though, in a city like that, when you were a serviceman. Most girls were afraid of you and more comfortable with guys who lived in the area for real, not just because they happened to be stationed there temporarily. Most girls liked to feel a little secure about who was putting his arm around them, kissing them, reaching for their private places. They wanted to know their date would be around for a while.

Some of the local girls, of course, didn't feel that way. But the more aggressive, bolder, braver guys got them. Pete was brave, but clumsy.

So they would head for T.J., or to the fights. Where was good ol' Pete now? He'd be interested to know Stanley had taken up boxing, "probly." That was a word that Pete used frequently: "probly"--his answer to anything. It expressed the transient nature of military life, the indefinite range of possibilities, the lack of personal control.

The war in Vietnam had loomed like an angry problem west of the P.I. Daily, soldiers were fighting there, dying there. How many this week? Over a hundred? How many injured?

While Stanley was stationed overseas, America's involvement was predicted to last only a number of months, or develop into a wider conflict with the communists. What would certainly not occur was an extended war without headway. At least that's what he was told.

He sipped at his last beer and thought sadly: People just don't want to think about it anymore. Why had it gone on so painfully long? That was the gag in the throat, that was the pain in the gut.

War, well, it's a terrible thing that goes on for a while and then it's over and those who survive are supposed to recover with the strength and character historically associated with this great nation. Of course, being strong and experienced, you win. But Vietnam is embarrassing to think about, because we know we could have won. Had we been the long shot, we could more easily live with losing. But us? The U.S.? Arguing over it and then pulling out so pitifully? <u>Don't send anyone if that's going to be the result</u>. Save them.

What happened? President Johnson had to quit because of it, and his successor wouldn't go either way--he messed around for years because he was more interested in staying in office than resolving the situation. That method didn't work either. Kennedy was the smart one. He decided to get out of there while the getting was good, but didn't have the chance. Johnson reversed that plan, and Nixon finally pulled us out.

Now the public's unsettled attitudes are directly related to the war in Southeast Asia. Nobody wants to remember it much, but there it is, on our minds, anyway. You can sense the anguish. At least Stanley thought so. And the kids see something is wrong. They know.

He looked out on the evening, at the lights of nearby buildings. He heard a TV in another apartment, heard the cars on the street, out front, felt the vibration of the city.

When you feel the vibration of a city you feel the essence of humanity, the rightness and wrongness of it, the love, the anger, the kindness, the unkindness, the generosity, the selfishness. It's palpable.

You could try to grasp it with both hands, and miss it. But you could sit in a worn chair that wasn't even yours, and feel the existence of life around you. Or drive through town, in its midst.

But it seemed to Stanley he understood life scarcely more than he had twenty years before, when he'd played with a plastic car in the dirt near his house.

Or only nine years later, standing on the deck of the *Salsbury Sound* in Cam Ranh Bay, watching fighter jets-- Phantoms--take off from the airport, and then return...from what? Reconnaissance? Air raids?

The "pig boats" rested peacefully in the water, bobbing, pulling against their restraining lines, one pontoon in the water, then the other, depending on wind direction, depending on what someone might be doing inside. At night one crew member had to stay in the seaplane, armed

with ammunition and a very serious forty-five in a holster.
Stanley did it once or twice. Not fun. There had been
attempts at sabotage; enemy frogmen could reach the plane
from shore. It was an interesting experience, standing
that watch. And it was frightening--alone, late at night,
when something banged against the hull. Only the waves,
hopefully--not the enemy in the water. It was so dark out,
and the ship had seemed so far away, listlessly brooding
nearby.

Back in the Philippines nights were spent quite
differently, as they were in Hong Kong, where Stanley had
taken a few days of "R-and-R," or in bustling Bangkok. But
in 'nam, not so. There was something so aberrant, so
bizarre about the war zone that it defied description.
Someone wanted to kill you, someone supplied with weapons
who would make you die, if he could. It was a feeling, an
awareness that didn't leave you. Here was this long
stretch of land, and from somewhere up north danger was
coming. Somewhere in the jungle, death was hiding.

Occasionally the crews went ashore, to sit in an Army
canteen, to place their feet on the soil of Vietnam, and
talk to the men who were there in the teeth of it--strange-
looking men who had seen things that made their faces
tight, made their eyes seem closed while open, made their

voices quiet, made their hands move secretly, as if they'd get caught if they grabbed the wrong fork, or the wrong cigarette, or the wrong beer can, made their jokes flat-- seen things that made their previous enthusiasm remote, made their thoughts wistful and distant.

One night ashore Stanley spoke with two black Marines who were headed to Hong Kong for R-and-R. They had been in 'nam a long time. They were ready to visit a place that was at peace, even if they themselves would not feel at peace. They were strong, capable-looking military men, but that distant look was in their eyes, they took everything with a measure of acceptance--a psychological trait necessary to maintain while they were at war.

The two men had a bag of bread and meat which they handed around under the table. You weren't allowed to bring food to this outdoor, dirt-floor canteen. You had to eat what they served or forget it--some sort of regulation. The Marines expressed dislike for the rule, saying: "This is better than the shit they got here." The bag of food was from someplace, anywhere, perhaps sent from home, or taken from a military kitchen that had better provisions. They didn't say. Simple food that tasted good. Stanley admired these sad-looking men. It was a paradox, though--

they were accepting the way things were without really
accepting them the way they were.

No beer left, his mind wandering, Stanley peed in his
sink rather than go down the hall. Then he lay on his bed,
drifting off to sleep with visions of seaplane patrols, of
being wakened early in his tiny bunk on the ship, having a
sleepy breakfast in the mess hall and suddenly being on
deck in the dark, before dawn, climbing down the side into
a power boat that took him and the rest of the crew to the
P5M that waited in the water, climbing up, loading
equipment and provisions and ammunition and the Jato
bottles, preparing for takeoff, hearing the engines warmed
up, putting on his flight helmet, checking the I.C.S.,
getting situated in takeoff position as the pilot taxied
the plane to its takeoff position and then the two gigantic
engines were roaring and the Jato bottles were in place
outside, on the doors, and the plane began that telltale
lunge forward as the South China Sea grew solid underneath
as their speed increased, with the sound of pounding, the
sound of the engines, and like a kick in the ass the Jato
bottles fired with that piercing noise that meant war, to
Stanley, because you didn't need Jet-Assist-Take-Off
bottles in the P.I. or in San Diego where the bay was

bigger--you only needed Jato in 'nam, and the plane was propelled as by an unseen hand, lifted like a glider from contact with anything but air, that thin substance that held you up, that substance the propellers grabbed, held on to, pushed away from as a mountain climber does to each rock and ledge on his journey, and you lifted upward, on your way.

Then you were powering through the beautiful sky over the greenish-grey ocean, over miles of growing foliage, unlike trees, exactly, unlike bushes, but growth that was green, and brown, and you didn't want to look at it because it was a tropical jungle at war, and Americans were being wounded there, and Vietnamese, and some had maybe died right where you were looking, so you turned instead to the sunlit sky and to the long horizon of sea to the east, where your western country was, a place you hadn't appreciated enough, wanted to return to so you could stride down a street in a city, go to a movie, play pool with Pete or sit on a rock on a road on a hill and see the country below, your country, and beyond, and think about how wonderful it was to be a part of it. And you saw the machine gun mounted next to you, pointed through the hatch into the day, waiting for use, waiting for use for use for use.

And you walked, keeping your balance, bent over, to tap your friend Bill Ryan on his shoulder, to see how he was doing at the radar scope, and you got yourself a paper cup of ice cold water, and it entered your body like a diamond sparkles in bright light.

And you leaned by one of the open hatches, your hand on the safety webbing that separated the outside from the inside, hearing the roar of the engines, feeling the hot strong wind that came in like a fullback pushing for a first down. You put your hand out into it, knowing it's first-and-ten with such power, then put your hand into the frayed pocket of your flight suit because you must be cool, man, and unafraid.

Then the pilot is bringing the plane down close to the sea, he must be checking something out, but you have your helmet off--you haven't heard--and the plane starts to turn, and it seems like only a few feet down, now, to that green-grey water, the plane begins to bank, and like a rocket something is in the water and goes past, below, and you turn around as the plane also turns, you stumble to your position and unlatch and swing the 50-caliber, ready on its mount, as Bill is suddenly there putting a helmet on you and you set up an ammunition belt as the loud low leaning turnaround of the plane nears completion and your heart is going fast and Bill is getting more ammo ready to feed into the gun and you hear the pilot talking and the flight captain is talking and the radio operator is saying "no response" and that means something and the flight captain asks you if you are ready and you reply "affirmative" and the co-pilot says you're close and it's on your side and then you see it, a small boat in the water with some smiling gooks and they wave and the pilot slows and the plane banks around the junk and you hear the radio operator tell the pilot there is still no answer to his I.D. request and then oh the gooks are pulling away some leaves on deck, some branches, and there are guns and oh shit they are pointing them now and you point yours and the pilot yells and you do not wait, you pull the trigger and whamwhamwhamwhamwham the gun starts firing loudly, banging around in your hands and your friend nearly falls from his kneeling position and you're sweating, the boat is gone past, the flight captain is yelling to someone and you are holding on to the 50-caliber that you have now fired at human beings and the plane is still going away and someone is cursing but you don't move from where you are and your legs shake but you don't let that affect your grip, so no problem, you and your friend are looking out the hatch leaning forward as the plane starts a gradual turn and you hear they notified the Marines and that feels <u>real good</u> and everyone is checking for damage and you are asked if you are okay and you reply "affirmative" and the plane is turning around, increasing altitude--you are not going in again you are just keeping track of the junk until it can be approached by the Marines when they arrive in their Swift Boats.

PART FIVE

When Stanley woke up his head hurt. It proved he was
getting out of shape. He could drink more beer when he was
in shape without feeling the hangover. And he'd noticed
muscle loss and the inevitable widening of his mid-section.

The bent cans were strewn on the carpet under the
window; he tried to keep from looking at them but did take
a glance. He hadn't even removed his pants when he crawled
to bed the night before.

Stanley put on and laced up his tennis shoes, drank
some water, wet his face at the sink, went out the door,
pulling a T-shirt over his head, checked to make sure he
had his keys, locked the door, tucked in his T-shirt, went
into the bathroom at the end of the hall, and, finally,
gritting his teeth and blinking at the sun's brightness,
found his way out onto the sidewalk of Union Avenue.

Almost fall in Southern California, with the wind from
the mountains cooled by the touch of a brief snowfall,
cooled by the cold wet rocks and sun-hidden crevasses,
blowing with power across the drought-weary, oil-price-
angry, summer-spent city to the waiting whitecapped
seagulled saltaired sea.

Stanley made his way to the corner.

He took some deep breaths, and by the time he was up the surprisingly steep street to the disturbingly distant corner he felt faint. But then he saw the small shape of Jim's Café and knew that the black coffee-bean water would wake him up and straighten him out.

It did do that. Luckily he had some money left.

L.A....city of hope, city of trouble, city of work, city of hate, city of love. Home of the Johnny Carson show since he moved from N.Y.C. Well, actually, it was in Burbank.

City of a park in the hills with a large zoo, with an observatory from which to watch and wait, from whence James Dean threw a tire iron in *REBEL WITHOUT A CAUSE*. City of Hollywood, of moviemakers, of newspaper stands, of girls with legs moving swiftly beneath soft dresses, walking to and from work, or store to store, shopping. Of men at magazine racks looking at pictures of girls while real live ones stride past, looking for clothes to buy and wear to attract men.

And of dissimilar people who walk the streets, their sexuality changed from the norm by some unknown and unseen force, their lives straining to adjust to its plight. Men behaving as women and women behaving as men. Made to hide this difference for fear of hatred and violence, or to flaunt it in wild desperation, risking the disdain of those with problems different and less obvious.

Who can spot a rapist on the street? Yet his actions are more heinous than those of people who are derided and dismissed every day.

City of laborers' long hours, of stoic citizens riding a bouncing bus to and from work, of bus stop benches bearing momentarily their weight, exchanging it for another's, while prices insidiously go up up up like a nightmare that does the exact opposite of what you want it to, while you try to wake.

Stanley's day, as he gathered himself together inside the café, was beginning its slow and probably uneventful journey toward night, a welcome time when he again could recline, tipping up a beer or two if he indeed felt better as the day passed and the awaited evening's respite arrived, and he could close out the day's waste, forget the lost day, the lost opportunity, and finally sleep.

What day was it? For a moment he couldn't recall. He had a refill and asked for a donut. Coffee was served in small cups there, so he could have many of them and not drink as much as somewhere else. The donut was sweet and stale, but it was food, and it helped fill the cave in his stomach--a cave that seemed to have enlarged since he lost that stupid fight.

2

The weeks began to flow by steadily. Stanley's life was more or less a series of getting up, plowing through, going to and fro, and lying down again. And the summer heat lingered.

He told his companions at the gas station that he would return to boxing, yet it didn't seem they believed him. Since most people didn't understand boxing in the first place, how could they be expected to comprehend a desire to return to it after a lack of participation? But he meant it. At least, he thought he did.

The Golden Gloves Tournament would be starting the first of the year. Plenty of time to get ready for that.

Or he could turn pro, make some money.

His cut was healed--the doctor had removed the stitches in August.

So what was holding him back?

Why wasn't he going to the gym and running and applying for a pro license, doing all the things he should be doing if he were to be doing it?

Why was he putting on weight? He was over middleweight now. Why had he been stopping at the liquor store on the corner and getting those bottles of beer and dry sausages at night? Because Amy left?

Why was it a relief to sit in the big chair and listen to the radio and chew the sausage and guzzle cold beer? That wasn't the way he wanted to live.

On one hot day, before work, Stanley was run out of his room, because the fan wasn't much help, and the wind through his car windows offered more relief. Normally he didn't mind hot weather--it reminded him of his months at Sangley Naval Station, all those fond memories...

But today he was hit by the opposite sort of memory. Sad, bad, evil. He'd driven aimlessly to the gym and cruised past, up Main Street, spotting the entrance, the big arch beside it that led to the parking lot, and felt a twinge of pain because a certain Cadillac was not in its proper place under the arch. A Cadillac which had been a fixture for years, always parked there in a preferred location. Its owner had been the gym's owner, Howie, who'd been suddenly and shockingly murdered earlier that year. Stanley didn't care for that memory.

It had happened on his birthday, too. An unsolved crime.

He'd liked Howie, a gruff and no-nonsense older man who ran the gym with an iron fist. He reminded Stanley of Humphrey Bogart. He had a heart under the gruffness, a soul. It took a certain degree of repeated association for Howie to reveal that side of him, however.

He'd always called Stanley "kid," even though Stanley was no kid, really.

But that was gone now, that friendship. Someone had killed Howie and left the body in the Cadillac on the side of a freeway.

The gym had kept going, of course. A new person sat in the office at the top of the stairs, Howie's fighters got new managers, the family grieved, Stanley grieved, and life went on. But today the sadness stirred darkly within, the hot weather lost its impact, and he returned to his room to wait to go to work.

3

September drifted along until something crazy and wonderful happened: two weeks of a sweet adventure. The day arrived when Stanley, remembering the evening at the Troubadour, decided he had to see that Rosy again. He didn't quite know how to go about it, but he was determined.

There was no mention of her in the paper, so one day he drove through the city, for awhile, then to the Troubadour. Middle of the day, not many people around. The bar in front was operating, but the club itself had not opened for the evening.

Stanley looked in the door and saw the place where she had been. It was empty except for a few workers setting up tables and arranging equipment on the stage.

He hesitated. Maybe he should have a beer at the bar before going in there. No, no more beer.

He took a deep breath and swung the door out and nearly strutted in, overflowing with nervousness and courage at the same time. He had to make the effort.

One guy seemed to be in charge. He was telling two other men on the stage what to do, how to set up the music equipment and hook up the wires, while he rearranged the seating area.

Stanley approached him. It was surreal being there now, with dust and the sunlight from the front and workers' voices and the sound of tables and chairs being moved--too different.

"Uh, excuse me."

"<u>Keep that fucker to the left</u>! No--farther!"

"Can you maybe--"

"What do you need, pal?"

"Uh, I'm interested in finding Rosy Sanchez. Do you--"

"Shit, I'd like to find her too! What a babe."

"Well, yeah, uh, it's just that I saw her here and--"

"Charlie, set it next to the drums!" Then:

"She ain't here, buddy. Bring the mike to the front!"

"Do you know where she is? I mean, is she singing anywhere?"

"How should I know? Check with her manager."

"Okay. Thanks. Good idea. But, uh, do you know who that is?"

Now the guy was losing patience. "No. Ask Marcia in the bar."

So that was that. Marcia told him: "Caliente Artists. Should be in the phone book."

He called the number, asked if Rosy was performing locally. No, not at the present moment. Well, how could he reach her? To his surprise, the woman at the agency gave him the name and address of Rosy's business manager. "You can write to her there, if you wish."

"Thanks."

It was a place on Wilshire, only a mile or so from Barry's gas station. Weird. Stanley drove by. A large intimidating building.

He made himself park.

Had to; he wasn't going to write her a letter.

He walked in the front entrance, feeling like he was dreaming, or something, like an action movie in slow motion. Only everything was moving too fast. His plan was to find out where he could see her perform, again.

There was a row of elevators in the lobby, people getting in and out. Busy, formal. He wasn't dressed right, that was for sure, but he had to get to the 10th floor.

There were guards in front of the elevators, there was a sign on a table in front of the guards.

People were showing little cards--badges--when they walked past the table to the elevators.

Stanley had no badge.

The sign read: "No Unauthorized Personnel Beyond This Point." Stanley veered away.

Those elevators were for certain floors only and he wasn't to reach them without specific approval. That was obvious. Maybe he should speak with one of the guards, ask to go up to the office.

He looked around.

Floors above 15 were serviced by an additional row of elevators. People were entering them without showing badges to anyone. No guards.

He got into an elevator, but could only select floor 15 or higher.

He pushed 18, and went up.

A woman with him in the elevator, a well-dressed woman, was going to 20. He stared at the floor, got out when they reached 18.

The elevator had moved rapidly. He felt sick.

It was a fancy hallway with glass doors with company names on them--okay. He walked to the left, immediately, for no reason.

Now what?

No sign of the other row of elevators.

He was nervous. <u>How stupid</u>. Bill Ryan would laugh at him.

But it occurred to Stanley what to do: the stairs. Stairs to the tenth floor.

He looked for the exit.

Naturally, it had a sign on it: EMERGENCY USE ONLY.

He reached for the knob, looked around, prepared for an alarm to go off, pulled the door open.

Silence.

He shot in.

Dark, cool, metallic, a breeze from below, somewhere.

He walked down the steps. One floor, two floors, three floors.

Then at 15 he saw the sign of all signs, in the stairwell, on the wall: RESTRICTED. NO UNAUTHORIZED PERSONNEL BEYOND THIS POINT. BUILDING CLEARANCE REQUIRED-- CODE 724. TRESPASSERS SUBJECT TO PROSECUTION. What the...?

A wide red line was painted up the wall.

This is ridiculous. I just want to meet Rosy Sanchez.

He walked past the painted barrier.

When he got to the next door, he tried it. Locked.

Oh, shit, they're all locked!

He went down another flight.

Locked.

He kept at it.

What if someone heard him? He might be judged a thief or something. Those guards had guns.

The tenth floor, at last.

Locked.

He kept going.

What was this? Would he end up in the lobby again?

He found a door that was open--a little.

It had a piece of leather around the knob, stuck inside the door so it wouldn't shut fully. Good trick.

Stanley pushed the door open.

A hallway. No, an office.

Shit, somebody's office.

Oh, well. He left the stairwell, entered the hallway.

He didn't see anyone. There was only one direction to go, so he walked along the hall, passed a couple of closed doors, feeling very uncomfortable.

Then he saw two girls sitting at desks. Young women. He didn't really know what to do, but he smiled at the girls when they looked up at him in surprise.

He threw up his hands, kept moving.

"Ha, ha, don't mind me, I'm just lost!"

To his relief, they both smiled and laughed. As he went further he saw an elevator door a short distance away. Stanley headed for it and pushed the 'up' button as one of the girls said, "That's okay, I'm that way most of the time myself!"

He nodded, forcing a laugh. "Yeah, heh-heh."

Where was that elevator?

"It happens sometimes," he said, trying to continue the conversation so they wouldn't become too interested in an explanation. They were both still looking at him. It was a weird place, an elevator right there in the office.

When the doors opened he stepped in, waving to the friendly secretaries or whatever they were, pushed the 'ten' button, the doors closed, and he was going up.

He was glad to be away from the stairs and out of that remarkable office, but he was still somewhere he wasn't supposed to be, and didn't know what to expect.

So he got out at the tenth floor. At least there was an ordinary corridor. Stanley walked one way, then the other, and found the right office. Right name, right number.

Okay.

He opened the door and walked in, realizing he had no idea what he was going to say.

Large waiting room. Must be a big company.

An efficient-looking woman sat at a desk behind an opening. She stood when he walked over.

"Excuse me."

"Hello," she said. "May I help you?"

Nothing to do but just say it.

"I'm, I'm looking for Rosy Sanchez."

She hesitated. "Yes?"

"My name is Stanley Larson. I..." He paused.

A tiny smile came to her mouth. It must not have been difficult for her to figure him out. "She isn't here. Miss Sanchez is a client but we don't generally keep her around." Then she laughed. "What can I do for you?"

"I saw her at the Troubadour, and I'd like to know when she'll be performing again."

"I see. As far as I know, that won't be for some time. She's recording an album."

"Oh."

"Would you like to leave a note? I'll make sure she gets it."

"Well, sure. Okay. But that's...don't you know where she is?"

"I'm sorry, I can't give you that information."

Stanley nodded. "Sure, I understand."

She handed him a pen and a sheet of paper. "Sit down over there, if you'd like." She indicated a couch and table behind him.

"Thanks." Stanley took the paper and pen and sat, wondering what to write. Oh, well. It's a note, what's the difference? The phone rang, thankfully, and the receptionist answered it, giving him a chance to relax.

He thought a bit, and wrote: "My name is Stanley Larson. I loved your performance recently at the Troubadour." Now what? "I hear you are recording an album. That's great. Good luck. I hope to see you again in the future. Stanley."

He returned the pen and paper to the receptionist, then asked for them back. He wrote the end of one of his poems, hoping he recalled it properly:

AFTER DISASTER

"The birds, no matter what some say, will sing.
The sun, no matter what some say, will shine.
The earth, no matter what some say, will turn.
And music, no matter what some say, will lift
    us up."

Stanley folded the paper and wrote his address on the outside. Hey, that Playmate had written back, hadn't she? As the woman took it he said: "Thanks a lot," and got out of there.

4

He was ten minutes late to work. Barry didn't like it, naturally.

"Don't take advantage of me."

"Sorry. Had some stuff to do."

As the afternoon progressed, the boss left, the kids from the school hurriedly passed by, he helped Mark attach a spotlight to his truck in the garage, he pumped gas and thought about Rosy, thought about the gym, thought about Sugar Ray Robinson.

The Sugar Man didn't come to the gym anymore. Too bad. Stanley had liked to watch him work out, to study his style.

A lot of the other exciting guys, the black guys, had shifted to a gym further downtown. Their spirit and determination was noticeably missing. Maybe that's why Sugar Ray had stopped coming in. Too bad.

He'd been there when Stanley started, showing him how to practice in front of the mirror, perfecting jabs and slips. They'd even sparred, although Stanley was reluctant to throw a punch at a legend.

"Come on--put it out there! Don't be afraid to swing," he'd told him.

How funny it had seemed--a man telling him to hit him.

But then, when he did try, Stanley couldn't hit him anyway--that is, not at first. After a while he could connect--a little.

But Sugar Ray stopped training there after a year or so--he was long retired, anyway--probably had other things to do.

"Gonna get some fresh pussy tonight."

"What?"

Mark had come out of the garage, a smile on his face. "Yeah, man. Got a date with a virgin!"

"Good luck," Stanley said weakly, trying not to be jealous.

That night he considered going to the high school track, to run--but he didn't go. He resisted drinking any beer, however.

From bed he looked at the crumpled picture of the Playmate tacked on his wall. She reclined on an oversized pillow, her hands behind her head, her large soft breasts staring back at him deliciously, her legs curled toward him, ready to be spread apart.

He reached down the front of his underwear, and began to rub.

He looked at the girl on the wall, imagining running his hands over her skin, kissing those arms. His rubbing increased.

He pulled down his underwear.

It didn't take long.

5

The next few days went slowly until the disturbed landlady slapped a letter on the front counter when he walked in: "Mail, piggy."

The return address was 6300 Wilshire. That building! No name, however. In his room he waited a moment to open it. Could it be from Rosy? She must have hated his corny poem. He opened the letter.

No, she hadn't hated it. "I'm glad you liked my show."

Liked? I said I loved it.

"Joyce at the office said you were cute. I want to see for myself. Do you ever eat at The Mission? It's Mexican food, on Beverly. Do come in Saturday, at noon. I'll be there with my friends."

Huh?

"P.S. Your poem, if it was one, was sweet. Rosy."

If it was one?

He checked the envelope again. Oh, let this be authentic.

Stanley risked being spotted by the landlady in order to go to Beverly Boulevard to find The Mission. He found it; little adobe-looking Mexican place, closed for the

night. When was Saturday, now?

6

But before Saturday there were a few spark plugs to replace in his '57, and points to be cleaned--with sandpaper. This he did between pumping gas for customers. He changed his oil, too. That, of course, had to be paid for. Barry would miss oil cans from the stock. Payday was prior to Saturday, also. There was a deduction--partial repayment of the bail deposit Barry had provided. That would take a few more paychecks. Fuck it, Stanley thought, it was my own fault.

He didn't blame the man who'd opened his car door, anymore, or the speeding police car. He had no one to blame but himself, as they say.

Friday night Mark wanted to leave early. Sure. He owed him one anyway, although Stanley couldn't remember what for, anymore.

So he worked alone; it was fairly busy, too. By closing time Stanley's feet hurt. Before he could close up, though, a white El Dorado pulled in. But they didn't want fuel.

"Where's the '10', do you know?" the driver asked hurriedly. "How do I get on the '10'?" He looked foreign, although Stanley couldn't guess which country.

"Go down La Brea, maybe five miles," he told the driver, pointing up the street to an intersection. "Turn left up there. You'll hit the freeway. It's not far."

"South on La Brea?"

"That's right."

"Left?"

"Right."

"You say right?"

"I mean left, turn left."

The men didn't laugh; they drove off, toward the signal at La Brea. He closed the place up with his usual routine, cleaning, sweeping, putting the cash in the safe, all the while hoping the men didn't plan to rob him.

In the morning his neck was sore; he couldn't figure out what caused it--sure hadn't been doing any sit-ups.

He felt nervous about meeting Rosy. Was he supposed to sit with her at lunch? Was he to look "cute," and leave?

Stanley took a shower in the bathroom down the hallway. The previous night he'd restricted himself to one-and-a-half beers. He shaved at the little sink in his room, put on Brut aftershave, rested on his bed wondering about the lunch, or whatever it was going to be.

He didn't even know if she'd actually be there. You never know with women--they're changeable. He imagined her sweet lips, her body that had moved so enticingly onstage.

Who were her friends? Girls, he hoped. But probably not. Probably six guys to guard her. Ha ha. He wasn't _that_ sexually aggressive. Amy had known that.

"You're the only one, Joe."

At ten he had cereal. He read in _A THOUSAND DAYS_ but couldn't concentrate. At ten-thirty he almost fell asleep. What if he'd missed the noontime gathering? He got up, put on a clean shirt, black Levi's, tennis shoes. Hadn't worn his boots in weeks.

Too early to go, yet. He played an old B.J. Thomas record. At eleven-fifteen he went out.

No landlady, thank God. Must be sleeping it off. One night she'd followed him to his room when he'd brought that black art student over. She'd actually knocked on his door, saying: "We don't allow that in here!" They'd waited quietly until she gave up--but it was an unromantic episode.

The girl had declined his offer to get into bed, saying, "We have to be more compatible." What did that mean?

"We're compatible," he'd said.

"I don't feel right"--so they kissed, talked.

No, he wasn't aggressive enough.

Stanley arrived at The Mission before noon, but didn't go in. Wouldn't do to appear desperate. Not that it mattered much. She only wanted to look him over.

Whatever takes place, he decided, I'm going to be cool. Not going to mess it up. Be aggressive, but not pushy. Let her do a bit of the work.

After driving around the block he went into the parking lot behind the restaurant. Going to sit here like a dope? No. Have to go in.

But he sat for two or three minutes, hoping she wouldn't see him there. But that wasn't cool, so he went inside.

Stanley had missed this spot, never been in it before. You had to place your order at the front, then sit at a table; not fancy. Well, she wasn't Linda Ronstadt, after all. He tried not to scan the place; he looked at the menu on the wall behind the cash register. But he heard voices, laughter. How many people was she with? He turned and looked. Not tough to find her. A booth, with four people. No men. She was there, listening to the woman across from her.

So he went over. She looked up as he approached. Her eyes seemed only half open. What was she thinking?

"Hello," he said. "It's me." Silence at the table.

"Oh!" she said, smiling. "You are the guy?"

Her friends looked at him curiously. He nodded.

Rosy said: "Hi! Sit down. Here he is." She pushed over. He smiled at the others, said: "Hi." They responded "Hello" as he sat beside her, uncomfortably.

"So you saw me?"

"Yes. It was good--very good. Wonderful."

Her friends laughed, for some reason. Rosy looked at him with those partly closed eyes. "I love praise."

"You deserve it." That made her eyes open.

"Well..." she laughed. He was feeling more confident. And he liked her accent.

"It's true. You sang wonderfully."

"Where was I? Oh, the Troubador. Fun place."

"Too small," the woman beside her said.

He nodded again. What else could he do?

"Rosy should be at a bigger place, like the Amphitheater," one of them said. The others agreed, laughing. He saw they were having margaritas.

"Someday," Rosy said, glancing at them. "Are you hungry? Stanley, isn't it?"

"Right." She waited. "No, I'm not hungry."

"Really?" She seemed to be flirting with him. "You can eat, can't you? Too nervous?"

The women giggled.

"Eat with us!" the one across from her said. Her accent was thicker than Rosy's.

"Okay. What are you having?"

"Huevos." They all laughed, like it was a joke.

Later he learned from Rosy that 'huevos' were eggs, in Spanish--which he'd vaguely known--and in addition a slang term for a man's balls. Apparently they found the double-meaning humorous.

After formal introductions he ate standard fried eggs, with hot tortillas and beans. The other girls spoke a little while Stanley grew more and more confident answering Rosy's many questions. He had to tell her where he worked, that he boxed, that he was a writer. He got in a few questions of his own:

"So, you're making an album?"

"Yes."

"Did you write the songs?"

"Yes."

"Is it fun?"

"Yes."

"I look forward to hearing it."

"It won't be finished for a long time. Don't you want to hear me before that?" One of her friends said a few words in Spanish; the others laughed. Rosy opened her mouth in mock protest, and then remarked: "Don't say such things! Stanley hasn't even asked me out." She turned demurely to him.

"I'm asking now," he said, to his surprise.

"Oh, you are?" Everyone was watching him.

"Let's go out. Would you like to go out?"

"Where?"

"To a movie, to the beach, anywhere."

"A movie. That's my choice."

"No," the one beside her, Ada, exclaimed. "To the beach!"

Rosy shook her head. "I'm too fat." She put her hands on her waist. "See?"

"Oh, Rosy!" "Oh, no, Rosy," they protested.

"Do you think she is fat, Stanley?"

"No." He felt his face redden. "She's perfect."

"Listen to that!"

"Do you hear, Rosy?"

She kissed him on the cheek. Then she put her hand on his face. "Ada, isn't he handsome?"

Ada agreed, nodding. "Oh, he must make the other mens jealous." The others concurred, laughingly.

"You will make him embarrassed," Sylvia, across from Ada, observed. "Stop eet!"

"Do we embarrass you, Stanley?" Rosy asked, innocently.

"Yes, you do."

More laughter. Ada took a sip of her margarita. "Well, are you going to the beach or to the movies?"

"To the movies, Ada, not to the beach. He doesn't want to see me in a bikini."

"Oh--I hope I will." Once again the women giggled. Rosy looked at him with those half-closed eyes.

"Do you?"

The woman across from him, Elena, pushed at his arm. "¡Por supuesto! He's a man! Of course he wants to." She looked at Rosy. "You have to watch out for him."

"Yes?"

Ada, finishing her drink, said: "And you must be very careful of her, Stanley. She's a bad girl."

7

Sunday he called her, but she was out. They were going to a movie that very night, *THE DEEP*. He'd found it was still playing, at the Vista, in east Hollywood. Rosy hadn't seen it. He had, but would watch it again--good things in that movie.

The only problem--Rosy hadn't given him her address. Stanley felt lucky to simply have her number. But, not aggressive. Should have pushed for her address. Was she putting him on?

The pond in the courtyard of the Cambria had long since dried up. Stanley looked at it as he left to have his car washed. No water in the city! They probably cut back at the car wash too. It was worth a try, though.

He wasn't going to mess this one up. She'd fallen into his lap--a pretty, sexy, "bad" girl. No one knew as well as he how many times he'd screwed up in the past, let girls slip through his fingers. Not this time.

After getting through the car wash, he felt like stopping at "The Little Orient," but didn't. The girl who'd reached down and squeezed him that time danced on Sundays. But he didn't go. Wanted to save his energy for Rosy.

His car was running well, thank God. But he had to have the address. He had enough cash. He had clean clothes. So he went back to his room to wait.

What if she didn't answer the phone, never got in all day, didn't really want to go out with him?

Two o'clock. He called again, downstairs. No answer. Why didn't she have a message machine? Lots of people had them. He walked past the corner store and headed east. <u>Lynn</u>. That was her name. Blonde. Had her in a class. Was it English? No, history. He'd hated history. No, he'd hated the professor. So smug. So cold. No, no, no, he didn't hate him. It was his own fault--not studying.

But <u>Lynn</u>, she studied. So proficient in class. They'd spoken a few times afterward, but he hadn't asked her out. What was wrong with him? She'd always smiled when she saw him.

And in the library he'd been standing near a shelf, holding open a book, when he felt something warm and resilient push at his arm. Turning, he saw it was Lynn. She'd put her breast right against his upper arm. Smiling, so near him, so cute.

"Hi, Stanley."

"Hi." Instinctively he put his arm on her back.

"What's going on?" She was standing very close to him.

"I got an 'A'. How'd you do?"

"On what? Oh, that test? Not too good."

Her back felt so strong. Was she a gymnast?

Why hadn't he pursued it? She was so friendly.

He went into a Chinese restaurant on 8th Street for a cup of decaf, but they didn't serve it, so Stanley had tea--which he hated.

What was his problem? Sometimes having sex was so difficult he couldn't reach orgasm. Embarrassing. For some reason he held back. It made him reluctant to pursue women.

Of course it might be related to the time he'd been kicked repeatedly at age twelve. He was playing football in a friend's backyard; just kids, but an eighteen-year-old neighbor had joined them. Stanley stole the football from him and ran for a touchdown. Enraged, the neighbor punched him in the face, kicked him in the groin several times, making him bleed.

The doctor stitched it up, said he'd be okay.

But...

Not this time. He wasn't going to run away this time.

Outside the Chinese restaurant he called Rosy's number again. No answer, so he returned to his room.

At four, a child--hers?--answered; Rosy came to the phone, full of life.

"Stanley? Hello!"

"Hi. How are you?"

"Fine. How are _you_?"

"Great. I called earlier, but nobody was there. I--"

"We were out, I'm sorry. Too many things to do. How are you?" she repeated.

"Great...do you still want to go tonight?"

"<u>Por supuesto</u>. You going to pick me up? What time?"

So he picked her up. She looked radiant. Her house was on Pico near Normandie, a little place with no yard in front. A new Firebird sat in the driveway. Good car for her.

"Oh, look at your car!" she exclaimed as they approached it. She was wearing a simple dress, not low-cut, but with bare arms and shoulders. Lots of lipstick. Big earrings.

He let her in; she didn't bother to cover her legs. As he walked to his door the neck pain returned.

"Stanley, don't drive fast and scare me," she told him after he'd revved it up. "Please."

"Okay." Putting the Chevy in gear he carefully pulled out onto the street. Rosy sat a discreet distance away. Not like some dates he'd had.

His aftershave competed with her perfume, but lost.

"¿De dónde es usted?" He'd learned it from George-- where are you from?"

"You speak Spanish?"

"No--un poco."

"Soy de los Estados Unidos."

"Uh...the..."

"Here, I'm from here. Los Angeles." She laughed, for some reason.

"I thought so," he lied. She waited. Talk, Stanley. "We have half an hour. Should we go right to the theatre?"

"I don't know." She waited, her hands in her lap, but her legs open. Talk.

"Want to stop...for something?"

"If you do." She looked at him.

"On the way? Coffee or something?"

"No, not for me." It was getting dark.

"No, we don't want to be late." <u>Talk</u>. "Is that your car in the driveway? Cool car."

"That's my sister's." She waited.

He couldn't think of anything else to say. His neck hurt, he felt sweat on his forehead. Almost to the theatre.

"You like your album?"

"What?"

"Do you--like--your album so far?"

"Oh yes." Radiant again. "The songs are turning out. I'm very happy."

"Good." <u>Be aggressive</u>. "Your friends were funny the--at the restaurant." She laughed, thank God.

"Were you nervous? I was."

"Really?" he asked, astonished. "You didn't look like it." She waited. "I <u>was</u> nervous." She waited. "I'm glad you invited me. I wanted to meet you."

"Why?"

"Why? You're kidding."

She turned to him, put her hand on his arm. "I'm not kidding. Why did you want to meet me?"

"Just--I don't know--when I saw you that night--I liked you." She squeezed his arm, took her hand away. He wiped his forehead. Fortunately they were near the Vista;

he turned the corner, found a place to park. "Here we are."

"Are you nervous now?"

"Yes," he admitted, forcing a smile. She waited. Should he kiss her? Too fast. But he wanted to. She seemed to sense it--they all do.

"You want to go in? We're early."

"No. Why don't you kiss me?" She <u>was</u> a bad girl.

He put his arms around her, he kissed her, she opened her mouth almost immediately, he moved his tongue inside, making contact with hers. It was a long kiss. At first her tongue waited, then responded. She pressed herself against him, emitting a kind of soft moan.

It was not easy watching the movie after that. They sat there, pretending interest. Even the breasts-inside-the-wet-T-shirt sequence wasn't important to Stanley, except that he was thinking of Rosy's. After a while he put his arm around her and kissed her; she put her hand on his leg. In the car he'd rubbed her shoulders but resisted moving his hands anywhere else--too fast. Now he put a hand on her stomach, slid it upward, but she stopped him. Before he could be disappointed, however, she whispered: "<u>Not here</u>." Meaning, he hoped, not here, but somewhere.

They watched the movie. Rosy left her hand on his leg, moving it back and forth a few inches, leaning her head on his shoulder.

Before the end she looked at Stanley with eyes that seemed to be glimmering in the light from the screen. "Let's go. I want to go."

Outside Rosy said she wasn't feeling well. "Maybe it was the popcorn." They got in the car. "I'll be fine tomorrow."

He drove her in silence to her house, parking in the driveway.

"Did I say or do anything to make you--"

"No, no," she interrupted. "Nothing you did, sweetie." She leaned against him, in the front seat, almost sadly. "It hurts," she whispered, patting her belly. "Really." So, he rubbed it.

"You're not upset?" Stanley asked, kissing her temple. She shook her head and put her hand on his forearm.

"It isn't you. Yo tengo problemas."

"What? You have problems?"

"Sí." She closed her eyes as he caressed her stomach. "I'm sorry." A car went by fast on the street. There were lights on in the house. The Firebird was still there, in front of them.

He dared to touch her breast, gently squeezing it. "Don't be sorry. It's my fault for not feeding you. Should have eaten first."

She opened her eyes. Then they got that low-lidded look. He kissed her. Great mouth.

She dropped her hand to his pants. "What's that?"

"Nothing."

"Let's see." She began to unbutton his Levi's, stopped, pulled open his belt, then pulled open the top buttons.

"I thought you didn't feel good..."

"I want to see." She got it out from his underwear, holding it. "Umm." She bent to look closely. "Very handsome." At least she didn't say "Not bad," like the dancer in "The Little Orient."

Shifting her body, trying to push back his underwear not too successfully, Rosy asked: "Should I?"

"If you want," he managed, hoping she meant what he thought she meant.

She held on to him, sliding her hand up, then down. "Oh, maybe not. We only just met."

"We didn't only just meet."

She laughed a little, sweetly, then repeated: "We did too--we just met." But she kissed him once, anyway. He

put his hand on the top of her head for encouragement.
Another car drove by, behind them. She must have heard
because she sat up, letting go of him.

"No?" he asked.

In answer she placed her hands on his shoulders,
smiled apologetically, kissed his mouth and whispered:
"Next time. I have to go."

8

Monday he thought about her, about their date, over and over. By the time Stanley got to work he was trying to will himself to <u>not</u> think about it. "Next time." The words wouldn't let him be, wouldn't leave him alone.

What to do now? Was he to calmly go back to work, pump gas, wipe windows, shove the spout into oil cans, shove the cans into the receptacle in the engine, lean on the car while the liquid poured and stare off into the current of cars on the street? Feel the wind strike him like a soft reminder of punches once received? Sit in the office looking out the large window as if between rounds, waiting for the bell so he could jump up and go out there, to go into practiced action? Watch the sun set and see headlights go on, turn on the ones for the station and wonder what to do what to do what to do?

He had to call her, take her someplace. Where? Dinner? Then to his crappy room? Sure, maybe she wouldn't mind. Probably she would. Go to a motel? In a way that was an improvement but tacky. He decided to ask the cowboy waiter--he seemed to know a lot about women.

After work Stanley made himself go to the high school track to run. Getting up and over the gate was more difficult than it used to be, and he only ran a mile. But it was better than nothing.

He slept well, got up early and went to the Hollywood coffee shop in search of the waiter from Texas. But he wasn't there.

"Cowboy? He's off today. What can I get you?"

"Ahh...Castillian omelette, please."

"More coffee?"

"Please." Couldn't ask that guy, he seemed gay. Not that they don't know stuff, they do. They understand women. But...no, Stanley just couldn't ask him what to do with Rosy next.

At noon he called her, planning to find out where she would like to go, but there was no answer.

The weather was beginning to cool off. Same thing every September, until Indian summer, which may or may not happen this year. Everything else was screwed up, why should that be any different? Not that he actually cared. What he cared about was seeing Rosy again.

He drove past The Mission but didn't stop. Even if she wasn't there, which was likely, it would be too pushy. Someone might tell her, if they remembered him.

Too late to go to the gym and still get to work on time. He thought of trying to finish his last poem, in his room, but that didn't inspire him. He wanted to be with Rosy. So he called again from another pay phone, but no one answered, and he went to his room after all.

Gus, the part-time maintenance-man/gardener was out front, sweeping. They nodded hello.

"No training today?"

"How could you tell?"

"You don't have your gym bag."

"Oh, right! Good eye, Gus."

Inside he slipped past the counter, up the stairs, into his room. That omelette had been good, but he still had to speak with Cowboy, ask for advice.

He drank some water, sat in the big chair, turned on the radio and closed his eyes. A Beatles song was ending, but he couldn't recall the title. And the DJ Russ didn't say, only shouted: "Time's a-changing, people," and played a commercial for Firestone tires.

At two-thirty he called from the lobby. Rosy answered.

"Hi. It's me, Stanley."

"Hi, lover. What are you doing?"

"Heading to work. Just wanted to talk to you."

"Miss me?"

"Well, yeah, sure."

"That's good. When am I going to see you again?"

She was aggressive enough for both of them.

"As soon as possible. How about, ah, Saturday?"

"How about tonight? When do you get off work?"

That surprised him. "Sure. Eleven-fifteen."

"Oh, too late. I have to go back into the studio around ten."

"No, I get off after eleven."

"Every night?"

"Yes. Until Saturday."

"Okay."

"Want to do something then?"

"Like what?"

"Anything."

"You call it."

"Well, we can go to the park and, ah, then have dinner, if you'd like."

"The <u>park</u>? Stanley. You're not serious."

"I'm serious," he tried to say lightly. "It's relaxing. Aren't you stressed out recording?"

"No. I love it." Then: "Here's what. We'll go to my manager's house. She's having a little party. I might even sing."

"Really? When is it?"

"I don't know yet. Maybe Saturday night. I'll let you know. Wait, you don't have a phone, do you?"

"No. Sorry."

"We'll have to change that. How can I reach you when I feel like it?"

"I don't know. At work. Want the number?"

"Give it to me." He did. He was sweating again. "I'll call you when I find out definitely. That okay?"

"Sure, okay."

"But you absolutely have to get a phone. It's the Twentieth Century, you know." She laughed, to his relief. "And by the way, you live alone, don't you?"

"Yes. Why?"

"Just asking. No girlfriends hanging around?"

"Had one, but we sort of broke up. She went back to school."

"School?"

"She moved. She went back to college."

"Oh. How old is she--nineteen?"

"No! She's, ah, twenty-two, I think." The office door slammed. He looked over but didn't see anyone. "Too immature for me."

"Are you kidding?"

"I'm kidding."

"Sometimes it's difficult to tell, with you."

"I know. You're not the first one to say that."

"And what does that mean--you 'sort of broke up'?"

"Nothing gets by you. We did, we broke up."

"Are you sure?"

"I'm very sure. And why do you care so much?"

"Why do you think, lover? I want you for myself."

"You do?" He was really sweating now.

"Did you enjoy our date?" she asked softly.

"What? Of course I did. What do you think?"

"Well, you never said it."

"I'm saying it, I'm saying it." The office door opened; the landlady came out, behind the counter. Stanley quickly looked away. "Listen, ah, I have to go."

"All right. But you miss me?"

"Yeah."

9

Her voice had sounded--what? Like another person.
Not much of an accent--that was it. And so <u>forceful</u>.
Stanley questioned the future of their relationship if she
was that forceful.

Work was boring that week, more boring than usual.
And Mark was mad at someone, or something. The boss was
the same.

At least it was cooling off. And the Wilshire
corridor wind picked up, flapping the little colored flags
strung above the gas pumps. The smell of gasoline, the
smiling customer thank-yous, the kids from the Catholic
school jauntily streaming by--boring boring boring, now--
while he waited waited waited for Rosy to call.

She did, though, Thursday. Luckily when Stanley was
there.

"Hi, lover. How are you?" she purred.

"Bien," he said, attempting feebly to promote a return
of her accent. It didn't succeed.

"Oh, good. Say, the party's on Saturday. Can you
make it?"

"Of course I can make it. At night?"

"No, in the morning! Just kidding. Of course at night, silly."

"Great."

"Let me give you the address. Unless you want to take me. I'd rather you took me."

He tried not to dwell on Rosy too much. It drove him to distraction. Simultaneously Stanley fought self-doubt. He remembered her soft kiss, in the car, that night. He'd felt it, sort of, but oh, it was over so <u>quickly</u>, he hadn't truly appreciated it. Maybe this Saturday. "Next time."

But what if he couldn't enjoy it? Amy hadn't liked doing it, and he didn't really care. It wasn't an act he particularly desired. Not that he could communicate that to anyone. No, no. The guys raved when a girl performed it. They bragged, they luxuriated in the memory. Not Stanley. Sometimes he couldn't even ejaculate. The girl would wonder what was wrong. What could he say?

But hope sprang eternal where Rosy was concerned. She had excited him. Maybe this time would be different.

He ran at the track, going a mile. The night was misty, but not cold. It wouldn't be cold out there until October, at the earliest.

But he _did_ dwell on Rosy. When he bought groceries at the corner the clerk asked was anything wrong.

"No, I'm fine." Must have been the expression on his face. "How's it going?"

"Can't complain," the clerk replied.

"Me either."

Friday morning he had cereal, worked on the poem, listened to the radio. He thought of her wanting to leave the movie, her hurting stomach, her breast as he squeezed it, her tongue against his, the lights on in the house--who was in there?--her asking him if he had a girlfriend.

Les, the DJ on KHJ, announced a giveaway of Fleetwood Mac's "Rumors." Just write a note, send it in, win the prize. What, no quiz, no question? Then he played "Don't Stop" from the album. Cool.

Would he have sex with her? Sounded very possible. Should he take a rubber to the party? What sort of party was it?

Work dragged on. The sun set, the sky turned from azure to pink to grey-black. An ambulance sirened by. Mark told an anti-semitic joke. Stanley didn't feel like laughing. His friend from creative writing class wouldn't have liked it.

"That's bad," he remarked after the punch line. "They're not like that."

"The fuck they aren't. Money grubbing."

"But Jews <u>have</u> to be careful--all through history people have beat up on 'em."

"Because they're money-grubbers."

"No, they're cheap because people have kicked their ass."

"I'll kick your ass."

"Try it, man. You'll regret it."

Mark nodded. "I'm gunna haveta kick your ass, big shot. Big boxer." He walked around the desk where Stanley was sitting, poking the chair leg with his foot.

Stanley pushed back, stood up. "Now?"

"Now."

"Over a Jew joke?"

Mark popped his open hand into Stanley's chest. "You're an asshole," he said with a rising voice. "You think you're so fucking good."

"That's bullshit." He stepped clear of the chair, loosening his arms. Mark pointed his chin at him. "You outweigh me," Stanley said.

"Faggot."

That did it. "Let's go outside." The adrenalin started. Mark backed out the door, bumping it as he went, smiling.

"Big shot," he repeated, in a high voice.

Stanley followed, working his hands a bit, moving his head around. Mark was too big, he thought. But probably doesn't know how to punch.

Outside they positioned a distance from the door. Mark stood solidly, still smiling, and put his fists up.

"I don't punch first," Stanley said.

"Faggot." Mark swung with his right and immediately went for a tackle. Fortunately Stanley ducked and moved away, but not fast enough. One thick arm caught him, and he nearly fell--but he'd just gotten away enough to avoid the tackle. Mark, in a crouch, grabbed at Stanley again. But he'd lost his momentum along with his opportunity. A left to the side of his head and a right to his eye slowed him even more. Stanley took a step back, but reminded himself he wasn't in the ring--had to be more aggressive. So he jabbed twice as Mark lunged, stopping him. Then Stanley threw as hard a right as he dared, not wanting to hurt his hand. It only bounced off, causing little damage.

A car drove in, the bell pinged. Mark growled--did they teach that in football practice?--and charged. Stanley lowered his head, felt the weight strike him, and fell backwards.

"Hey! Hey!" the driver of the car yelled.

Mark hit with his left and his right as Stanley sat on the ground. Pretty good punches, Stanley thought, as he tried to crawl away.

The driver began honking his horn, then drove off, not wanting any part of it.

Before he could get to his feet Stanley had to duck another punch. Without being set he tossed a body shot, then another. Mark didn't care. He swung again but Stanley blocked it, and then he did get set. One-two-three, all landing. Mark looked surprised and hurt--a good sign. He charged, going back to basic football. Stanley pivoted to his right, punched, pivoted again, punched again. Basic boxing.

Mark looked tired--another good sign. But Stanley was tired, too.

"Had enough?" he heard himself say, ridiculously.

"Fuck you!" Mark swung wildly, missing once--as Stanley stepped backward--but landed the follow-up. It stung.

Be aggressive. He tried an old gambit: "jab and drop one to the body." Sure enough Mark was open, expecting the second punch to be at his face. Pow. He grimaced, lowered his hands. Stanley tried a right uppercut, always good if it landed--but it didn't. Mark had leaned a little to one side as he saw it coming. Fucking athlete, Stanley thought. He punched with his left, a bad version of a hook, and moved away. Too tired now; get back, rest. He bounced a bit on his feet.

They both waited a second. Mark was now squinting. "You're dead," he panted, and ran forward. But Stanley sidestepped again, letting Mark stumble on, stop, and turn back. Another car drove in. They looked over at it.

Two women, their mouths agape. Mark gestured dismissal, turned back to the fight.

"Oh, come on, this is stupid," Stanley panted. "You can't beat me. Forget it." Mark dropped his arms to his sides. He wasn't smiling now. The women drove off.

"You can hit, alright."

Stanley didn't say anything. They were both sweating, breathing heavily.

"We'll call it even," Mark said quietly, and walked toward the water fountain.

Lucky. _You were lucky_. He put ice on his swollen face, later, in his room.

If he'd gotten you down he'd have...His hands hurt, too. _Blockhead_. _What was he so mad for_? Oh yeah, Stanley thought. The joke. His Jewish friend from college owed him, now.

Stanley drank from a bottle of beer, feeling lucky. Mark could have killed him. All because of a dumb joke.

The next day was Saturday. His hands hurt more than his face, which was still slightly swollen and bruised. Stanley splashed water on it, went down the hall to the bathroom. Thank God he didn't have to go to work today. The two of them had hardly spoken the remainder of the evening, certainly didn't shake on it.

Even? Yeah, call it even, Stan, you out-of-shape, lucky, self-righteous bastard. After returning to his room he drank a glass of water, looked in the mirror again. Oh shit, _Rosy_. What's she going to say? Bruised under both eyes. Thank God they aren't black, although they may be by tonight.

Stanley ate at Jim's. The cook never said a word about his face--he was used to seeing him like that. Only this time there was no report in the paper.

As the day progressed Stanley became increasingly distraught. He felt guilty having been so pious. Where did he get off? Same shit in the military, criticizing others for their biases. Who did he think he was? Mark was right.

He'd have to make up a story as to why they had fought. Rosy would ask. She asked about everything. But Stanley didn't want to lie.

By afternoon he didn't want to go to the party. He'd look like a fool, with two black eyes. She'd be embarrassed. The other guests would want to know what had happened. Let's see..."My co-worker got mad at me because I wouldn't laugh at his joke." "Did you win?" "Sort of." "It doesn't look like it." "Well, I hit him more than he hit me."

But he did go. He showered, shaved, dressed--even put on a sports coat. But he couldn't shake the feeling of guilt.

Rosy was all smiles until she saw his face.

"What <u>happened</u> to you?" she asked from her doorway, concerned.

"Well..."

"You were sparring today?" She touched his face, compassionately.

"Well, I, yeah, yesterday. Not too much."

They walked to his car.

"Not too much?"

"That's what happens."

"That's what happens?"

"Actually, it was a real fight. At work."

"¡Pendéo!"

Now what does that mean?

Her manager Shauna lived in a three-bedroom oceanfront house in Malibu. By the time they arrived Stanley had foolishly told Rosy everything. She didn't like it.

"But he's just a kid!" Now that's funny, he thought, as he parked behind the garage, next to a Mercedes and a red Corvette.

"Well, he's a big kid."

Shauna let them in. "Greetings! Welcome." She was 30ish, black, tall.

"This is Stanley."

"Hello!" She didn't mention his marked-up face.

"Hi. Glad to meet you." They shook hands.

"Nobody's here except Cindy and Donna and Frederick."
They walked past a fountain to another door, into the house
itself, and then back to the living room. The ocean was
right outside; a stereo played Roberta Flack.

Three people were on couches, holding drinks in their
hands, all looking at Shauna and her new guests.
Throughout the introductions nothing was said concerning
his blackening eyes and red bruises. Classy.

"Frederick works for the record company," Rosy gaily
announced. His wife, Donna, smiled and stared. "Cindy's
an old friend."

"Watch it."

"Oh, not <u>old</u>."

"Have some wine," Shauna insisted. "Sit down."

Stanley looked at the surf, beyond the deck.
"Beautiful place."

"Thank you. Sit, sit." He sat. Rosy went with her
to the wooden bar leading to the kitchen. She spoke
quietly as Shauna poured wine into glasses. For the first
time Stanley saw the tight-fitting blue dress Rosy had on,
the big earrings, the silver bracelets.

"How long have you known each other?" Cindy asked.
She was wearing a white sunsuit with yellow flowers, but no
earrings.

Before Stanley could answer Rosy said, "Not long. He swept me off my feet."

They all laughed, except Stanley. "My, my," Cindy remarked.

"Sounds like love at first sight," Donna intoned casually, sipping from her glass.

"It was," Stanley offered, at last. Rosy handed him a glass, sat down beside him.

"How wonderful," Cindy giggled, not caring if it were true or not.

"Should we go on the deck?" Shauna, still standing, was asking them all, but looking at Rosy.

"No, not yet, please," Rosy replied, wiggling closer, putting her hand on Stanley's leg.

"Okay." Shauna sat beside Frederick. "A toast to the new album!" They all held up their glasses, then drank.

"Halfway finished," Rosy blurted, and took a sip. Frederick nodded, Stanley nodded, Cindy smiled and nodded.

"It's going to be great, I know it is," Shauna responded, her eyes happy. Stanley noticed she was wearing designer jeans and a blue shirt that read "Great Expectations."

"Here, here," Frederick added.

"When will the record be finished?" Stanley asked. "I want to hear it."

The others looked toward Frederick, who raised his eyebrows and answered: "Soon. Within a month or two."

On the deck, later, sitting in lounge chairs, Rosy and Stanley ate from plates on their laps, and watched the waves.

"Delicious," he commented. "Really." He was feeling better. The wine helped.

"Do you like my friends?"

"Yes. Of course."

She ate her chicken, holding it daintily in her fingers.

Cindy came onto the deck. "Will you be spending the night here, lovebirds? Shauna wants to know."

Her mouth full, Rosy shook her head. Then, after swallowing: "We haven't discussed it, honey."

"By all means, discuss it. Excuse me." She returned to the house.

Stanley ate a forkful of rice, nearly tipping his plate over. Rosy laughed and took another bite of chicken.

"What do you say?" she asked.

"Spend the night?"

"Yes."

"I'd love to. But, you mean, together?"

"Uh-uh, no. You sleep on the beach! Certainly together."

Blood rushed to his head. Should have brought a rubber. Maybe she's on the pill.

"Have you talked it over?" Cindy shouted from the glass doorway.

"We're staying," Rosy shot back.

"Oh boy," Cindy said, retreating into the living room.

Frederick and Donna said goodbyes and left. Shauna and Cindy joined them on the deck, drinking wine. Shauna smoked, Rosy hummed to the music playing inside, Stanley tried to act nonchalant.

After a while the phone rang; Shauna went in to answer it.

"Nobody tells me anything," Cindy said to no one in particular. "I'm always in the dark."

"What are you talking about?" Rosy asked her.

"Suddenly there's this party, Michael's in Vegas, I have to come, nobody tells me anything."

"You didn't have to come."

"That's what I was told."

"You did <u>not</u> have to come."

"Rosy wants a party, I <u>have</u> to come. That's what--"

"Stop it, Cindy. Be nice. What's Michael doing in Las Vegas?"

"Business. Motown people there. Diana Ross at Caesar's Palace."

"I'm sorry, but--"

"Well, I'm <u>not</u> driving home. I'm staying too." She got up, took her empty glass inside.

"Don't worry about her, she'll be fine," Rosy whispered.

Stanley put his arm around her. "So <u>you</u> told your manager she was having a party?"

"What makes you think so?"

"Nothing." He kissed her mouth, pulling her close.

10

In bed upstairs, with the sea breeze flowing through a window, with Rosy's soft hair touching his face, he entered her. Sensual, she gasped as though hurt--but she wasn't hurt. She began twisting and turning like an animal; Stanley had to ask her to slow down.

Then he placed his hands on her head and pulled her body toward his thrust, wanting to get deeper into her. He kissed her sweet face, her luscious lips. First, her knees were up, then down, her legs wide, then closing onto his. She wouldn't stop changing position. Was she faking it? No, impossible. He saw in her eyes that was impossible. Then he heard her yearning moan, almost imperceptible. He bent lower to kiss her dark nipples--had to get at both of them.

Then, before long, she began to climax, and then he did. He couldn't stop it if he tried, though he knew he should. But he couldn't.

"You just about broke my diaphragm," she whispered, returning from the bathroom.

"Yeah, sure."

"Really."

In the morning he discovered she was kissing him under the sheet. It woke him up.

"Hey!"

"Hmmm?" She maneuvered up to his face. "Awake?" They kissed. Her hand held him, tenderly. "Hello. It woke up first--wanted to play." She slipped down under the sheet, kissing at him, sucking at him.

Shauna, dressed, her hair back, her brown skin vibrant, peeked in the door after tapping. "Time to eat, lovebirds." She closed the door. No secrets in this house. Rosy yawned luxuriously, politely covering her mouth with her hand.

"Want to eat?" he asked her.

"No. You go. I'm worn out."

"Yeah, sure."

"Really."

Cindy was at a table in the kitchen. Smells of toast, coffee, salt air struck him when he walked in.

"Hi, Stanley. Sleep okay?"

"Yes, thank you." He saw the glass doors were open, the sun splashing off the blue Pacific.

"Coffee there," she pointed. He went to a small black pot, poured a cupful in a mug that read "Have a nice day." On the side was a small drawing of a giraffe. "Where's Rosy?"

"Upstairs--wants to sleep." He sat. Cindy chewed on a piece of toast, looked out the doors; they listened to the waves breaking.

"I'm leaving," Shauna said, descending the staircase. "Make yourselves comfortable, please."

He wanted to ask her where she was going, but didn't. "Thanks for everything, Shauna."

"No problem," she laughed. "Sorry I have to rush out- -brunch with a client." No wonder she was wearing a skirt and blouse.

"You look good," Stanley observed, feeling a distinct friendliness toward her.

"Thanks. Stay a second. Cindy can lock up when she leaves."

"Okay."

Shauna disappeared into the garage, her keys rattling, her heels clacking on the pavement. They heard the electric door open, a car start up and drive out, the door closing behind it.

"She moves fast, doesn't she?" Cindy asked.

"I'll say." He drank his coffee. "How long has she handled Rosy?"

"Oh, they--let me see...more than a year, I think."

"Bet she'll be good for her career."

A sea gull landed outside on the railing. They both watched until it flew away.

He ate scrambled eggs that were warm on the stove. Cindy went out to lie on a lounge chair, Stanley went upstairs to check on Rosy. She was just out of the shower, partially dressed.

"Hey," Stanley said. "Scrambled eggs, toast, fruit--"

"Bueno. ¿Como está?" She pulled her dress on, tilting her face toward him simultaneously. He kissed her and smiled.

"Me? Muy bien."

"I hope so, all the work I did!"

"I did some, too."

"Sí...take a shower, honey." She went downstairs.

In the car on the way back to town Stanley was quiet. It all seemed too good to be true--the evening, the morning, how she'd made him "come." Rosy filled him in on her struggle to sign with a good manager, the contract, the style of music for her album, the comparisons with Linda Ronstadt.

"I'm sleepy," she finally sighed, her head against his shoulder.

"Want to just go back to your place, call it a day?" She didn't answer at first; her eyes were closed. Then:

"What do you want to do?"

"I don't know. We can ride around."

"How boring."

"Stop at The Mission?"

"No. Too noisy."

"Walk on Hollywood Boulevard?"

"Yuck."

"The park?"

"No!"

"A museum?"

She looked at him. "Now I know you're kidding."

"Hey, I almost forgot--you said you were going to sing last night. What happened?"

"Oh, not enough people there. It's embarrassing unless there's a lot of people. Too much like an audition, or something." She put her head back on his shoulder.

Eventually she decided to change clothes and ride around more. He waited in his car. When she came out in a revealing top and jean skirt, Stanley wondered if he wasn't falling in love. It <u>had</u> occurred this rapidly before, he remembered. But what about her? Could she fall for him? Not likely, the life she had, was destined to have.

"Let's go, honey," she purred when she got in.

Stanley concluded he'd best not mention it. Might scare her. Might drive her away.

"Who's in there, anyway?" he finally asked.

"In the house? My sister, her daughter, my brother, off-and-on. Not now. He's in jail."

"Oh. Sorry."

"And a friend, a musician, but he's moving out."

"A friend?"

Rosy hit his arm. "¡Sí! But we're not together anymore. He's not good to me, like you are."

"But he still lives there?"

"Once in a while. Oh, it's too complicated. Where are we going? How about your place? Show me your place."

"I was afraid you'd suggest that. Please, it's only a little dump. I'd rather not take you there."

"Who's there?"

"What? <u>Nobody</u>."

"Really? Don't lie."

"Rosy, I'm not lying. I'm ashamed to take you there."

"Alright. We don't have to."

"After I make more money, after I turn pro, I'll move to a good apartment."

"After you turn pro? You're going to?"

"Have to. What else can I do? Sell drugs?"

"Not funny. Don't joke like that."

He drove past the Cambria to let her see the building.

"It's pretty!"

"Yeah, but too old inside."

At the corner he turned left, toward Hollywood.

"Are you hungry yet?"

"No."

He drove past MacArthur Park and the lake. "There it is."

"What? The park? Forget it!"

"Just kidding. How about a movie?"

"How about a motel?"

"Are you kidding?"

"Yes. I'm not that wild."

"'Bad,' your friend said."

"Who said? Ada? She's crazy."

When they drove past Barry's he pointed it out to her.

"Just temporary."

"Stanley, do you think I care? I don't care where you work. I don't have a lot of money either. Really."

"There's a good spot," he said as they passed the Art Museum.

"Shut up!"

"Lots of nice paintings in there."

"You've been?"

"Sure."

He parked on Sunset near the Strip, and kissed her. He wanted to say "I love you," but resisted. Instead he said: "I love the way your tongue feels."

She laughed. "I bet you _do_."

"I mean--no, I don't mean that," he laughed too. "Like this," he said, and kissed her again, a long time.

They walked along the Strip, went into a bookstore, had lemonade at the "Old World" restaurant. Rosy admired and bought an embroidered skirt--one she might perform in, she said.

"What do you write?"

"Mostly poems. A few short stories."

"Try to get them published?"

"Yes, but they were sent back."

"Don't worry. I sent demos to a whole lot of places. I almost gave up. You just need the right match."

"What?"

"The proper match. You and a magazine. You and a publisher."

"I understand." They returned to his car, headed east.

"Not hungry yet?" he asked her. "I am."

"Let's eat."

"How come you don't have an accent over the phone?"

"Ha! I know. Don't ask me. Everyone says that."

"I like it, like now."

"You do?"

"Of course."

They were in the steak house near his apartment. Rosy ordered soup and salad only; Stanley had steak.

"They know you here. You come here often?"

"Used to come here with that girl I told you about."

If she minded she didn't show it. But she asked: "Was she as good as me?"

"Absolutely not," he replied, and felt guilty.

At her door they kissed goodbye. He put his hands on
her back, then moved them lower, rubbing her.

"Don't. You'll get me too excited."

"Sorry. Can't help it. I like your...behind."

"Say it. <u>Ass</u>."

"I like your <u>ass</u>."

"It's not too big?"

"No, it's not too big."

11

All he had to say to Barry when quizzed about his black eye was: "A little sparring," which was true enough. Barry had seen him come to work with black eyes before, so he let it go.

Mark didn't show up until six, which was his new time--six to nine. School had started. He looked tired, most likely from football practice. Stanley didn't say anything to him, although Mark nodded vaguely in greeting as he went to change in the locker room. Funny. It's funny, Stanley thought: Mark's face is hardly bruised at all.

He'd called Rosy but there was no answer. Working on her record, no doubt. Wow--she was great. They'd made plans to see each other this weekend--like his schedule with Amy. That was funny, too.

As usual, business picked up in the early evening. Stanley offered to get the food for them, and went to Del Taco at 7 o'clock. He wanted to call Rosy, but didn't. Too aggressive. Had to find the proper balance.

"Let's be friends," he said to Mark, handing him the take-out tacos.

"Might as well," he replied. Stanley gave him his change. But no handshake.

It was good enough. <u>I don't care. I don't care what he thinks. And I don't feel like shaking his hand, either</u>.

At nine Mark got in his truck without saying goodbye, but must have thought better of it--he honked and waved to Stanley as he left.

After two or three customers there was a quiet interval. Stanley ruminated on those words: 'might as well.' Good words. Important words for humans to use. Have to put them in a poem.

He called anyway. The niece answered. Rosy wasn't in yet. Message? Yes, tell her I called.

Glen Campbell's "Southern Nights" was on the radio as he parked outside the Cambria. Stanley let it play, listening to all of it.

Nearly midnight. He went inside, a bag of drive-thru cheeseburgers in his hand.

"Halt!" the landlady shouted as he walked through the door. He kept walking. "Three things, there are three things. Do you wish to know them?" He reached the stairs. "One, two, three things." Stanley kept going. She stopped talking, this time.

It disturbed him slightly Rosy hadn't called the station. Maybe she was working late.

But...why hadn't she returned his call? Didn't she feel the way he did? She'd certainly been passionate enough. Maybe she hadn't gotten his message.

He ate his two cheeseburgers and thought about her body, and quite a few of the things she'd said. One beer and Stanley went to bed, determined not to worry. Isn't that what Duke always said? "Don't worry, it gets you into trouble."

At dawn he woke; couldn't sleep. But couldn't call her this early, either. He had breakfast at Skinny Jim's, trying not to listen to the morning banter. It was critical of Jimmy Carter, anyway, and he liked Carter. Give the guy a chance, can't you?

He went to Elysian Park to run that fire road, after waiting for his food to digest.

Rosy, you are my posy. What was that from? A movie he saw once. But he couldn't place it. What is a posy? A flower. Yeah.

God was watching him, he knew. <u>I mean, He's omnipotent, isn't He?</u> And omnipresent.

"Please help this to all work right," he prayed as he ran.

After a shower Stanley dressed and drove to a pay phone, not wanting to risk the landlady eavesdropping. Rosy answered.

"Good morning! How are you?"

"Fine," he answered. "How do you feel?"

"Tired. We were in the studio all night."

"All night?"

"Just about."

"Well, get some rest. I just wanted to talk to you. No big deal."

"Okay. I'm going back to sleep. Will you be at work later? I--"

"Yes, after three."

"Uh-huh, that's good. There's something I have to talk to you about."

"What?"

"Not now, I'm too tired. I'll call you after three, at work, okay?"

"Okay."

Trying not to worry didn't do it. He couldn't try that hard. Conjecture didn't help, either. Reading *A THOUSAND DAYS* did, partly, but he couldn't read for three hours, so he went to work early.

"Hey, kid."

"Hi, Barry. I'm early."

"No shit. What's up?"

"Just couldn't stay away."

"Ha, ha. Anything wrong?"

"No," he lied.

Stanley changed his voltage regulator, and one plug that wasn't looking good. Barry said he'd leave since he was already there. Why not?

The cars came in, the cars went out. The phone rang, but it was a call for the boss. The kids came by from school, they got ice cream from the machine. A woman wanted to know how to get to Laurel Canyon. He told her. He drank a soda. Larry wouldn't approve--he had to turn pro now. But it worried him--some guys didn't fare so well. Some had smashed-in noses, squeaky voices. Pro bouts were more severe than amateur ones. Some fighters kept at it when they should quit. Would he do that? Or would he win, as he hoped?

She called at five forty-five, just before Mark drove up. She was crying, or on the verge of it.

"What's wrong?"

"I'm so sorry. Don't be mad, please."

"About what? No, I won't be mad."

"I like you a lot, Stanley. But--you know I told you I had a boyfriend?"

"You said he left."

"Well, that's true, but..."

"What?"

"He came back. We talked it over."

"You're going back with him?"

She didn't answer. She must have been crying.

Mark walked in, saw the look on his face, and went out.

"This just happen?"

"We--we've been discussing it for awhile. I didn't know...I'm sorry. Please don't be mad."

"I'm not mad," he lied.

"I care a lot about you. If it wasn't like this..."

"Like what?"

"With him."

"You don't want to see me anymore?"

"It's not that. Can't you understand? I love him."

It was Stanley's turn to remain silent. Then she said: "I had a good time with you, you know that."

"I thought we had a good time."

She was audibly crying, now.

"Don't cry, Rosy. I understand."

"You do?"

"Yes, naturally. Don't worry about it. Worrying can get you into trouble."

She laughed and said: "That's for sure."

They were both quiet now.

Then he said: "Don't lose my number. Call me if you break up again."

"Okay." She was sniffling a bit. "I'm sorry."

"You don't have to keep saying that. I understand."

"Okay...goodbye, then."

"Goodbye." He hung up, went into the locker room.

You're such a pussy, Stan. Such a pussy.

PART SIX

It was October before he seemed to realize it--not as warm, now, though summer lingered in L.A. There were sublime evenings, beautiful skies, and early in October it rained some; people were excited about that: perhaps the drought was over.

Also in October he was fired from his job--falsely accused and convicted without trial of stealing money from the cash register, a little each evening.

As if he would do that! Where was he supposed to have spent it?

He'd been taking it for weeks, the boss said.

First he was let go for a few days, and when the cash stopped being taken, Barry had no alternative but to can him. So he said.

Who had done it? Had it really been missing in the first place? What was the truth?

Now he was out of work, that much was certain.

Had the boss been unable to take Stanley's independent thinking? Had he made the whole thing up in order to fire him?

<u>Good luck getting the remainder of your bail deposit, asshole</u>.

Sure, he'd snatched a few cans of carburetor cleaner, of gas booster. But Barry never seemed to notice.

He couldn't collect unemployment because he had been fired for a "bad" reason. But he hadn't been convicted in a court of law--only in the boss's mind.

Perhaps Stanley should have taken it somewhere, to a city agency. But where? And how? And what good would it have done? So he had to look for another job.

He didn't like to work at most jobs. Most jobs made you talk to people. At the station at least he could confine the conversation to automobile subjects.

He could go to a newspaper and try to get a job.

Yeah, sure. No degree, no experience.

He'd have to lie to get another gas attendant job.

Maybe a warehouse somewhere downtown. But he'd done that, hated it.

Drive a cab?

He could ask his father for some money. His father lived in Riverside, not too many miles east of L.A. But they didn't talk much.

He had to do something pretty soon.

2

During his lifetime Stanley had been accused of being simplistic. Perhaps he was. Perhaps they were right. Perhaps they were wrong--his college girlfriend, his English teacher, his so-called parents. How was he to know?

Rosy had fallen into his lap, a blessing, and been snatched away, a curse. Was that it, or was it the other way around?

Thinking he was falling in love--was in love--and that she too was possibly falling in love, was that simplistic?

Being fired for a theft he hadn't committed, being unable to defend himself--was that simplistic?

Thinking he could become a world champion, or close to it--was that simplistic?

Hoping Rosy would come back to him after she found out her boyfriend was no good--if he was no good--was that simplistic?

Staying in an apartment building with a crazy landlady--was that simplistic?

He dug out his dictionary: "Tending to avoid complexities." Bullshit. He didn't avoid them. They followed him, they haunted him.

So, he spend his last paycheck, he took out money from his bank account, he drove to see his father and borrowed $500 from him, most of which went for the drunk-driving fine. Luckily his insurance covered the accident. He looked in the newspaper for work, and by November he was behind in his rent, he stopped reading the JFK book, he wasn't shaving often, his clothes were not as clean, his car broke down, he took to riding the bus, and he had run after a man in a fancy car who had almost hit him in the crosswalk, who got away, fortunately for both of them.

He went to those peculiar places, early in the morning, that provide labor for transients on a day-to-day basis. You sit in a room waiting until your name is called, you work where they take you, you get a day's pay and most guys go to a cheap bar and to a cheap hotel, and Stanley would get a cheap supper and cheap beer and some corn chips to munch. That was his day. He didn't have to do it every day. That was a luxury--he could go when he felt like going, not go when he didn't feel like going. But the work undermined his confidence, weakened his spirit.

One day you'd pick up trash around the hospital, another you'd clean out the storage room of an appliance store, the next you'd sweep and mop the dance floor of a downtown club.

But you had to get to the labor office early, or to one of them, because there were many men there, and not as many jobs. Sometimes he was too late, would sit there for hours, and finally the man in charge would say: "No more jobs. Come back tomorrow."

He had coffee in the morning, when he didn't go downtown to the day-labor office, at the old hut on Seventh Street. He felt more like those regular "cup-of-mud-whatdayasay-have-ya-been-to-the-racetrack-lately" customers than ever before. He didn't want to end up like that. He wanted to be somebody, to do something, to live a rewarding life.

George said he'd appealed to Barry to take Stanley back, to no avail, that Barry was convinced he'd been stealing from him. George guessed that either Mark or Harold, the mechanic, had done it. No more money was missing now, naturally.

"He's too smart for that, whoever it was."

"Probably Mark," Stanley offered. "Kid with secrets."

"Yeah? What secrets?"

"They're secrets, how am I supposed to know?"

"Come on, Stan, let's take a look at your car." He'd dropped by to visit, with this in mind.

"Naw, screw it. The fly-wheel's broke--you can't fix that."

"Please, let me take a look. Don't be so stubborn."

Stanley was lying on the bed. "I really appreciate it, I do. But--"

"Come on." He kicked the bed frame. "What the fuck's the matter with you?"

Stanley sat up, put his feet on the floor. "Hey, I'm alright. I'll be alright."

"Come on then." George went to the door.

"Okay, let's look at it." They went downstairs.

George connected his battery to the Chevy, but it still wouldn't start. "Probably need a new generator," he said.

Sometimes he stood on a street corner early in the morning with other men, waiting for a car or truck to come by, the driver looking for workers. After an hour or so most of the men had been picked up for a day's work, or a half-day's work. He didn't get many jobs that way because the men in the cars, in the trucks that pulled up, were familiar with the laborers and always took the ones they knew. They were choosy, they took who they knew had worked well before, who had given them a good day's work before, and Stanley and a few of the other men were too new, and even if you got in the back seat right away, or climbed into the bed of the pickup, the driver or his partner would yell for you to get out, would motion to someone they knew to get in, and when they had how many they wanted, they left.

The day-labor companies exacted a fee from the employer, and took out tax from the check they paid employees. On the corner, however, neither was the case, and once Stanley realized that, and felt bad about not paying taxes, he stopped going there. It just wasn't right. Not unless he figured out how much he owed and sent it in at tax time, and that was a difficulty he didn't feel like accepting.

3

During this time of dismay Stanley heard a religious program on his radio late one night. A man was discussing the benefits of faith and he asked a question that so penetrated Stanley's consciousness that the next day the question was still with him.

It seemed to be a simple question, but in light of his situation Stanley wondered if it wasn't exactly the question he was supposed to hear, God's way of touching him. The man on the program had said: "If you are feeling unhappy, if you are feeling unfulfilled, if you are feeling lost, if you are feeling far away from God and His promises, then ask this question of yourself: Who moved?"

Who moved? Had God moved, or had he?

It made him think that was why things had been happening to him like they had. Losing the fight, losing Amy, not having the guts or whatever it was to go back to the gym, losing his job, being disappointed so in regard to Rosy, just generally broke, pissed off, perturbed, dismayed. Was this the result of "separation from God," as they say?

Had he moved away from God? How was he supposed to know a thing like that? Then Stanley realized something

significant. He'd pilfered items from the gas station,
feeling justified due to his low salary. But it <u>was</u> theft.

Maybe the boss had known, and made up the missing
money story to lend support to firing him. But it didn't
matter much either way, did it?

And where <u>was</u> God, anyway?

He was supposed to be everywhere, but how could you
see Him?

"I know You're here--that is, You're supposed to be
here--" Stanley prayed in his room the day after hearing
that question on the radio. "What I need is, I need some
help. I need You to help me. I'm sorry I stole those
things from Barry. It wasn't right. I'd like to box
again. I'd like to find a job, I'd like to get closer to
You. I'm sorry if I moved. I didn't mean to. Amen."

4

November hit the southland like Jesse James and his gang, startling the faces of Palm-tree land inhabitants as it charged in with cold weather, rain, and threatening dark-skyed nights, hitting the streets with chilly boots and clanging spurs, causing fear, discomfort, downcast eyes, the inadvertent scrunching in of shoulders, and sickness.

November charged in like a band of robbers, hostile and greedy. Its grey days and chilly nights produced concern instead of relief, automobile accidents, drugstore overcrowding, mudslides. Many people found themselves unable to escape a sense of foreboding, the feeling that something was wrong, that some strange fate lay in wait, that they were going to pay for something, _were_ paying for something. And cruelly, in addition to the harsh weather, the Los Angeles Dodgers, who strove valiantly, making it to the World Series, had fallen short of victory.

When November snow fell in the mountains to the north, and word spread that water would be in greater supply, in spite of bringing a sense of relief it served to remind Angelinos of the preceding months of drought, pointing to their dependency on the laws of nature, on the laws of

Heaven, over which they obviously had no control. They coughed, they sneezed, they complained bitterly.

Stanley saw this and felt this, heard it at coffee shop counters, on busses, on street corners, on the radio.

Nevertheless, one day, idly walking around Westlake, feeling that characteristic wind which often whipped through the area, Stanley thrilled at its sudden coldness, embraced its promise of newness, of change, of a second chance. He started a poem, but couldn't finish it:

"O double-sevens, where is your gift?
Nineteen seventy-seven, where is my victory?"

He walked along the edge of the park, not wanting to venture onto the grass or near the paths because it reminded him of his boxing days, days he longed for, days he knew were growing distant. But he had prayed, so he waited.

He spent time in a small bar on Alvarado, and heard the arguments of the poor, hostile Chicanos who didn't have the chances he had, yet were struggling on, had not given up, had faith, had hope.

November marauded, disrupted, stretched inexorably toward the last of the year, taking everyone and everything with it.

And what about the oncoming year? What was he going to do?

The prospect of getting a regular job again, of finding a girlfriend, again, of simply trying to get into shape, again, overwhelmed him, consumed him. But he had to do it.

One night Stanley found himself at the track, sitting in the stands, looking at the field. New green grass had sprung up and been freshly mowed. How many times had he run around it? It was a familiar place to him. But he wasn't going to run tonight. He didn't have his running shoes; he was wearing work boots.

Why had he come? To find what he had been. If he could be that again, he could box again.

Stanley prayed, asking for help. He didn't know what sort to ask for, so he merely asked for help, hoping that God would provide what he needed.

At the end of his prayer he heard a noise, and when he'd said "amen," looked up and saw the sprinkler system starting. He took it as a sign from God. The water sprayed over the field, the sprinklers turning slowly in rhythmic plan. He felt that funny feeling that accompanies the unusual. Sure, it was simplistic. Sure, the grass

didn't need any more water. But it had to be a sign, a
signal. God was letting him know that everything was going
to be okay, that by hitting a low point, and seeking His
help, Stanley had done what he was supposed to do, and the
fountains of life were going to reopen for him. It had to
mean that.

In the morning he went to The Mission for breakfast.
Rosy wasn't there. The place looked the same:
comfortable, unpretentious, smelling of Mexican-style
cooking.

The waitresses spoke in Spanish to each other. They
seemed to be having a good time. He ate eggs with avocado
and hot corn tortillas that he covered in salt and butter.
He felt close to God.

The smiling owner wasn't there that morning, but a
friendly, hard-working girl who must have been his
daughter. She moved through the café with authority and
ease, greeting people, taking money at the register,
speaking with the waitresses, joking with obviously regular
customers.

Stanley thought, as he ate his breakfast, hey, I could
keep coming in here and get to know her, like they do, and

maybe see Rosy, and she would see the daughter of the boss liked me and I could talk to her and sit with her again and--

Forget her, Stan. <u>If God wanted you to be together, He'd make it happen</u>.

So he finished eating, hoping she might walk in...but she didn't.

5

Thanksgiving came and went, but not without Stanley feeling thankful. He'd prayed, he was expecting an answer.

Riding the bus to Westlake, his jacket pulled tightly closed, the sky darkening, he was weary, having loaded firewood onto pickup trucks most of the day. But he had a check in his pocket.

He still hadn't finished that poem. What was the promise of '77? What was the victory? In a burning flash the loss of his last fight hit him. Something...something ...what did it mean?

He'd lost his first two fights, taken off, came back-- so what exactly was the problem? Sugar Ray Robinson had lost fights, had even killed a man in the ring. What's more horrible than that?

The bus rocked and rolled, passengers boarded, sat, got off. Then it came to him. He was afraid of losing again. He didn't want to fight if he was going to lose again--too painful.

As soon as he realized it, Stanley was free. He could risk it, he could take another loss. Big deal. So? It wasn't the last fight that disturbed him, it was the next. He had to risk defeat. That's what he'd been avoiding.

Well, screw it. He was willing to lose again.

Whether he won or not, he wanted to fight.

"Don't hassle me, man."

"Who's hassling you?"

The first man held a bag of food from Burrito Village. The second, taller man, a Latino, was grabbing at it unsuccessfully.

"Lay off. It's mine," the first exclaimed.

"One burrito. You said I get one burrito." He reached for the package again.

Nervous now, the first man put the food behind him. "Lay off, cocksucker."

"Give it to me."

They had gradually worked their way to the corner of Western and Hollywood. The second man was becoming increasingly furious.

"Since when d'you keep the shit?" he asked.

The first, smaller man, began coughing.

"You sick?"

"Got a chest cold."

"Hand it over or I'll call the cops."

"You say--what?"

"I will, asshole. Hand it over."

"No, *urgg*," he coughed and spit.

The second man got a hand on the bag. It tore as they each pulled.

"Son of a bitch!" A taco spilled onto the street. "Here." Letting him have it, the first turned away, spitting phlegm.

"One burrito." The tall man dug into the torn bag, extracted his booty, returning the crumpled package.

"I was goin' to give it to you. Look at this shit."

"I don't trust you, amigo."

"Look at this shit." The smaller man attempted to salvage two remaining tacos. "What do I say to Besse?"

Standing erect, the other man said nothing.

"She paid for this."

"Tough."

Stanley stepped onto the curb from the crosswalk, maneuvering around them. His foot grazed the spilled food.

"Watch it, buddy," the tall man warned.

"Thanks, yeah," Stanley replied as he avoided the mess, passing by.

"What do I tell Besse?" the smaller man repeated.

Stanley got in line outside the walk-up window. Two women inside were dispensing items, taking orders.

"Ask him," the tall man pointed at Stanley.

The smaller man thought it over, walked behind Stanley, cleared his throat.

"Hey, buddy."

"Yeah?"

"Can you help us out? We need another taco. He dropped it."

"You dropped it," the tall man said.

"Sure," Stanley said, digging out a dollar from his pocket. "Here."

"Thanks, man. Appreciate it."

Later, on the bus down Western, Stanley looked to see what was at the theatre near Clinton Avenue. A movie he'd not heard of. Didn't want to go there without Amy, anyway.

He switched busses on Wilshire and traveled east, past the gas station, to Union. His steak burrito was getting cold, so Stanley ate it, sitting on the bench, after leaving the bus.

George was getting a new generator for him. Have to pay him later. But I need my car to get to the gym, to the track. Cold wind struck his face. He hurried to finish the food, concerned about catching cold. Don't get sick now. Have to turn pro--Larry would be pissed.

He did sit-ups in his room, jogged on the street and
exercised his hands until George installed the generator
for him. It worked. He drove to the track, then, and
drove to the day-labor office.

He'd paid the kid back who worked at Barry's on the
weekend. Now he had to pay those stupid parking tickets.
He wanted to call Rosy, but didn't. The landlady began
cutting up the courtyard plants again, now that they were
growing back. Things were fairly normal.

There was the driedsweat-coated full-length mirror on
the wall, and the pictures of the good old fighters of the
past, and the life-size cardboard figures up higher, on the
walls, of past World Champions. Stanley felt the coolness
of the place, the coolness it always had in winter,
coolness that waited all morning until the gym opened at
midday, coolness that remained between the old green walls,
until enough guys worked out, and the old rattling heater
finally produced enough warmth, coolness that made Stanley
feel lonely, made him think of all the fighters in the past
who'd trained in cold gyms, ran on cold mornings, waited in
cold dressing rooms, sat in cold cars outside arenas, tried
to get warm by moving around, throwing punches in those
gyms, running ceaselessly on those mornings, shadowboxing
in those dressing rooms, tightening, relaxing their
shoulders and hands in those cars.

He said hello to the old black man, Rip, who
customarily sat by the doors, and went swiftly into the
dressing room area with its lockers, ancient weight scale,
exercise table, low benches and, further back, shower room.
He sat on a bench and put his bag down.

Voices came from a nearby cubicle. Stanley hadn't bothered to see if Larry's room was open--he knew it wouldn't be. Too early.

"Hey, Stan the man!" It was a white trainer by the name of Johnny Nemo. "Whatja doin' here?"

Stanley smiled at him as he walked by. "Hey, Johnny."

"Coming in again?"

"Yeah, guess so."

"Alright! Good to see you." He proceeded through the door, into the gym.

So he worked out, got the kinks out. Not easy. He took it slow. The big bag felt hard--he didn't punch it much. He shadowboxed in front of the mirror, used Johnny's speed bag two rounds, loosened up. Duke came in as Stanley was heading for the showers.

"Hey, Duke!"

"Hi, champ. Finish your workout?"

"Yeah."

"Long time no see."

After showering, Stanley felt good--happy. <u>Not going to be afraid to lose</u>.

The first month, he'd go to the gym one day, go to the labor office the next. Then to the gym, then to a job. His neck hurt, his back was sore, he couldn't touch his toes. No matter. Time, just need time.

Stanley was driven. down the hall agreed he should turn pro. Stanley felt enthusiastic; he'd overcome a barrier, a fear barrier. He strived, he began to hit the bag harder. But his neck still hurt. Larry recommended Dr. Placer, the chiropractor.

"Make an appointment. It'll help."

It did. Dr. Placer cracked his neck. Twenty bucks for fighters.

"Feel better? Walk around."

He walked around the table, out into the reception area, rolling his neck. "Yeah!"

The new year came, the old year passed away. Stanley wore sweat clothes, undergarments, rain gear when he ran. <u>Can't get sick</u>. He drove to Riverside, borrowed another $200 from his father.

"Can't you find a gas station job?"

They were in his well-furnished apartment. His father sat on the couch, Stanley in a chair.

"Not likely, because I was fired."

"Hell, you don't have to tell them that!"

"No, I know. Maybe I'll try it."

"Don't try it, do it."

His father was a salesman, living alone for years since the divorce. Oily hair, thin, bespectacled.

Stanley nodded, knowing he wouldn't lie.

"Don't worry about paying me back anytime soon," Mr. Larson said, lighting a cigarette. "But you have to get a real job."

"Well, I'll make money boxing."

Silence. Then his father chuckled, flicking an ash into a small red tray. "Haven't got that out of your system yet?"

Returning to Los Angeles, Stanley played the radio loudly, the oldies station. Out of my system? He didn't understand. He meant well, he always meant well. But he didn't understand. Bobby Darin's "Splish Splash" blared from the speakers. The freeway was crowded going both ways: rush hour. Someday he'll see--someday he'll say, "Good work, son."

He'd said it once. When was that? A baseball game? No, he hadn't gone to any of Stanley's games. His father had moved out already. Shit, it's been a long time. Oh, yeah...the art contest, elementary school. The volcano

erupting, hot lava in every color in the world. First

place. <u>Where is that painting</u>?

8

Gradually the workouts became more vigorous. Larry wanted him to start sparring, but he knew from experience not to, yet--Larry always urged him to spar whether he felt like it or not, but Stanley wanted to get stronger, first. He'd laid off in the past, and come back; he knew to be careful.

"That's how you get into shape."

"I know, Larry. But I don't feel ready."

It was an unrelenting process of running, eating well, drinking water, training, telling himself not to fear defeat.

January became February. Rainstorms hit the southland with a vengeance. People got sicker, traffic got snarled, the sky was hidden behind storm clouds and pouring rain. Stanley bought extra vitamin C, took it unremittingly; he didn't get sick.

He also made a plan to carry on professionally, making money, until mid-year, and call Rosy. Perhaps, by then, she'd have broken up with her musician "friend."

The State Athletic Commission provided forms, addresses, a "check list" for applicants: four passport photos, x-rays at a free facility, fingerprinting at the

Sheriff's office, eye exam and physical. Stanley did it all.

The ring doctor was pleased his cut had healed.

"Glad to see you're going pro, Stan. You'll do well, I believe." The doctor didn't have much of an office, but he had enthusiasm.

"Hope so."

"Just throw a lot of punches, remember? I always tell you that."

It was true. The doctor had said that for years, after he saw Stanley fight.

"More punches, that's the key. You can hit. Don't wait. Throw a lot of punches."

"I will, thanks."

Rosy Sanchez, meanwhile, completed her album, "Special Love." She thought about Stanley often, regretted returning to her boyfriend, but kept at it.

She went to The Mission frequently, but didn't see him. Of course he wouldn't go in there! She'd put a stop to their relationship. It was over.

"Why do I hurt men?" she asked Elena one day in February, over margaritas. "What's wrong with me?"

"I don't know. That just happens, you know."

"Does it? Do you hurt them?"

"Me? I have. It just happens."

"No, I do it, I don't understand why."

"They hurt <u>us</u>, don't they! They're worse than we are." Elena smirked, drank, waited for Rosy's response.

But Rosy didn't respond. She wanted to call that number he'd given her. She wanted to hear his laugh again.

As if sensing her thoughts, Elena said: "Stay with this guy. He's going to be rich, you'll see. That boxer won't be able to take care of you. Right?"

"How do you know?"

"Get off it, Rosy!"

"My album can sell, when it's released. I don't need Rick's money."

"You're dreaming. Even if the album <u>does</u> do well, you--"

The owner's daughter, Carmen, had approached their table. "How are we doing, ladies? Need anything?"

"Hóla," Elena said.

"Hóla, Carmen. No quisieramos nada."

"Bien. Wish I could sit with you, but I'm busy."

"Sit and <u>dish</u>," Elena urged. "Cheer up Rosy!"

"You need cheering up?" she asked Rosy.

"No, she's crazy."

"What's the matter? Rick?"

"No, he's--"

"She thinks he's too possessive," Elena interrupted.

"I'll come back. Don't go anywhere." Carmen left.

"Thanks."

"What? You are so depressed it scares me."

The screening committee had approved, Larry and Stanley signed the application, and in late February the long awaited temporary license arrived in the mail. No photo--the permanent one would have the photo on it. Stanley held it and carried it in his wallet with fear and excitement.

He was sparring now. George came to watch a few times, Duke smiled his near-toothless grin, wiping Stanley's face with a towel between rounds. Larry pushed pushed pushed.

His hands were sore, his feet were sore. He soaked them in salts after each workout.

Lonnie helped him. Lonnie hit hard, but worked easy with him. Pow. The worst was his body shot right below the heart. How could he do that, how could he always find an opening? Stanley never saw them coming. Pow. Right above his stomach, taking his breath away. He'd have to wave Lonnie off, pace the ring, try to breathe. When they'd resume boxing, Stanley would try to jab and stay away, but Lonnie would get in there close, again, and pop that left to his heart. But he took it easy on him.

Lonnie was also preparing for a fight, in France, with a middleweight contender. Sammy was going with him. Stanley wished he could go too, fight his first pro fight there. But Larry set it up outside of town.

"Just target practice, Stan. These fighters in Bishop don't know much. You'll do well."

"Where is Bishop, anyway?"

"Toward Reno. A few hours away. Tony's going with us. Turning pro too."

"Cool." Stanley bounced in front of the mirror, shaking his weary arms. His old green T-shirt was soaked in sweat.

"Let me look at that." Larry turned him, held his face, examining a slight bruise under his left eye. "It should be alright. Little mouse."

9

He got a haircut in the barbershop under the gym--a haircut by the same barber who had cut his hair for years. After that Stanley felt more like a fighter, but let his sideburns grow longer than usual.

The mouse below his eye got worse, so Larry wouldn't let him spar for two days.

Good. It was a needed respite. His muscles had to develop. Just over three weeks until the fight.

"Four rounds. Nothing to it. Target practice."

"How many fights has he had?"

"Don't know, Stan, but I told them it was your pro debut, so they'll put you in there with a comparable opponent."

"Hope so. Remember my amateur debut, with that dude who fought so much as a junior?"

"Oh, well." He laughed his characteristic relaxed laugh.

"He had twelve fights or something."

"This is a dinky arena, don't worry."

That evening after he left the gym Stanley drove south further than usual to see the "Jesus Saves" sign mounted high on a church. Maybe that was simplistic, too, but he liked the concise brevity of the message. The sign had been there for many years, and he hoped whoever owned it would keep it from being removed, like so many other landmarks in Los Angeles.

To his surprise, as he drove around the church, there appeared another, identical sign, on the other side. He'd never known there were two. Funny how God can reveal things to you gradually.

The familiar fear of dying returned. Happened every time. Irrational, perhaps, but constantly imposing itself, constantly lurking in the back of his mind as the fight neared. Sometimes it was strong, sometimes weak. This time it wasn't so bad. And it normally diminished as he thought about it, confronted it, resisted it.

Four rounds. He could handle that. Amateurs went three. Not too much more--one extra round. All he had to do was jab, anyway, to get through it. And land some good right hands to win it. Maybe he could knock this guy out, finish it early.

Steak and vegetables at the restaurant. Rosy had remarked that they knew him here. Touching, how she'd cried, on the phone. Guess it meant she felt some love for him, didn't it?

He didn't have any coffee, didn't have any beer. And the waiter didn't talk much--he knew Stanley was a private person. Must have wondered, though: what happened to those women?

In his room he listened to Simon and Garfunkle's "Bridge Over Troubled Water"--always calmed him prior to a fight. Great song.

10

He returned to sparring two days later--the old
routine: gloves on, laces tied, bouncing up and down
outside the ring, Duke pulling the headgear over his head,
strapping it on, making sure the cup was secure around his
waist, telling him to warm up more even though Stanley
wanted to save his energy for the sparring session, being
signaled into the ring, nodding at the other guy, Larry
standing outside the ropes rinsing the mouthpiece off,
demanding Stanley work hard because his bout was coming up,
overhearing instructions by the other coach to his fighter
to "avoid this guy's right hand" which always pissed
Stanley off, but, sure, it was fair, and on went the grease
over his face and in went the mouthpiece and he was
breathing deliberately as they walked around, not looking
at each other until the bell sounded--

--both moving forward, touching gloves, beginning to
throw punches, ducking, slipping from side to side, getting
hit in the nose, Larry saying nothing, watching--

--in a tree outside L.A., years ago, the sturdy wood
of a supportive branch beneath him, the clean blue-grey
empty sky above him...wearing cut-offs, no shoes, feeling
warm in that summertime sunshine sprinkling through the

branches and the soft leaves...barely close to maturity, just into the Boy Scouts, just into the tempestuous teens, loving pocket knives and Tarzan books and thinking about things, wondering about the girl who lived across the way-- in a tree on a secluded street, northeast of L.A.--

--that young kid, that plan-dreaming boy, trying to keep from gripping the branch or the tree trunk because it's braver to be there, up in that jungle, that foliage, without having to hold on like a typical civilized individual...that kid now in the middle of a beat-up ring, holding his gloves up, keeping his head down, thinking what punch to throw, waiting to block whatever came his way, feeling wonderful...

--getting hit with too many left hooks, for some reason, and that sudden right slapping against his side, powerfully, trying to block it with his elbow, wanting to keep his glove up at the same time, leaning against the sagging, worn ropes--Larry yelling, "Get out of there!"-- pushing away, sticking, circling, stepping in with two jabs and missing with a right and a left hook both, taking a hard hook, waiting for that fucking bell--

--panting, sweating, Larry pouring water over his face, telling him to be more aggressive, applying more grease, Duke watching from below, the bell--

--not _too_ tired, feeling loose, going to the body, scoring well with his right, circling again, seeing a slightly concerned expression on his sparring partner's face, ducking the incoming jab, going to the body again, getting nailed by a sharp right hand--yikes--knowing he has to be more aggressive--

--using an old trick: changing the timing on a follow-up right, hitting sharply before the guy can block it, pivoting in order to escape a counter-punch, knowing he needs to land another one to impress the guy, looking for a chance, finding it by faking to the body but going higher, _pow_, and seeing that look of respect in his eyes, _his_ coach yelling "Don't wait," but Larry saying nothing because he can see Stanley's doing okay, the other guy's trying to 'not wait,' to land a few, but in a bad position now, trying too hard, thinking it's the way to go but Stanley lands a stiff jab, throwing the pro off stride, Larry yelling "More than one!" meaning don't just throw one, throw several shots in a row--the hardest thing to do when you're tired--and Stanley was getting tired, and mad, also, because this guy wasn't going to spar easy, because he was upset, or something, coming on strong as if he were in a real fight, Stanley backing but still taking a couple of good ones that don't bother him too much, thank God, and

his jab is still working which makes the pro even madder
since he isn't used to that, had been in there with more
experienced boxers and withstood their jabs, but Stanley's
got a great jab--

--in the third round experience prevailed as Stanley
tired and suffered the ire of a mean professional who
wasn't going to be embarrassed by a punk who thought he
could fight, by an amateur/almost pro who had popped him a
few sneaky punches, and Stanley absorbed a wicked
combination, retreated, to no avail, stung by recurring
blows--why didn't the guy hold off a little or why didn't
his coach tell him to?--oh fuck it it's boxing so Stanley
drew on his reserve, his second wind, getting one or two
through, occasionally, and slowed the guy up a little, by
the end of the round--

--"That's enough," Larry said, after the bell,
thanking the other fighter who didn't bother to look over,
but his trainer did, briefly, before giving his fighter a
stern look.

He went to The Mission that night, his eyes black-and-
blue. After placing an order at the front, Stanley sat
down at a table. The waitress promptly brought him a
Corona, no lime, as he'd asked.

"Can I have a glass, please?"

"You don't drink from the bottle? What's the matter with you?"

When she brought it she said: "That's a bad one. Who hit you?"

"Boxing."

"Oh! My uncle did that. What's your name?"

"Larson."

She shook her head. "Never heard of you."

"I haven't turned professional yet. No, wait, I have. But I haven't had a fight yet."

"No fights?"

"Well, no--I mean, yes, twenty or so as an amateur."

"Do you like it?"

"Uh-huh."

"My uncle did too." The waitress continued her work; Stanley tried to remember exactly how many fights he'd had. In a few minutes she returned with a plate of hot chicken and rice, a roll of tortillas, a smile on her face.

"Carmen knows who you are. You went out with Rosy!"

That threw him, but he recovered quickly. "Yes, I did. Who's Carmen?"

She indicated the woman at the cash register. "Right over there."

"Sure, I've seen her. She knows me?" He felt emotionally invigorated, happy.

"Carmen!" the waitress hollered. "This one?"

Carmen looked; Stanley hoped he wasn't blushing, and waved. She smiled, then pointed at him. Several customers watched.

"When's the last time you saw Rosy?" the waitress asked. Stanley busied himself with his dinner, feigning nonchalance.

"Oh, well--not for a long time. Last year."

"She comes in a lot."

"I know," he nodded, putting a forkful of rice in his mouth, feeling his heart pound.

Carmen was walking toward them. She spoke, in Spanish, to the waitress, who went back to work.

"How are you? Oh, your face! What happened?"

"Training--boxing."

"You must have lost."

"No--" he had to laugh "--just training." But in a way, she was right. "I have a fight coming up."

"Oh. Rosy told me about you. Good luck."

"Thanks." He took another bite of food. What to say now? "Three weeks from tonight, as a matter of fact."

"Will it be on television?"

"No, it's in Bishop. No TV."

"Too bad."

11

His birthday, March 9, came and went. Not many knew about it. Stanley never bothered with it much, anyway--an idiosyncrasy of his--and was happy when March 10 rolled around. Big deal. 30.

Lonnie sparred with him regularly, and with others, preparing for his ten-round fight in April. Little Tony was training hard; Larry was also getting him ready. An odd thing, though: Hershel's noticeable absence from the gym. Stanley didn't feel like asking about it, and no one said a word. Maybe he'd quit. He did have a wife and young child--perhaps he was working a lot of overtime.

As fight night approached the training sessions intensified, the miles at the track increased, and stepping on the weight scale became a daily procedure. Two pounds heavy, one week to go. No problem. More running, more sparring. He saw Burnett--the black pro who'd overdone it--in the gym, but didn't spar with him. One day he asked Larry:

"Why did he do that, anyway?"

"Don't worry about it. Some of these guys just don't know how to work. It's not personal."

"I think it was."

Larry chuckled: "After a few fights you'll be able to handle him. Keep your mind on your condition."

One pound gone, four days to go. George said he couldn't make it to Bishop due to school; Stanley didn't feel like having his friend see it, anyway. What if he lost?

The "team" would go up in two cars: Burnett, the overdoer, would drive Stanley and James in his car, Larry and Sammy would go up with Tony--more comfortable. James had one pro fight, was looking for another win. He was a happy-go-lucky black welterweight; Burnett was outspoken--a "big mouth," some called him--pretty good record, full-fledged middleweight.

The final few days passed uneventfully. Stanley was at 154, junior-middleweight limit, the day before the trip. He just moved around, throwing punches, jumping rope.

"Eat a good meal tonight, have yourself a little ice cream," Larry told Stanley after his shower. He always told him that before a fight, but Stanley never ate ice cream, believing the sugar was bad for him. Maybe so, maybe not.

He was hungry, though, and ate an extra portion at the steak house, telling the waiter his bout was the following night. He wished him luck, didn't charge him extra.

Stanley slept well, but woke up too early--nervous. The morning was crisp outside--looked like more rain. He had three scrambled eggs, hamburger patty, at Jim's when it opened. The coffee was difficult to resist.

What to do? Read, rest, listen to music. He finished *A THOUSAND DAYS*. Good timing. It ended before the assassination. Better that way. Too painful to address, no doubt, for the writer, who had worked with J.F.K.

Stanley's morning was not very well-defined. He lazed about, played Linda's album:

> "--so he's hanging on to half her heart
> But he can't have the restless part
> So he tells her to hasten down the wind
> He agrees, he thinks she needs to be free--"

Yeah, that's what happened, alright. Fuck it. Life goes on. His life has to go on, too. Yeah--go forward, keep going, have faith.   He added to his "double-sevens" poem:

> "O double-sevens, where is your gift?
> Nineteen seventy-seven, where is my victory?
> And yet, I rejoice, having held her--
> Sweet success in a year of defeat."

He'd be getting more money than usual for a four-round match: $750. Larry couldn't say why, but that's what they'd offered. Larry got one-third, common manager's cut.

After tax, tithe, the cost of a new pair of trunks Larry had gotten him--red ones, oddly--Stanley might have a few hundred left.

The thought that he'd die in the ring returned, vigorously. To assuage it Stanley tried to reach his high school friend, Andrew, but he wasn't in--had to just leave a message about the fight. Andrew had an answering service--he was an actor.

James Dean had died on the verge of great success. It happened sometimes: unfulfilled promise. Screw it. "If I die, I die. But I'd rather shoot pool."

He played an old Eagles number about Dean, but it sounded morbid--Stanley turned it off.

After eleven he packed his bag and drove to the gym, parked his '57, waited for Burnett, early. Couldn't go upstairs--not open yet--so Stanley waited on the sidewalk.

He thought of meeting that cute Maria, showing her the gym, going to the Forum, kicking her out of his room. Son-of-a-bitch. I'm so sorry, Maria.

Nice Buick. New. James was inside, happy as ever. Burnett shook hands, for some reason.

"All ready?"

"Let's go."

It took a lot longer than three hours. Burnett talked; they stopped for gas a few times. Luckily Stanley was able to sleep. James was excited, laughed at every wisecrack Burnett made--and there were quite a few: he ridiculed Stanley--being old to turn pro, being white, being quiet, being--what did he say?--a "slow-starter."

"Gunna let him put you down like that?" James asked, giggling.

"Why not? It's all true."

Stanley didn't care what Burnett said--he was only doing it to edify himself, to elude his own fears. Or because he didn't like Stanley, didn't like any white people. It was understandable.

"Whose car is this?" James asked.

"My old man's."

"Must have a fine job!"

"Contractor."

Stanley didn't know what that was, didn't care. He stared at the passing scenery, recalled his prayer at the track, the sprinklers going on, the year past.

Have to think of the future, he told himself. Let God's grace into your life. Ignore the Burnetts of the world. Focus on tomorrow. Get through this match, write a poem about Rosy Sanchez.

Arriving in Bishop, nearly twilight, cold, the three pioneers ate small meals, quietly. <u>All talked out, asshole? Thank God George isn't here. Too much pressure</u>.

Sammy and the others pulled up outside; they walked into the Sizzler. Larry was smiling, happy.

"We'll shoot over to the auditorium, check in," he said. "You all get over there in a half an hour."

"Sit down and eat," Sammy told Tony. He gave Burnett the directions. "We'll meet you over there. Don't get lost."

Tony looked pale and distressed. Nothing to do about it. He got a cheeseburger but only ate part of it.

"You better not drink that shit," Burnett advised, referring to Stanley's cup of coffee.

"I know." But he drank it anyway.

Nearly dark, when they found the auditorium. Only a few people there, yet. A temporary ring set up, folding chairs. <u>Just a dumb basketball court--my pro debut! I hate basketball</u>.

Then the worst part: after undressing, weighing in, the once-over by a young doctor, the proffering of licenses--the bad news:

"Come in here a second, Stanley." Larry took him into a small office near the locker rooms. "This is Manny, the promoter."

"Hi!" Manny had big hands, a big smile. They shook. "How are you doing? You the light-middleweight?"

"That's right."

"Well, there's a little problem. Our light-middleweight can't make it. He called just a second ago."

Stanley, stunned, finally asked stupidly: "There's no fight?"

Manny's big smile. "Hector will take his spot, if you agree." He pointed to Hector, standing by the wall, who smiled, too. Stanley looked at him, then at Larry.

"Now, he's a middleweight," Larry told him. "You don't have to do it, but..."

I'll say--a heavy middleweight.

Hector shrugged his shoulders as if to ask, 'Why not?'

"It's the best we can do," Manny said, apologetically. "But we'd hate to have you not fight, after coming all the way up here."

What a pal.

"Okay," he said, feeling cold all over. "Sure."

That was that. If Larry didn't object, fuck it.

"Looks like he's been around," Stanley remarked when they were outside the office.

"Three pro fights. You'll be alright. You're ready."

Stanley felt queasy, a sense of peril, then forced it away. Three fights isn't much. Not to worry.

Well, I want to get paid. Stanley had found a secluded spot on the grounds, outside, away from the auditorium entrance. People were filing in, buying tickets. He sat near a tree on a ledge close to the wall. Have to do it; three hundred bucks after taxes and expenses.

Inside, the other fighters sat and waited. Larry sipped, now and then, from a small brandy bottle. Tony moved his position from the floor to a bench, then back to the floor, leaning against the wall.

"Don't get suited up until I tell you," Larry said, walking a few yards up the hallway, listening to the scraping of chairs inside, the excited voices. When he returned he told them: "There's one amateur bout first-- after that, I guess you're up, James."

The black welterweight was sitting on the floor, near Tony. He lifted his fist in response. "What's that Duke says? 'Knock him stiffer than...'"

Larry laughed. Burnett, lying on the bench, asked, "What? What's he say?"

"Stiffer than a 'wedding prick,'" Larry drawled, and laughed. The others did too, except Tony, who appeared not to understand. Burnett stretched out, chuckling.

"Knock 'im stiffer than a wedding prick," he repeated.

Stanley strolled in, sat on the bench. "When do we get ready?" he asked. A piercing scream shot through the hallway, two young boys ran by, talking loudly.

"Slow it down, fellas," Larry ordered.

They slowed, grew silent, stared at the group.

"What're you doing here?" one asked.

"What are you doing here?" Burnett countered. They didn't answer; it was a stalemate. James chuckled. The boys hesitated, panting, and then ran on.

Stanley closed his eyes, leaned his elbows on his knees, wondered why they weren't getting their stuff on. Not that he was in any hurry.

Fifteen minutes later all the fighters had boxing shoes, trunks, cups, hand-wraps, robes and grim faces on, except for James, who was smiling, bouncing up and down on his feet, swinging his arms. The small crowd was cheering, yelling inside. Sammy appeared.

"Let's go," he said to James, who lost his grin, momentarily. "Knocked him out fast."

"Oh," he said, and tossed a punch, looking at his bag nervously.

"Where's your mouthpiece?"

"In there."

"I'll get it," Little Tony offered.

"Get it. Give it to me," Sammy told him.

Larry grabbed up the taped, worn container of water bottles, Vaseline, medical supplies. When Tony handed the mouthpiece to him, Sammy picked up a towel, nodding his head at James. "Come on, son." They went up the hall, leaving the three lonely boxers to themselves.

James lost--a close decision. The crowd applauded, naturally. Larry had returned prior to the announcement, to take Tony inside. "You're up next," he said to Stanley, but not before taking a slug of brandy.

James came back, alone, smiling. "Almost beat the bastard!" He was covered in sweat. He removed his robe, retrieved a soap dish from his bag, picked up a towel from the pile, and went to the showers--silently.

Neither Stanley nor Burnett said a word.

What was there to say? Sorry?

The two kids ran through again, full of energy, as before.

"Get away from here," Burnett growled.

Stanley loosened up, did knee-bends, fought the fear. He was glad, now, that Burnett had overdone it--he was prepared for anything.

By the time James returned from the shower room the bout was over. Larry came in, shaking his head. "Turned him over. Stopped it."

"Stopped who? Tony?"

He nodded at Stanley, giving him a serious look. "Don't think about it. Do what you have to do." He took up a towel, wiped Stanley's face. "Warm enough?"

"Yeah." He felt weak, as usual, didn't want to go in.

"What happened?" James asked in a high voice, as he began dressing.

Larry didn't reply. He rubbed Stanley's shoulders. The crowd cheered. "Let's go. Where's your mouthpiece?"

"In my pocket." They went down the hall, James finished dressing, Burnett loosened up, threw punches, ducked imaginary ones, bent his head from side to side.

Not much of an audience. Must be another event in town. The chairs weren't filled, although some people were in the stands. Little Tony passed by going the other way, with Sammy, head down, eyes blank.

"Get up there," Larry instructed, his voice a bit too loud. Probably the booze. Applause. Hector was in the ring already. One glance revealed to Stanley a different countenance than the one he'd seen in the office. Now Hector wasn't acting so nice.

Gloves came on. Pro gloves--smaller than the amateur ones. No rosin box. Cheap setup. Vaseline on, mouthpiece in; Stanley saw a young blonde girl looking up at him.

The announcer announced. 158? They'd added four pounds to hide the disparity. 161 for Hector. Ha. Must have subtracted four pounds. What bullshit. "Making his professional debut...Stanley Larson." No similar statement about Hector, of course--only that he came from Nevada. Didn't even mention his record.

Robes off, meeting in the center of the ring. Instructions. No holding? That's a laugh. Hector glowered, made Stanley mad rather than intimidated. Asshole. They shook hands--gloves--barely.

Then the tough part: trainers climbing out of the ring. The usual thought: What am I doing here? Then, the bell. "Stick him," Larry said.

Stanley lost the first round, no doubt about it. Slow-starting Stanley. He missed with his first jabs--not in close enough. Hector charged, aggressively, threw a combination, one punch severely stung. A moment later he did it again, making Stanley retreat. <u>Don't get knocked out</u>. Larry yelled: "Stick him, stick him!" Always paid to follow his advice. So he jabbed back, landing a few times.

But Hector kept charging--'macho,' like almost all Mexican-Americans--forcing Stanley to hold on; the referee pushed them apart. "Don't wait!" Larry hollered.

It was a long three minutes. Hector punched so often Stanley had to cover-up more than usual, didn't have time to return fire. But he was in good shape, made it to the bell.

Larry was all over him. "You can't wait with this guy. Too jabs, right hand, jab on the way out. Stick him!" Funnily enough, Stanley smiled.

"Okay."

More grease. Mouthpiece rinsed, Stanley taking those important deep breaths. Mouthpiece in. Bell.

He lost the second round, most likely. But Hector missed with many of his punches. Stanley "made him miss," as Duke would say.

He stuck, he followed with the right hand, he jabbed his way out, he circled. Hector charged, got a little wild. <u>You don't hit as hard as Lonnie, tough guy</u>. Another long three minutes. Hector was proficient at ducking, so Stanley tried an old trick: initiate the right hand, but go immediately lower. Hector had ducked, was surprised to be hit in the mouth. It worked.

Before the bell Hector landed a solid shot to his chin. Momentary blackout. Still on his feet, Stanley did what he had to do: don't retreat, throw any possible punch. That worked too. It landed, fortunately, but without much power. Hector stepped back, however, surprised again, his tempo interrupted.

Larry was kinder this time. "You're doing fine. Keep sticking--don't let him in." He wiped his face with a towel. "Want a rinse?" Stanley shook his head.

Sammy stood just outside the ropes, impassive.

He might have won the third round. Big as he was, Hector wasn't smart enough to stay away, continued to move forward, couldn't block every jab. As long as he kept sticking, Stanley could prevent that onslaught of punches, and follow up with one of his own. But he had to move more than usual. This guy was as tall as he was--no advantage there. His arms were larger--no advantage there. He was also in good shape--no advantage there. But Stanley was quicker, smarter.

Still, it was a long three minutes.

"It's yours to win," Larry said--code for: "You're losing, get going."

He won the last round, no question. Hector had tired at last. All that running, training, exercising paid off, in Stanley's case. He finally got in a few body shots. At one point, maneuvering, leaning against the ropes, Stanley sprang forward, ducking under and out, as his opponent threw a punch in the vacant air, over his head, and fell awkwardly against the ropes--where Stanley had been a second before. The crowd cheered.

Stanley tried to follow up, landing a good left hook for a change, making his opponent cover, for a change. Larry was screaming something--Sammy too. His opponent didn't charge. How much time left? They met in the middle, both swinging, both connecting. Stanley got stunned, must have done the same to Hector, who held off, stepping back. Larry yelled, Sammy yelled.

So tired, now. Have to punch--his gloves are low. The audience was noisy but Stanley didn't hear it. He struggled forward, making the 'three jab, right hand' approach. It worked. Hector, for all his experience, couldn't fully defend against it: he blocked one jab, slipped the second, but was hit with the third. Stanley was close, then, and his right hand struck; Hector's knees buckled. Stanley had to keep swinging, but his arms were weak. One left landed, one right missed, his opponent backed up. Stanley advanced wearily. <u>Now's the moment</u>. Bell.

Big cheers from the audience; they liked it.

The referee signaled it was over--a formality.

The fighters hugged, smiled, Stanley waved to the crowd, looked at the blonde girl near his corner. She was on her feet, clapping.

Larry took his mouthpiece, put the robe over his shoulders. Based on Larry's facial expression, however, he must have lost. They waited for the judges to compile scores.

Stanley felt happy--he knew he had fought well; he liked that last punch. But his head was sore. <u>Fucking little gloves</u>. He took a rinse, spit it in a bucket.

The announcement confirmed Larry's demeanor.

Decision for his opponent.

"Good fight," Burnett said as he headed toward the ring. Must have watched it from the doorway, Stanley thought.

"Close decision, don't worry about it," James said, smiling. "I thought you were going to get him."

"Yeah--almost." Now Stanley felt less happy. James was entering the arena to watch the next fight, but turned to yell: "They're cheating us, you know that?"

Stanley looked over his shoulder. "What?"

"Tony figured it out. They're cheating the shit out of us." He walked back to Stanley. "You fought a middleweight, right? They lied! There was a junior middleweight--_I_ had to fight him. And Tony--"

"There was?"

"Right, and Tony fought my guy. They told him there wasn't no lightweight."

Stanley hurried through his shower, dressed, packed his bag, went in to watch. Burnett was bearing in on his opponent furiously. The guy _was_ bigger--a light-heavyweight, maybe. Red hair, pale skin. As Stanley watched he realized they had indeed been screwed. _Burnett should be fighting Hector, not this guy. I should have_ fought the light-middleweight. Neat trick, all the way

down the line.

The over-doer was over-doing it, hustling, taking

advantage of every opening. The redhead fought well, but

by the end couldn't fend off the attack. Decision for

Burnett.

In a tiny office afterward Sammy handed out their

checks, and said: "Follow us to the motel. After we get

situated we can eat."

Tony lingered, holding his check, as the others filed

out.

"Why'd I fight a welterweight? Why'd you let 'em do

that?"

Stanley stopped at the doorway to hear the reply.

"First of all, you didn't fight a welterweight. He

was 142. And--"

"No, that's what they said he weighed! None of us

fought the right guys. You--"

"Take it easy. There's nothing we can do about it.

Take your money, get back in the gym on Monday."

Sammy was calm; Larry frowned, but said nothing.

"They lied, man. You should have protected us. You

probably got something for it!" Little Tony didn't know

what else to say; he went out the door, muttering. Stanley
looked at the trainers.

"Did you know?"

Sammy laughed. "'Course not. You heard what they
said. They told you the same thing they told us. In fact,
I knew <u>nothin'</u> about your fight, I was with James at the
time."

"You didn't know? You didn't know what?"

"Settle down. I didn't know you had to fight a
middleweight."

Silence. Then:

"You should have won that fight, anyway."

"How could I? He was too big."

Sammy shook his head, standing. "Should of done like
Burnett--kept at him the whole time. You waited too long,
like always."

"What do you mean? I went after him. I did
everything I could. He was a middleweight!"

Sammy continued to shake his head, started to walk
out. "Forget it."

"What do <u>you</u> say?" he appealed to Larry, who held his
hands up, palms outward.

"You mighta gone after him more." His speech was slightly slurred. "But--you fought good--I don't agree with Sammy." He stood up shakily. "Come on."

"Okay, okay. Set up another one. When we get back to L.A., set up another one right away. You'll see!"

Larry laughed his laugh. "Sure thing, champ."

"Your ride's here, Stan!" It was James, calling from the passageway.

"What? What ride?"

"Girls, man. Said they're waitin' on you."

In fact, there was a car outside with three women in it. Stanley stood, with his bag, at the open exit. It was dark and misty--he couldn't see who they were. The driver waved, opened her door, climbed out. She looked familiar. Another door opened, a passenger got out. It was Rosy.

HASTEN DOWN THE WIND Copyright 2004
Paul Le Mat

Cover Design and Art by Steve Montiglio

PROFILES IN COURAGE John F. Kennedy Copyright 1955 Harper and Brothers, New York, NY

"Hasten Down The Wind" Copyright 1973 Warren Zevon, Warner-Tamerlane Publishing Corp.
and Darkroom Music/BMI

"Heart Like A Wheel" Copyright 1974 Anna McGarrigle, Capital Records

All Rights Reserved.

Except as permitted under the U.S. Copyright Act of 1976, no part of this may be reproduced or
distributed in any form or stored in a data base or retrieval system without written permission from
the publisher or author.

Third Edition April 2010

Library of Congress #137507211
TXul-173-098

Printed in Great Britain
by Amazon

47403095R00210